LIES THAT BIND

LIES THAT BIND

an Anastasia Phoenix novel

by diana rodriguez wallach

Entangled Publishing, LLC
2614 South Timberline Road
Suite 105, PMB 159
Fort Collins, CO 80525

Entangled Teen is an imprint of Entangled Publishing, LLC.

Visit our website at www.entangledpublishing.com.

Edited by Alycia Tornetta
Cover design by Clarissa Yeo
Interior design by Toni Kerr

ISBN: 978-1-63375-902-2
Ebook ISBN: 978-1-63375-903-9

Manufactured in the United States of America

First Edition March 2018

10 9 8 7 6 5 4 3 2 1

entangled teen
an imprint of Entangled Publishing LLC

For Jordan, Juliet, and Lincoln

"Remember, remember!
The fifth of November,
The Gunpowder treason and plot;
I know of no reason
Why the Gunpowder treason
Should ever be forgot!"

English Folk Verse (c.1870)

PROLOGUE

Four years ago…

We traveled light. Many people probably claimed the same, but after moving nine times to three separate continents, we truly had perfected the art of packing. Our moving van was filled with the basics—kitchen table, sofa, mattresses, area rugs. The "stuff" we shed. I'd never kept a karate trophy. My sister and I likely painted pictures when we were little, but they were probably recycled into coffee filters by now. We bought clothes for every season and every culture, but if you weren't going to wear that polka dot bikini in Morocco, then there was no reason to bring it. Thrift stores loved us. We'd dropped belongings in secondhand shops from Singapore to Boston.

Only this move was different. We weren't pit stopping in Beantown until my parents completed another chemical project. This was the real deal. We were relocating to the Dresden Chemical Corporation's main headquarters in Massachusetts, and we were staying until I got my high school diploma.

We stepped onto the curb in front of our new brownstone

in Brookline, an almost suburban-like neighborhood on the edge of Boston.

"Okay, *darlings*." Mom always called us that, no matter how many times we asked her to stop. "It's a walk-up, but we're only on the second floor, which isn't bad. And compared to our place in Madrid, it's massive."

"You have your own rooms," my dad reiterated yet again—it was the main selling point. Well, mine at least. I'd never had my own door before.

"Dad, I'm staying in the dorms," Keira reminded him. "You sent in the housing check."

"I know, sweetheart, but in case you change your mind," he hedged.

My parents were having a hard time with my sister "going away" to college. They traveled so much for work, you'd think they wouldn't even notice that Keira was gone. But they were adamant on keeping her close. First, they insisted she enroll in the University of Miami, down the street from where we were living; then they forced her to transfer to Boston University when we decided to make the move up North. Keira could have objected to the transfer more, but I knew she never felt comfortable in Miami. She was an A-cup swimming in a land of D-cups, and every time she stepped a flip-flop onto the white sand beaches, her pale skin bubbled like bacon left too long on a griddle. The seven-year med program at BU was renowned, and the fashion in the city focused more on Patagonia fleeces than on cleavage mini dresses. Still, Keira refused to be a commuter kid. She really wanted to eat dinner in a dining hall in her flannel PJs with a roommate that doubled as a new best friend. (We watched a lot of teen movies.)

"So this is it," I said, staring at the second floor of the three-story brownstone. A large bay window protruded with cracking white paint around the glass. The building was constructed of bricks that likely dated back before the Kennedys moved into town, and there were two pale pink rose bushes on either side of the stoop that made the air actually smell like the L'Occitane shop at the mall.

"Yup, we're home." Dad threw an arm around my shoulders.

Mom pulled a set of keys from her pocket, which hung on a bare ring, no keychain, as the rev of a sports car zoomed up the otherwise quiet street. A blazing-red Corvette stopped short at the curb.

"Right on cue," Dad said.

"He's so humble," Keira joked.

The door opened, and a long leg stretched from the impossibly low car. Out stepped Randolph Urban, his gray suit unwrinkled despite the cramped, ostentatious quarters.

"Welcome to Boston," he said, greeting us like a politician at a rally. "It's so lovely to have you in my city. And before I forget..." He reached into his car and pulled out an elegantly wrapped package with silver paper and a white satin bow. "For my friends. Welcome home."

He hugged my parents like the extended family that we were, then turned his big smile toward me. "Anastasia, you get more beautiful every time I see you." He squeezed me tight, his white beard scratching my neck, the smell of his woodsy cologne rising up from his skin. I associated that smell with him as much as I associated the scent of pine needles with Christmas; it was an essential part of who he was. It made me want to buy my dad something from the men's fragrance department.

"Keira." He nodded. He didn't hug her, and she wouldn't have let him. My sister wasn't a fan of overt displays of affection. She and our mother had that in common. But they looked nothing alike. Keira was the spitting image of our father with his pointy nose and pale brown hair. I, however, shared my mother's thick, dark locks and full lips.

"How were your travels?" Urban asked.

"Easy to fly when you don't have luggage," Dad said. "Moving van was already waiting for us when we arrived." He nodded to the yellow truck behind us. Dresden paid for every corporate relocation—burly men came to our house and packed each drawer down to our underwear (which, while embarrassing, was still better than packing it ourselves). Then they transported it to wherever in the globe we were headed, unloaded it, and restocked our drawers in our new accommodations before we went to bed that night. It was the least the company could do considering it was the cause of our countless change of address forms. Honestly, they would save a lot of cash, and trouble, if we all kept our stuff in the big brown boxes. We knew it would end up back in those cardboard containers eventually, so why pretend?

"Fantastic." Urban turned to Keira. "Would you like the movers to unload your belongings in the dormitory?"

"You know, I think I'll skip the hairy men unpacking my shower shoes, but thanks," said Keira. "Not exactly the impression I want to make on my first day."

"Suit yourself." Urban shrugged. "For you." He held out his package to my father. "A gift."

"Randolph, I think we're past housewarming presents by now." Mom smiled politely.

"It's our ninth move," I noted.

"Sorry Miami didn't last longer. I know it's hard on our Dresden Kids, but at least you have each other. I'll have Donna send you an email with a list of other Dresden Kids in the area." He smiled like this was a generous gesture when it was really standard procedure.

My parents might be the ones with the jobs, but the Dresden Kids were my coworkers; we were forced to be friends out of corporate obligation and a universal understanding that no one else understood us. We moved unpredictably, from one country to the next. We spoke too many languages, we embraced unusual curriculums, and we had little other acquaintances because it seemed pointless to exert the effort. For Keira and me, it was even worse. Our parents were technically everyone's bosses, which meant Dresden Kids had to be our friends or at least pretend they were. My entire life was filled with faux relationships, and I didn't want that anymore. Boston was going to be different. I was going to make real friends, who went to my school and who shared my interests. This was my home now.

Still, I couldn't be rude to Urban.

"That's great. Thanks," I replied.

Then my mom tugged the tape on the silver package he offered and slid out a gilded antique picture frame. Her brow furrowed when she glanced at the image, her eyes flicking to my dad, who for a moment looked equally puzzled.

"I had the coordinates framed. I know this place is very important to you," Urban explained.

My parents nodded with tight smiles that I knew were fake. Maybe they didn't know what the coordinates meant?

"Of course, yes," Mom said, as if finally getting it.

She turned the frame toward Keira and me. Displayed under the glass was a piece of fabric with latitude and longitude numbers stitched in black yarn below embroidery that read: *The Phoenixes* with a crimson rose cross-stitched above it. For a billionaire like Randolph Urban, it was a very Etsy housewarming present. But I didn't see what was so confusing; it was clearly the longitude and latitude of our new home. Maybe my parents didn't like embroidery? It was a bit Southern Country for their tastes.

"Thank you so much," Mom said, awkwardly hugging Urban. He whispered something in her ear, and she smiled wider, almost too wide, like the second runner-up in a Miss Universe pageant trying way too hard to look thrilled.

Then my dad took the gilded frame from her hands.

They never hung it up.

CHAPTER ONE

I expected the fire, but not the noise.

The constant irregular popping of firecrackers boomed in every direction, reverberating off the aging stones and mixing with the rattling drums and honking tubas. Drunks had to shout to be heard, their slurred cheers freezing in visible puffs warmed only by the countless torches. Marchers filled the street, each holding a flaming stick that when too sizzling to hold was simply dropped and abandoned at their feet. There were unattended torches littering the cobblestones, which led me to believe the UK was in serious need of a public service announcement on the value of not playing with matches. I'd already burned the rubber of one sneaker, but at least that foot was warm. Even with long johns under my jeans and wheelbarrows full of fire rolling past, my teeth were chattering and my nose was running.

I guess this is one way to celebrate a holiday.

Not that we were in England for fun. These days, I strove for ordinary. I actually dreamt I was walking through the halls of Brookline Academy the other night, laughing with

Tyson and Regina, my former best friends. We were talking about going to karate then binge watching a new TV show. Honestly, I wasn't sure if it was a dream or a memory. It was so normal. But when I woke up, the dark of night still cloaking my room, there were tears trailing down my cheeks as if my subconscious had just lowered the old me into the Earth. I couldn't fall back asleep, sniffling and wiping at my eyes as I realized Tyson and Regina were probably visiting colleges right now; they were sending out applications and writing essays about how tutoring saved their lives. Their entire worlds were going on without me, while I stayed immersed in a toxic realm my parents created. It was a life I didn't want.

But I also couldn't ignore it. Marcus's brother was in danger. At least, we thought he was in danger. That was why we were at this festival, searching for Antonio. I owed Marcus for helping me find my sister in Venice, but more than that, I wanted to help him. I *needed* to help him. He was sort of my boyfriend (we never actually talked about it). So officially, he was more like my adventure junkie companion, or the guy who saved my life, or a fellow Dresden Kid whose family might be as twisted as my own. He was also the reason I stayed entangled in this world of spies and Department D and didn't run away with Keira. But once Antonio was found safe (he *had* to be safe), Keira and I had a decision to make. Only I wasn't sure I was ready to admit what that decision might need to be.

I breathed into my wool scarf, warming my face as we cut through the dense crowds clogging High Street, fast food wrappers crunching under my sneakers. Surprisingly, even across the pond, parade-goers still relied on hamburgers and pizza to absorb the fountain of alcohol pouring down their throats. The air smelled almost as strongly of ale as it did of smoke, and oddly pubs were open, but their windows were boarded shut. In fact, every storefront within walking distance of the main parade route had nailed plywood to its windows — not to protect from fire, given that cheap wood made for excellent kindling, but to protect from the attendees. There were drunks swaying atop the iconic red phone booths, hanging out of windows, and hovering in doorways, all with pints dripping down their frozen hands.

I tightened my grip on Marcus's black leather jacket.

"Don't worry. I won't lose you," he said, wrapping his hand on top of my mine and squeezing it tight as he pulled me through the hordes of people glowing in a red fiery light that flickered as if the parade were being held on Mars, not in England. But what else could you expect on Bonfire Night? Every November fifth, towns throughout the United Kingdom celebrated the demise of one of the country's most infamous villains — Guy Fawkes.

Being an American, this name, and holiday, meant absolutely nothing to me. I imagined it would be like celebrating the Fourth of July in Germany or Cinco de Mayo in Boston. Wait, we do celebrate Cinco de Mayo in Boston. I had a picture of my sister, Keira, with Craig Bernard and Luis Basso at a pub to prove it — that was a week before the two criminal spies kidnapped her from our home. Still, I had never heard of Guy Fawkes until Charlotte, my best friend and complete tech genius, explained the unusual celebration as I booked my train ticket.

Turns out, Guy tried to blow up Parliament more than four hundred years ago, but he sucked at his job. He got caught, in the bowels of the historic seat of government, holding a match about to light enough barrelfuls of gunpowder that it would have been seen from the New World. He was branded a terrorist and mutilated in the town square. (It was standard procedure back then, though Guy somehow managed to hang himself before they got to the really gory bits.) Afterward, the country began to annually mark the day of his screwup with open flames that screamed, "Yay! We saved Parliament! Long live the King!"

Only hindsight had a way of shedding new bonfire light on the situation.

Today, Guy has been twisted into a bit of a folk hero, at least to hackers like Charlotte. That creepy mask with the curled mustache that's the face of the hacktivist group Anonymous? That's Guy. He's the poster child for anarchy—*Fight the power!* And all that. Because ultimately, Guy's stance against the British government's treatment of Catholics has been given validity. Priests were being killed, Catholics were being forced into hiding, and senseless laws were being passed. There were now as many people who viewed Guy as a freedom fighter as there were those who viewed him as a terrorist.

"I think that's the inn." Marcus pointed to a tiny ceramic sign adhered to the rounded gray bricks of a home so adorably British it deserved its own postcard. Windows, glowing with reflected torchlight, were rung with red bricks that contrasted with the gray stones that made up the rest of the structure. There was a burnt orange shingle roof with dormer windows, bushes still blooming with pastel flowers from an unusually warm October, and trees dripping overhead with emerald and golden leaves. In the background, high above the parade, stood an imposing castle. Because what self-respecting European town didn't have a castle? They're like McDonald's restaurants in the United States—old, plentiful, and often overlooked.

Honestly, the bed and breakfast seemed much more fitting for a honeymoon than a single guy, alone, running for his life. Unless none of that were true.

Not long after we rescued Keira from Department D in Italy, Antonio stopped returning Marcus's phone calls. Their parents hadn't seen or heard from him in weeks, nor had he shown up to work—for his job at the Dresden Chemical Corporation. Antonio worked in sales for the engineering firm my parents created and used as a cover for their espionage underbelly, Department D. We didn't know if Antonio was aware of his link to a criminal organization that specialized in "fake news," but we worried that even if he were oblivious, he might be targeted by those lethal spies because of Marcus's assistance in saving my sister.

Allen Cross, my parents' old friend and our lone Dresden ally, even called Antonio to warn him of the danger, but he got his voicemail. So it was possible Antonio got the message and took off in time, or it was possible the voicemail was too late and Marcus's brother was shackled to a sink somewhere just like my sister had been. Then there was the third possibility that I tried not to say aloud (too much)—maybe Antonio was a bad guy working for the enemy.

I knew Marcus wasn't considering this possibility, and I couldn't push the idea, not after he traveled with me from Boston to Italy when we were practically strangers. He never told me to give up on my sister, and he refused to leave my side even when Luis Basso pointed a gun at our heads in Cortona. In fact, Marcus rode a motorcycle down that mountain in Tuscany and saved our lives. I couldn't abandon him now, and I couldn't question his faith in his brother—even if every step I took in this quaint English village raised my anxiety level to that of a gazelle galloping past a lion's den.

There was something too convenient about this lead.

After weeks with no activity on Antonio's credit cards, bank accounts, and passports, Charlotte suddenly uncovered a registration for a B&B at the Guy Fawkes festival in Lewes, England—only an hour and a half from where we were staying in London. And it was in Antonio's real name. This didn't sound like a guy hiding from super spies. We all debated the lead being a setup—it was practically wrapped in caution tape—but in the end, Marcus was willing to walk into the trap gagged and blindfolded if it meant saving his sibling. I knew how that felt, and I couldn't let him take that walk alone.

I squeezed past a young couple with a toddler, all three dressed in black and white striped shirts and red neckerchiefs to show the family's allegiance to one of the bonfire clubs. Unlike the giant cartoon balloons and celebrity performances that filled American parades, this celebration consisted of locals dressed in costumes that ranged from early Michael Jackson chic to inexplicably offensive. First, there was a group that looked like convicts who'd escaped from a nineteenth-century prison, hence the black and white striped shirts and cherry knit hats. Then there was a troop wearing what could only be described as train conductor uniforms bedazzled for a moonwalk; they were only missing a sequin glove. There were Victorian women in silk hoop skirts and bonnets. There was a guy dressed like Captain Hook.

Then groups shifted toward political incorrectness, like that troop dressed as American Indians in flowing feathered headdresses with war paint on their cheeks. There was a club holding burning crosses, and another hoisting anti-Catholic "No Popery" signs. But all of that paled in comparison to the spectacle before me now.

I yanked Marcus to a halt and gawked at the famously

pale British men and women sporting a Zulu African theme with their faces painted completely black. My jaw fell, the taste of smoke souring my tongue. This would cause a riot in America. There were actual babies in blackface being pushed in strollers and a guy pulling a long string of firecrackers that popped like gunshots as they walked. My wide eyes darted around, expecting to see another horrified expression, only I noticed all of the faces in the crowd were white. And not just Caucasian, they were British. I hadn't heard another American voice since I'd arrived, let alone any other accents.

"What is it?" Marcus asked, noticing the tight wrinkles on my forehead.

"They're in blackface." *Isn't that obvious?*

"Oh." He cringed at the scene. "Things are a little different in Europe."

"Clearly." My face continued to twist as I imagined how Tyson would feel if he saw this. It was hard enough being black in New England; I couldn't imagine what he would feel like here.

Just then a giant papier-mâché float of the American president, wearing a sombrero and riding a cactus, rolled toward us, presumably a statement against our immigration policies that would be burned in effigy at midnight. Tonight there would be dozens of sky-high fires lit throughout the tiny village, which consisted of narrow streets lined with Tudor buildings, constructed hundreds of years ago, mostly of wood, surrounded by hordes of people, many of them drunk. And there wasn't a police officer or fire truck in sight.

"This parade has taken an odd turn," I said.

"If you think this is bad, you should see *Las Fallas de Valencia*. Puts this little fiesta to shame."

"So Spaniards light things on fire, too?"

"Bigger than this," he said, proudly adjusting his posture. "Maybe I'll take you someday."

Then he leaned toward me, his dimples aimed like a weapon. There was smoke and literal fire encircling us, firecrackers sizzling in every direction, and hordes of bodies shoving us together. All I could see was his smile; I didn't get to enjoy it often enough. We met the day before my sister disappeared from a claw-foot tub of blood, then we fought side by side in Italy, and even when I did get Keira back, I was confronted with the fact that my parents might be alive, my dad might not really be my dad, and Marcus's brother might be in mortal danger. It was a rather extreme way to start a relationship.

Marcus reached for my waist, gently resting his hands and sending a warm tingle through my body. "Thank you for coming here, for helping me."

"Dresden Kids stick together." I repeated his infamous line. Though I wasn't the only Dresden Kid who wanted to help. Keira fought to join us. She wanted to somehow repay everyone for what they sacrificed to find her, and while I understood, I'd begged her to stay with Charlotte and Julian. I'd already lost her once, and I'd sunk into a funk so deep it left me bedridden and nearly institutionalized by Charlotte's parents.

So while I was the little sister in our tiny family, and while I realized she took care of me and protected me from social services for years, I felt our power dynamic shifted the moment I found her in Venice. It was now my job to protect us, and I needed her safe in London.

"Once we find Antonio, it'll be okay. We'll all be okay," Marcus said, his voice so monotone it was clear he didn't believe his words. Keira and I were living under assumed names. Marcus and I were taking online classes, because high school was a dream sequence we couldn't actually live out. Charlotte was hacking databases against a criminal empire. And Julian was funding the entire anarchist operation. We were all so far from okay that normal was a fantasy that kept me up at night.

"Antonio is fine," I assured him, my voice as flat as his.

He nodded, trying to force himself to believe. Then he pressed his forehead to mine and sighed, his whole weight leaning into me. I closed my eyes, my cheekbones feeling the flutter of his hair. He needed a trim. We all did. We didn't exactly have time for stuff like that anymore.

"I have to find him," he whispered.

"I know."

He exhaled against me, the heat of his breath warming my chapped, red cheeks.

"This has to end eventually, no?"

We both knew there was no answer to that question, and he really wasn't looking for one. He needed something else right now. So I shifted my lips toward his, barely a flutter, and we kissed in a way so sad and desperate that the sensation was instantly familiar—only now I was on the other side. Marcus moved his fingers to my hair, and I could feel him trying to forget the world, forget his fears, forget where he was. I knew what he wanted. I had been there myself not too long ago.

I grabbed at his neck and pressed hard against his mouth, moving my tongue until I felt a change within him, the strike of a match. He pushed me against the boarded-up window of a village shop, the splintered raw wood sticking to the wool of my coat as his mouth moved with a new excitement. I moaned slightly, and he slid his hand behind my head, gripping my hair, protecting my scalp from the hard wood, and pulling me closer.

Around us, crowds continued to push past, and I could feel torches glowing brighter, hotter, closer.

Much closer.

I cracked open my eyes and was startled by a man standing inches away, a fiery stick in his hand and a creepy grin on his bearded face. I jolted, pushing Marcus—visions of Department D, deadly spies, and endless threats of setups flashed in my head. Panic spread across Marcus's flushed face as he noticed my reaction.

Then he turned toward the stranger.

Only then did the man move the torch closer, illuminating his face.

That was when I recognized his familiar features—the dark hair, the double dimples, and the near-black eyes that ran in their bloodline.

"Hola, hermano."

CHAPTER TWO

The beer was warm. Not that I was a beer connoisseur, but given that this was my first taste of the bitter alcoholic refreshment, I would have at least preferred it as cool as the Rockies. Don't tell me that Skittles don't taste like a rainbow, either.

I sat in an English pub at a sticky wooden table that reminded me of the bar Charlotte and I went to in Boston, when we were first searching for my sister. Lately, we'd been searching for Antonio. Now, here he sat, right in front of us. Smiling.

"I'm so glad you're okay." Marcus looked at his brother like an exhausted dad whose kid walked in three hours past curfew, his face showing a mixture of relief and annoyance. "Where have you been?"

"Everywhere." Antonio shrugged.

After a massive brotherly hug, where Antonio swore he randomly spotted Marcus while he was mid-beer-chug standing atop a crimson telephone booth, we agreed to save our questions for the pub. At least here, we could hear one another speak. Then Antonio insisted he couldn't talk until he had a drink—hence the warm dark beer. Now we waited for answers.

"It's a long story," Antonio began, casually scratching his beard. He was twenty-five and had the look of a guy who bartended at a seedy rock show with cheap posters papering the walls. His beard was bushy and black, his head was full of thick, spiky dark hair that was intentionally messy, and his muscular arms were covered in two full sleeves of black tattoos that ran from shoulder to wrist. He didn't exactly fit the stock photo image of a corporate sales guy.

Antonio took a big swig, froth clinging to his facial hair like a grown-up milk mustache. "No, it is not a long story. What happened is—I'm done. I am done with Mom and Pop. I'm done with Dresden. I'm done with everything." He burped into his fist.

"I've been trying to track you down for *two weeks*. Did you get Allen Cross's message?" Marcus asked. I could tell he was trying really hard to sound cool and detached, but there was an obvious undercurrent of pain in his voice. Marcus had spent weeks thinking his brother might be dead. I knew what that felt like. It was the same panic I experienced when my sister disappeared, and now it turned out Antonio was fine the entire time.

"*Sí.* Cross left a voicemail about your sister." Antonio turned my way. "I'm glad she's okay."

"Thanks." I nodded, assessing him. He made me uneasy.

Then I realized it was his eyes. When I first saw him, lit by fire from a torch, I thought he looked like his brother, with identical features, but I was wrong. Yes, Antonio's eyes matched Marcus's in size, color, and shape, but Antonio's were guarded. He looked hardened, like someone used to bad news.

He exhaled a stale puff of beer breath. "Cross said I might be targeted, and that was all I needed to hear. I do not want this life anymore; I never did. So I went to stay with friends in Paris, then Brussels, then London. Now here." He flicked his hand around the pub full of locals hiding out from the festival. Firecrackers continued exploding outside, leaving a layer of crimson confetti snow throughout the streets and inside the pub, sticking to our shoes like toilet paper. "I met a girl whose family lives in Lewes. I'm a big fan of fire."

"So you've been partying?" Marcus asked, openly offended now. We both knew we should be thrilled his brother *wasn't* in danger, but we weren't. Marcus had worried so much, for weeks, and it turned out Antonio was living the good life the entire time. A phone call would have been nice.

"I've been laying low…with some *friends*." His grin was wide, and his eyes so close to winking that the needle on my douchebag detector instantly jumped.

He looked like a guy Keira would date, like a guy who would brag to his buddy about what a "great time" he had. There was a half-naked woman tattooed on his arm next to a giant snake, so my assumptions weren't completely out of line. The first time I saw Craig Bernard stroll into our Mother's Day party dressed like Kurt Cobain, I knew he was bad news; then he kidnapped my sister. Now Antonio was drinking and partying and leaving me with comparisons to assassins that made my arm hair stand on end.

"You said you didn't want 'this life.' What life?" I asked, trying to sound casual, though my question was anything but. If my instincts were right, then it was very possible that Antonio worked for Department D, and I was moments away from watching Marcus's entire faith in family, fairness, and puppies get obliterated.

Antonio's dark eyes swung to his brother, then back to me. "What is it you want to know?"

He peered at me as he said this, like he knew his brother wouldn't ask the hard questions, and he was right. Marcus had a bull tattoo on his neck, inches from his face, that Antonio talked him into—I'd say that meant his brother held a lot of influence. And while I didn't want to shatter that bond (I was quite a fan of sibling togetherness these days), I also didn't want to invite any more spies into my life.

I looked at my pseudo boyfriend, my eyes begging him not to be angry at me for asking the next question, but I had to say it. He knew that, right?

"Do you work for Dresden or Department D?" I asked.

Antonio's jaw flexed. He didn't seem surprised. Instead, he seemed to be gauging whether anyone within earshot was listening to our conversation. He reminded me of Allen Cross in that Roman cathedral when he first told me about Department D, and the fact that this comparison entered my head, right after a comparison to Craig Bernard, told me I was right.

Antonio sat back in his wooden booth with a resolved look, like he knew he was busted and was tired of lying. "Do I look like a sales guy to you?"

I turned to Marcus and watched every flush of pink siphon from his already pale face. I winced, painfully realizing this must have been what I looked like when I learned, definitively, that my parents were spies. I sat in that cathedral with Allen Cross, and I knew in my soul that this truth was coming—I'd discussed the possibility and analyzed it from many angles—but still, hearing it out loud, without question, dissolved everything I thought I knew about my life. All at once, my family, my past was put into a blender and pureed. Right now, Marcus's brain seemed to be turning into that same blended sludge.

I hated being right.

"So you work for Department D?" I pressed, not wanting to twist the knife but needing to make sure there wasn't any confusion.

"I *used* to work for Department D," Antonio corrected. "I don't anymore."

"Since when?" My forehead wrinkled. I wasn't well versed on the espionage world, but it didn't seem to be an easy business to retire from. Allen Cross couldn't get out.

"Since I got a message from Cross saying that the organization was kidnapping the children of employees, since I found out my brother ran around Europe like an *idiota* trying to help a girl he barely knew." He flicked an accusatory hand at me, like *I* had done something wrong. He really did not want to start pointing fingers now. "My job was to clean up messes that people left decades ago. These are not my problems. I don't care about government leaders or old conspiracies. I have wanted out of this *mierda* since the day I joined. What happened to your sister was a good excuse."

So he just quit? My head cocked. This wasn't a normal job where you simply put in your two weeks notice. Allen Cross couldn't get out even with decades worth of experience and close ties to upper management (i.e. my parents). But even if Antonio was telling the truth, it still meant he was a spy who worked for the enemy. Did it really matter whether or not he liked it? He still *did* it.

"You worked for them?" Marcus finally piped up, reason returning to his brain along with the color in his cheeks.

"*Sí*, but no more." Antonio chugged the rest of his beer

and gestured at a waitress for another. I had a feeling he'd down a six-pack before this conversation was over.

"What about Mom and Pop?" Marcus asked, his voice wobbling like he didn't really want to hear the answer. But I was glad he was asking the questions, or at least I was glad that I didn't have to. "Do they work for Department D, too?"

Antonio gave a look that said, *Do I really need to say this?* Marcus's eyes stayed blank. Yes, apparently, he had to say it.

"Of course they work for Department D," Antonio replied. "Who do you think recruited me?"

That was when the pin was inserted into Marcus's chest and deflated his last bit of hope like a day-old party balloon. His leather jacket sagged on his shoulders, his body shrinking three sizes. He hung his head, as he breathed through his nostrils like the action required effort. Marcus's parents were spies. That lifetime we spent thinking we were Dresden Kids was another piece of disinformation. We were Department D Kids all along. Both of us. Actually, I was worse. I had *three* parents who worked for the company.

Randolph Urban was my biological father. The man who kidnapped my sister shared my blood. The CIA confirmed it. My mother had an affair with him. And with that knowledge came such a conflicting set of emotions that most days thoughts collided in my head like particles in a Swiss research facility. My mother betrayed my father. She cheated on him. For how long? Did she know I was Urban's daughter? Did the father who raised me? Had Urban ever suspected?

He always showed me more affection than Keira, hugged me more, complimented me more, and I had assumed it was because my sister wasn't the touchy-feely type. Maybe there was more to it. After all, he had been sleeping with my mother at the time, so he must have known it was a possibility. But somehow, she kept it from him; otherwise Luis Basso wouldn't have sliced me open to run a paternity test. Urban didn't know I was his daughter until then. I was positive, simply from the way he clung and doted over Sophia, his granddaughter. If Urban knew the truth, he would not have let me be raised by another man. He was way too arrogant and entitled to relinquish his claim. In fact, I half expected him to pop out of a bush any moment and plant a flag on my head that read "URBAN" in CAPS LOCK.

Only I didn't want to be associated with him, let alone belong to him. He made me hate myself. He made me feel I needed to somehow prove my love for the only real family member I had—my sister. Keira and I were not "half" anything. We were sisters, the kind who would travel around the world to rescue each other and the kind who would do anything to protect one another. It was our parents who put us in danger. So if the mom and dad who raised us really were alive, I wasn't sure I ever wanted to see them, because that would mean facing a betrayal so profound it would scrub every happy memory Keira and I had. At least when they were dead, we were comforted with the knowledge that they'd loved us. If they were alive, and willingly abandoned us, it would all be gone. Everything. Who they were, who we were. What kind of people would we be after that?

I choked back a dark wave of emotion as I placed a hand on Marcus's arm, seeing in his eyes the same betrayal that only comes from being lied to by a parent.

"I'm so sorry," I said, offering whatever comfort I could but knowing words wouldn't fix this.

Then Antonio let out a disgustingly wet burp that quickly undercut the severity of the conversation. "It's not as bad as you think." He wiped his mouth. "*Si*, what happened to your sister was horrible. It is why I left. And your parents were bad people, *lo siento*," he apologized, though I wasn't sure for what. "But me, Mom, and Pop, it's not like that."

"What's it like?" Marcus's head shot up.

"Mom and Pop know about Department D, but they do not work for them. Not really. Their time is spent in the lab, biomedical research. This is true. Their connection is that their contracts, their jobs, are gotten through—how you say?—*back channels*. Department D does a job for the Prime Minister of France, and in return, France gives Dresden a new biomedical research grant."

"So they're not spies?" Marcus straightened his shoulders.

Antonio shook his head, giving him hope, dangling it like a shiny toy. If he ripped it away, if it turned out he was lying (which given his profession was very likely), it would only devastate Marcus more, make him feel stupid, and make him feel more betrayed. I warred with an urge to protect him mixed with a desire to not badmouth his parents and ruin any relationship we might ever have. I wasn't a girl saying I didn't like his mother's pot roast; I was a girl thinking his mother might deserve a life sentence in prison. There were boundaries I wasn't sure I wanted to cross.

"No, of course they're not spies." Antonio smiled like a salesman. "They know about the other side, but they do not touch it."

Marcus nodded, face lifting, as an eyelash-fluttering waitress brought Antonio a fresh beer. He gave her a dimpled grin, overtly staring at the cleavage in her tight T-shirt. She blushed, practically glowing from the attention. Then he watched her butt as she walked away, gulping half his pint in a single sip.

"I thought you said your parents recruited you?" I carefully picked at his words in a way that wouldn't make Marcus too defensive.

"*Sí*, my parents recruited me, but I was no spy," Antonio explained. "They called me a...a...fixer. With technology, old missions from long ago were coming back. You call them cold cases, *verdad*?"

Marcus and I nodded.

"I made this new evidence go away. I made the cases cold again."

"So...in your work...did people ever get...*hurt*?" I squirmed as I said it, not meeting Marcus's stare.

Seriously, was there a tactful way to ask someone if he was an assassin? I wasn't sure, but this would have to do. After everything we'd gone through in Italy, I couldn't *not* ask the question. My own parents were dangerous criminals.

"I do not *hurt* people," Antonio responded, using my word, but looking like he knew exactly what I was implying. "Burglary, bribery, evidence tampering. I was down here." He held his palm low to the sticky wooden table. "Randolph Urban, he is up here." He lifted his hand toward the rustic beams wound with white Christmas lights that lined the Tudor ceiling. "That is where the big stuff happens."

"And Mom and Pop?" Marcus asked.

Antonio waved his hands around aimlessly. "They are nowhere." He gestured toward the scattering of crowded high-top tables behind him. "They are back in a hospital. Totally separate."

Marcus's whole demeanor changed. His breath evened,

his smile returned; it was as if a tidal wave of relief swept in and flushed away his doubts. I could read his mind: *This isn't so bad. My family's okay.* And that made sense, *for him.* Only I didn't grow up with a lifetime of trusting Antonio. He didn't teach me how to ride a motorcycle or pick up girls (it was clear where Marcus learned how to work those dimples). To me, Antonio was a spy who worked for the same company as my parents, the same people who kidnapped my sister.

"What are your plans now?" Marcus clapped his hands once, like it was time to catch up on lost time now that the tough questions were over. "Because you need to call Mom and Pop. They're worried."

"I can't. I do not want to work there anymore, and I know they will not understand." Antonio emptied his pint glass, then gestured to the waitress for another. Despite the packed house, it seemed the blond barkeep was dancing on her toes, waiting for him to look her way again. People loved this guy. I didn't need to know him to see that. He was the guy everyone wanted at their party. Only I couldn't shake the feeling he was too charming, his answers too perfect.

"You said they don't work with the criminal stuff," Marcus reiterated, his eyes pleading with his brother to confirm it again. And again. And again.

"But they benefit from it," Antonio went on before turning to me. "And ever since what happened to your sister started making its way around the organization, people are nervous; loyalties are divided. A lot of staff loved your parents, so if they are alive..."

"How do you know about that?" My eyes narrowed. I'd found out in Venice, from Craig Bernard, somewhere between kicking his jaw and dislocating his knee.

"Everyone knows. Half the company went to your sister's memorial, to *your parents'* memorial. Now Urban is in hiding somewhere, the whole company is in chaos, and our parents are trying to rescue what is left of Dresden Chemical. It is a mess." The waitress placed another pint in front of him, biting her lip and shifting her chest his way. Antonio licked his lips, openly enjoying the view. Judging by the smirk on Marcus's face, he'd seen this type of interaction a lot. I had a feeling the Rey brothers might have quite a reputation in Madrid, if not the world, and I wasn't sure how I felt about that. My brow furrowed. We never really talked about ex-girlfriends, partly because I had no exes to speak of. *But Marcus...*

"So where are you going now?" Marcus asked, chuckling at the flirtatious scene. "What's your plan?"

"Yo no se." Antonio shrugged, eyes still on the waitress. "I don't make plans."

"You should come back with us." Marcus smiled like this was the greatest idea ever.

"What?" I snapped, my tone was so severe the waitress cut me a sidelong look and left the table, like she knew this was about to get ugly. I didn't mean to insult his family, or at least, I didn't mean to be so obvious about it. But the last thing our band of misfits needed was a secret agent with an identity crisis. I just got my sister back. For all I knew, Craig Bernard was Antonio's best friend. Maybe they went to Department D spy school together. Did Marcus really expect me to ignore all of that?

"I know what you're thinking." Marcus rested his hand on my forearm. "But *por favor,* this is different. Trust me."

It wasn't Marcus I didn't trust.

I pulled at the tense muscles on my neck and stared at the wood grain in the table. Of course, I knew Marcus would do this for me. He *had* done this for me. He'd risked his life for my sister. Was I really going to turn away *his* brother?

But what if Antonio was lying? What if he still worked for them? What if he was a bad guy? Marcus had to realize that this was a blimp-sized fear I couldn't overlook.

"Marcus." I wriggled, not wanting to say it, so I let my voice trail off, "What if…"

"What if I'm lying?" Antonio finished my thought. "I'm not, but I guess that's hard to prove, no? If you don't want me around, *hermano*, I can find somewhere else to go. Not sure where, but…"

Seriously? A guilt trip? How was I supposed to compete with that?

Marcus turned to me once more, his chocolate eyes pleading. I had to say yes. If I didn't, I'd be a complete hypocrite. Besides, Charlotte and Julian were cyber gods, so maybe they could dig up dirt on Antonio. Even if they couldn't, it wasn't like we planned to stay in London forever. Keira and I were in some quasi-version of witness protection—we had fake passports issued by the CIA, but we tried to have as little contact with the government as possible so as not to accidentally lead them to our presumed-alive parents. Because even if all this were true, and even with an epic-sized case of resentment for our mom and dad, we still didn't want to be the ones responsible for sending them to a supermax prison.

My secret plan was to find Marcus's brother, then go off the grid with my sister. Keira and I would relocate with new identities that we wouldn't share with anyone—not Randolph Urban, Department D, the CIA, or even our friends. If no one knew where we were, then no one could track us down. We could have normal lives. Keira could get a job at a hospital. I could go to college. We could leave this entire nightmare behind us.

Now I was staring at Antonio, and he was safe. Nothing was keeping me tied to Department D anymore.

Nothing except for Marcus.

I flicked my finger against the full pint glass in front of me. The idea of leaving him was like leaving a vital organ. He not only kept me sane, he kept me alive. With him I got to be a girl with a crush on a boy. I could be myself. How could I ever have that with anyone else? If we ran, I'd be lying about who I was, where I was from, what I was running from, and even my own name. No one Keira and I met from that day forward would ever truly *know* us. No one would make me feel like he did. No one would look at me the way he looked at me.

"Okay," I agreed, turning to Antonio. "You're Marcus's brother, so of course, you should come back to London with us, until you figure out your own situation. And, obviously, don't tell anyone where we are. I don't want Department D showing up at our door."

Antonio nodded. "*Perfecto.* Your secret's safe." Then his dimpled grin lit up the bar. "Let's drink! My little brother tried to rescue me today! This calls for shots!" He shouted an order of Irish whiskey to the adoring waitress, then switched to Spanish and began rattling with Marcus about cities seen, girls met, and parties attended. Antonio kept playfully swatting his little bro upside the head as the two of them laughed louder and harder than I'd ever heard Marcus laugh before. Mostly because we didn't have much cause for giggles; we'd been in survival mode since the day we met. Now, Marcus had his brother back, and it was like I was meeting him for the first time. This was the real him, the one who existed before I sucked him into the land of bloody tubs and deadly threats.

The brothers chugged beers and downed shots with half the pub as the waitress periodically sat on Antonio's lap, and Marcus routinely nudged my shoulder encouraging me to drink up, join the party.

Only I didn't. I couldn't. We were in a bar in Europe, amidst a festival of bonfires honoring an infamous traitor, drinking pints with an admitted former employee of our sworn enemy.

I was the wrong Phoenix sister for this situation. If Keira were here, she would have been dancing on the tables with a torch in her hand, screaming, "Remember, remember the fifth of November!" Instead, I was sulking in a wooden booth that I couldn't help notice looked like a confessional pew at a church, worrying that my pseudo boyfriend seemed happier with his brother than he ever had with me, while simultaneously realizing I may not have many more days to be happy with him.

Maybe Marcus was right earlier—this was all ending. Between all of us.

And it would start the moment we got back to London.

CHAPTER THREE

L ondon might be famous for its candy apple double-decker buses, but "Minding the Gap" on the Tube was a much faster way to get around. The next day, I found myself zipping underground beside Marcus and Antonio as they rattled in Spanish, and I tried not to eavesdrop on every word. I knew what it felt like to want a private reunion with a sibling. That train ride out of Venice with my sister would go down as one of the greatest experiences of my life—Keira was alive, seated next to me, holding my hand, and I could finally tell her everything I'd wanted to tell her since the day she disappeared. I could tell her I was sorry for being such a brat after our parents' funeral. I could tell her how much I respected her for what she'd sacrificed, both professionally and personally, to make sure I didn't end up in foster care. I could tell her I loved her, something I not only didn't tell our parents before they left, but something I never said before, ever.

So I tried to drown out Marcus and Antonio by singing a Coldplay song in my head and alternating my gaze between ads for male pattern baldness and retro patterns on the subway's cushioned seats that looked a lot like dad sweaters from the 1980s. I rested my head against the rumbling window behind me, a travel bag tucked between my legs and a cobalt blue pole.

We were headed to Julian's flat. With Antonio. A guy who worked for Department D and was recruited by his parents, *Marcus's* parents. And I had to pretend I was okay with that, because any word otherwise would make me a complete hypocrite. My biological father was currently in hiding from the U.S. government because he created Department D and kidnapped my sister; his philanthropic entrepreneur cover was officially blown. And the parents who raised me helped him start the criminal espionage organization, and they might still be alive. Really, did I have any right to judge someone else's family?

All I could do now was try to protect the people I cared about, and I could only think of one way to do that.

Keira and I had to stop looking for our parents.

They were the prize everyone wanted—the CIA, Randolph Urban, maybe even Antonio. We were pawns meant to lead them to the hidden palace of the king and queen. *But* if we stopped moving in their direction, if we stopped looking for them, then no one could use us, follow us, trick us, or trap us. Maybe if we went back to being boring citizens, under assumed names, with no one knowing our location, acting utterly oblivious to criminal underbellies, then we would simply *be* normal again. We'd all get what we wanted. Keira and I would get to have lives free from crimes that were thrust upon us. Our parents would get to stay gone, without us being responsible for their cells on death row or their tombstones in the ground. And maybe we wouldn't even have to face them. Maybe that was the kindest thing for everyone. Because if I were being really honest with my darkest thoughts, I wasn't sure my sister and I could look them in the eyes and walk away. They were our *parents*. Back from the dead. If they were alive, betrayal or not, there would always be a part of us hoping for the golden retriever and the picket fence. We'd be hoping for that right up until it got us killed.

I bit my lip as I watched the happily reunited brothers. Antonio was twisting his muscular forearm, displaying a new tattoo near his elbow. Marcus was examining it, dimples flaring. He loved his brother, and I loved that about him; it was how I felt about Keira. (Most days. Some days I still wanted to attack her for using all the hot water.) I wasn't sure I could cut ties with him, if it were even possible. Even if we moved, even if I put an ocean between us, my heart would still be with him. Could I live a life like that?

I pressed at my temples, pulling the skin around my eyes. There was no easy answer. Our parents took away our choices; now they were taking away our friends—Marcus, Charlotte, Julian, Tyson, Regina, and all of Keira's friends back in Boston. We'd lose everyone if we went into hiding.

I stared at the reflections of the passengers in the subway glass across from me, all reading, sleeping, chatting. Mindless. Then my eyes caught on a woman. She was staring at Antonio. When she noticed my gaze, she glanced away, snapping her focus to a book in her lap. Her long blond bangs fell to her high Slovak cheeks, though I could tell she wasn't reading; she kept peering at me from of the corners of her eyes. Then she looked back at Antonio. Given his instant connection with the waitress at the pub, it could have been flirtatious, but something felt off. There was no seduction in her movements—no licking of lips or batting of lashes. Not even a hair flip. Instead, she looked like she knew him, like she was trying to get his attention, only her blue eyes were cold.

I'm reading too much into this. I've been running and chasing and fighting so long, the paranoia has set in. I think every flirty blonde on a train is a secret agent...

I kept staring, glaring at the distinct strawberry birthmark near her forehead, right at the part in her hairline. Despite my gawking, she refused to glance my way. It took effort to ignore someone this much, but she did it. And so did Antonio. He didn't acknowledge our interaction at all, even though my gaze flicked between the two of them. This from a guy who had the waitress showing her cleavage before he even got his second drink last night. He knew exactly how to tell if a woman was flirting, and he reveled in it, but right now, he was focused on Marcus, completely oblivious.

At least, he pretended to be.

Julian's flat looked exactly how one might imagine a billionaire's bachelor pad in London to look: shiny, glass, and modern with décor that would impress the Beckhams. It was located in the South Bank, near the Tate Modern, and its design of crisscrossed red beams up the gleaming exterior intentionally contrasted with the Zen garden in the courtyard in a way that fit the modern-art theme of its neighbors. An added bonus was that many of its residents were foreign, which made the presence of Marcus, Charlotte, and I barely noticeable, except to the doorman. He smiled at me when I returned like there was no one else in the world he'd rather see. (I often bought him Starbucks. Even in England, people enjoy a nice caramel macchiato.)

I stepped onto the terrace, the view featuring the River Thames and almost every skyscraper in London. In fact, the image of Charlotte in her thick wool sweater, sitting with her laptop on an outdoor sofa with blue-gray cushions coordinating with the British sky was so picture perfect that #nofilter was practically spelled out in the clouds. She was surrounded by professionally tended gardens, an enclosed glass porch, and a fully stocked bar with marble counters.

"You're back!" she cheered, jumping up to greet me. Behind her was St. Paul's Cathedral, where Princess Diana was married.

"I am." I glanced around the rooftop. "Where's Keira?"

"Enjoying the steam shower." Charlotte grinned.

"She's not staying here now, is she?" I asked, concerned life had changed in the twenty-four hours I'd been gone. My sister and I insisted on rooming at a hotel. We said it was because we didn't want to inconvenience Julian, but really, we wanted our own space. And we suspected Charlotte and Julian wanted theirs as well.

"No." Charlotte shook her head. "No one's staying here."

"Oh, really?" I raised an eyebrow. "*No one?*"

She instantly blushed.

Charlotte had rented a flat in London, though I doubted she'd seen much of it. She and Julian were joined at the computer. Not only did they track down Keira and me in Amsterdam, after we were living under assumed names provided by the CIA, but they also found Antonio. They kept pretending that their relationship was purely professional, and they thought that since they didn't hold hands around us, we wouldn't notice the little smiles they gave one another, the longing looks, nor the time I caught them walking out of Julian's bedroom while he was tucking in his uncharacteristically wrinkled dress shirt. They'd make terrible spies. But we let them pretend. They seemed to be enjoying their "secret," and I recognized that a lot of their reservations might involve me.

My father ruined Julian's life by helping to orchestrate the fake terror plot that halted his journalistic career and made him a national laughingstock. In return, Julian wanted to use me to expose what my father did to him. It took some effort to trust our benefactor, but now I really did believe Julian wanted to help my sister and me. In a way, we were warped kindred spirits. Julian's father, media mogul Phillip Stone, worked with Department D for decades, and he didn't lift a finger when Julian was targeted by his enemies. Just like my parents didn't help me when Keira was kidnapped, assuming they weren't dead. Still, it was odd to think of him being with Charlotte. After Keira disappeared, Charlotte became my family, my person. I owed her a lot.

Charlotte's fingers flicked over her keyboard, then she lifted her skinny silver laptop from the outdoor sofa and looked at me with eyes tight with worry.

"What is it?" I asked, body tensing.

"It's not bad. *Exactly*," she reassured me, swiping her finger over the mouse pad. "I got something weird yesterday. I haven't shown it to anyone."

Not even Julian? Now, I really was worried.

She showed me her screen, and displayed was a photo of me—with Randolph Urban.

I was about six months old, wearing a pink eyelet dress and a white crochet hat with a rosy flower. I was sitting on his lap. He was smiling, his beard so bushy and white he looked like Santa Claus after a South Beach diet. My tiny fist was reaching for his beard in an adorably sweet gesture, so perfect, the image could have been a Christmas ad for Macy's in the underworld. *"Yes, Anastasia, there is a spy ring…"*

"Where did you get this?" I asked, eyes wide.

"My inbox. It showed up yesterday morning from a junk account. I'm trying to trace it, but so far nothing." She shrugged. "I think we know who it's from."

Urban sent me a baby photo? Why? To manipulate me? To pull at my heartstrings? What did he think I would do? Run off and find him? *Oh, Dad! Forget all about that whole kidnapping thing! I hardly noticed my sister was missing! Let's make another Christmas card together! XOXO!*

"Why would he do this?" I asked, almost rhetorically.

"Because you're his only living child." She tilted her head.

Urban's daughter died not long after giving birth to Sophia. That was why his granddaughter became his universe. Sophia was all he had. Until now.

"No." I shook my head aggressively. "He's *not* my father."

"I don't think he sees it that way. He's clearly reaching out."

"I don't care. It doesn't matter." I backed away from the laptop, which now felt like a dirty bomb.

"Anastasia, the man's gone off the grid, abandoned his home, and his company is all but destroyed, all because he found out your parents might be alive and you might be his daughter." Charlotte green eyes gave me a severe look. "He built up a highly lucrative empire over a lifetime, and lost it because of you. And he's *still* sending you baby pictures."

My mouth clamped shut. In Venice, the CIA Director said I made Urban act erratically. It was why I thought they gave us new passports and fake names, so the government could track us, because they thought eventually not only the parents who raised me, but *Urban's* biological impulses would win out. They believed his narcissistic desire to claim me as his property would supersede his self-preservation instincts. Urban would make a mistake because of me. Turned out, they were right. I wasn't sure how I felt about that. He was sending me baby pictures, at the risk of his own freedom. Meanwhile, my real mom and dad quite possibly walked out and left Keira and me to suffer in the wake of their mess without so much as a glance in return.

Of course, Urban also kidnapped my sister.

"Don't show that to Keira," I warned.

Last thing I needed was to remind her that I was related to the man who abducted her. I didn't want her to question where my heart was. If anything, this was further proof that we needed to leave as soon as possible, before anyone else could twist our emotions—not Urban, not our un-dead parents, and not even Marcus or Charlotte.

"I see the gang's all here," said a voice with a strong British accent. Charlotte snapped her laptop shut and subtly nodded in agreement. Our secret was safe.

Julian stepped through the glass doors of his terrace with Marcus and Antonio in tow.

"I guess everyone's met Antonio?" I nodded to Marcus's brother, trying to sound casual as I shook off my interaction with Charlotte.

"Not yet, but welcome to the party," Keira quipped as she joined us outside. Her hair was still wet from her shower and tied into a dripping bun at the base of her neck, recently dyed back to its natural color—a pale gingerbread, rather than Lady Gaga platinum. She said the roots were "too hard to maintain," but really, I thought she simply wanted to erase everything connected to her time in captivity. It was what we did after our parents' deaths—I chopped my hair while she bleached hers. Since then, I'd let mine grow back, and for a while, it felt nice to see my mother's reflection in the mirror. Now I was itching for the scissors, for more reasons than one.

Antonio turned to Keira, and their eyes met. If I thought he was flirting with the waitress the night before, I hadn't seen him really trying, because the look on his face right now would have made any dad reach for a shotgun.

"I'm Antonio." He extended his hand, his gaze stripping her naked. "*Mucho gusto.*"

"Keira," she replied, grasping his palm. Her posture, which seemed constantly slumped these days, instantly straightened, and her cheeks flushed.

"I've heard a lot about you," he continued, still holding her hand.

"You, too."

"Don't believe it all." He tilted his head seductively, scratching his hipster beard with his eyes brooding and his lips pouting in a way that even had me thinking he looked like a Calvin Klein ad.

Like I didn't already have enough to deal with...

I grabbed my sister's arm. "*Eh hem,*" I interrupted, breaking their eye contact. I hadn't had a chance to tell Keira that Antonio worked for Department D, and I was betting that knowledge might make him look a lot less like Johnny Depp. "The shower at the hotel doesn't work?"

"Julian's is bigger," she replied, her lashes fluttering at Antonio in a way I hadn't seen since Boston. She was even smiling. *Great, the one thing that makes her happy and I'm gonna rip it away...*

"Welcome to my home," Julian said, graciously lifting a bottle of champagne from a silver ice bucket and popping the cork. Charlotte immediately began filling crystal glasses like a hostess.

"While unfortunate circumstances may have brought us together, I'm honored to be in your company," he added as Charlotte handed us each a glass. "Welcome to London. Cheers!" He raised his flute, and everyone took a sip.

The sun was setting, streaking the skyline with blood orange bursts as the damp air grew colder. It was London in November, and we would soon need to take our little reunion inside if we didn't want our teeth to clink louder than the glasses, but for now we enjoyed the champagne bubbling in our chilly hands. I watched as Keira and Antonio glowed with the excitement of having just met, leaning into one another and accidentally touching as they spoke. Keira tossed back her head, laughing.

The longer I wait, the worse this will be.

"Can I speak with you?" I nudged Keira's shoulder.

"About what?" she asked, not looking away from Antonio.

"In private," I insisted.

"After this drink." She sipped her champagne, her entire body looking relaxed for possibly the first time since I'd rescued her in Venice.

We had to leave. Fast. Urban was sending me baby photos. Marcus was twirling my heart, and now Antonio had Keira giggling again. If we didn't get out soon, we never would. We'd stay trapped in a spy world forever. Or worse.

"How about now?" I gripped her elbow and guided her away.

It was time we talked.

CHAPTER FOUR

"What is with you?" Keira asked, tugging her arm from my grip.

We were standing in Julian's enclosed glass porch, with everyone still in view. Including Antonio.

"He's a spy," I said.

"Who?" Her face twisted.

"Antonio. He used to work for Department D. He admitted it."

"What do you mean, *used to*?" She picked at my words.

I did my best to explain Antonio's story, but I could see the doubt in her eyes.

"He wasn't a *spy*? Not really." Keira clung to what she wanted to hear, just like Marcus, just like most people. But being wrong about Antonio wouldn't mean a bad date or unanswered texts. It was life or death.

"He *worked* for Department D, the people who kidnapped you."

"But he didn't have anything to do with what happened to me, did he?"

"No," I admitted. Antonio had confirmed that much at

the pub, and for some reason, I believed him.

"And he said he quit the second he learned about my kidnapping?"

"Well, yes," I continued, not liking her simplistic line of questioning. He was a criminal—that meant run the other way. It didn't matter if he had dimples.

"Then what exactly are you holding against him?" she asked. "You must not think he's so bad if you brought him here."

"I brought him here because of Marcus." I pointed to the terrace.

Antonio was mussing his brother's hair as the two of them laughed in a way that said, "I won't let you get away with anything." Even Marcus's smile looked different around him, brighter, and they whispered a lot, shared a lot of looks. Maybe Marcus would be happier if I wasn't around?

"Antonio doesn't look so bad," said Keira.

"Of course you'd think that." But my irritation wasn't really for her.

"Does it bother you that Marcus is happy?" She raised an eyebrow.

"No," I lied.

Of course it bothered me. We'd spent countless nights lying in hotel rooms post-Venice, discussing the exact face Marcus would make when he wanted to kiss me, how exhilarated I felt when I was on the back of his motorcycle, and how my body seemed to tingle every time he got close. Now, it turned out all those smiles he gave only glimmered halfway; he had a whole different wattage reserved for his family. Maybe I did, too. Maybe I acted differently around Keira. After all, I was about to leave *him*. I was choosing her.

"I've been thinking about this a lot." The image of me sitting on Urban's lap flashed in my brain. He was sending me baby pictures. He was reaching out. And Marcus was pulling away, toward his brother, who worked for the enemy and flirted with my sister. "It's time. We need to leave."

"London?" she asked.

"Everyone."

Keira shook her head. "No, we've talked about this." Actually, we *argued* about this. "We have the CIA; they can protect us."

"Do you really think that's what they're doing?" I grunted. "They're using us to get to Mom and Dad."

"So you admit they're alive?" Keira shot me a look.

My sister was 100 percent convinced our parents would return to us with arms wide open. Maybe it was because she'd been responsible for me for several years, maybe she wanted that weight off her shoulders, or maybe she just wanted all of this to mean something. If we went into hiding, then all of her suffering—months in captivity, years as my guardian, a medical career lost—was for nothing. But if the end of this damaged journey led to a parental loving embrace, then in her eyes, maybe it was worth it.

I didn't share her view. Not just because I had a third parent in the equation, but because I refused to let my hopes lift any higher than the gutter. I was done being blindsided by pain. What I had right now, in front of me, was the sister the world thought was dead. I got *her* back. If protecting that miracle meant walking away, even from Marcus, even from our parents, I was willing to do it. I couldn't lose her again.

"Mom and Dad are either dead or they abandoned us. I'm not sure which is worse," I said bluntly. "But if they are alive, we don't know how many people, how many lunatics, think we're walking maps to their doorsteps. They'll use us, and they'll hurt us. Again."

"Then we'll stop looking for them." She shrugged like it was easy. "Why do we need to go anywhere to do that?"

"Because everyone on that terrace is somehow connected to Department D, Marcus and Antonio especially!" I stared at the gray sky, aggravated. Did she think I *wanted* to do this? I was about to walk away from a guy I cared about because of our parents, because of things that *they* did. *They* committed crimes, *they* had an affair, and *they* put us in danger. All we could do now was survive. "As long as we're linked to them, we're not safe. Especially if Mom and Dad are alive. We have to go off the grid."

Keira kept shaking her head, water droplets splashing from her hair onto my cheek. "You really think we can disappear and never wonder about them, never hope we bump into them, never try to find out the truth?"

"*I* can," I replied honestly. I hoped I never saw any of my parents ever again. But my sister started this mess by asking these very same questions, by ordering a DNA test. Maybe this was her way of admitting she couldn't keep her end of the bargain, even if it meant our lives. "I almost lost you, because you wanted to know the truth. And I'm not blaming you, but Keira, *they're not worth it*. If Mom and Dad are alive, they left us. They hurt us. On purpose. Why should we give them a chance to hurt us anymore?"

"But what if they're in danger? What if that's why we haven't heard from them?" Her voice was small.

"They were criminals. They can handle themselves." My jaw tightened.

I couldn't be expected to worry about the hypothetical safety of the people who did this to us. I had to worry about our own, and the longer we stayed here, the greater the odds that the next communication wouldn't be a photo emailed to Charlotte. It might not even be from Urban. Clearly, the espionage world knew how to get to us. It wasn't safe.

"They're still our parents," Keira stated.

"Try telling *them* that."

Her shoulders slumped at my words, all of the buzz from having spoken to a cute guy gone. She was visibly curling back into herself; it was the same hunched posture she'd sported every day since I found her in Venice, as if the weight of this situation, her entire ordeal, pressed on her every minute of every day. We had to stop this cycle of pain.

"Hey! What are you two talking about so seriously?" Marcus yelled from the terrace, smiling widely. At me.

"*Sí*, get out here!" Antonio waved a glass of champagne at Keira, then threatened to dump it on Marcus's head. They chuckled, dodging one another, each hoisting a menacing glass of bubbles like mischievous boys. Like brothers.

Keira stepped toward the sliding glass doors, glancing over her shoulder. "Are you going to tell them, or should I?"

My stomach rolled. Why did I let myself get so attached? I knew it was going to end. It always did.

I followed Keira out, praying for a meteor so I could put off the conversation. Only before astrological intervention could strike, Keira lifted a silver knife and tapped it against a crystal flute. "Everyone, my sister has an announcement."

Her hazel eyes dared me to reconsider, and she knew forcing me to face Marcus was the only way that might happen. My cheeks flamed with heat.

"*Que?*" Marcus looked at me.

Charlotte strolled over, ears perked.

My gaze flicked between the two of them; the thought of never seeing her or Marcus again was like being told I'd never see my feet again. I needed them. They were essential for moving forward. Charlotte's eyes fixed on mine, and instantly she knew. Maybe she knew the second she showed me that photo.

"It's time." I hid my gaze in the setting sun, away from their faces. "For Keira and me…it's time to go."

I heard Charlotte huff, like she was annoyed at having been right.

"What do you mean? Go where?" Marcus asked, as though he didn't understand, as though the language barrier between us was suddenly heightened.

"I don't know where, just away, from Department D." I was now willing the sunset to blind me, so I wouldn't have to see their expressions.

"I'll go with you," Marcus offered.

When I didn't respond, Charlotte stepped closer.

"I don't think you're invited," she answered for me. I turned toward her, dizzying black spots in my vision from the brilliant glare. "It's true, isn't it? If you want to get away from Department D, you can't lug around a guy whose family still works for the company. Or a girl who hacks their communications, who receives *all their messages*."

She was hinting at the baby photo, but I wasn't leaving because of the photo. This had been my plan for awhile, but Urban reaching out didn't help. "I'm sorry. I just don't see another way for us to get away from the danger."

Tears welled in my eyes. They were all looking at me like after everything they'd done I had the nerve to leave them behind. But it wasn't like that. I wanted to stay, I wanted to be with them, but there was a reason programs like Witness Protection existed: because sometimes disappearing was the only option.

"I understand your position, but might I offer an alternative suggestion?" Julian piped up, and everyone turned his way. "Running off, starting over, it is a viable choice. But so is coming forward."

I rolled my eyes, stifling a groan. I knew exactly what he was going to say. He'd said it before. More than once.

Julian held up a manicured finger, predicting my reaction. "Hear me out," he insisted. "I know you've been resistant in the past, but maybe the time has come. If you tell your story to me, I can protect you, help you perfect your image. I promise I will put your safety first, and believe me, it is not a kindness that will be afforded to you should your story get out through alternative means—"

"What do you mean?" I asked. "Are you saying you'll report on it anyway?" It sounded like a threat.

"No." He shook his head. "I would never publish your story without your permission. I'm too invested, in all of you." He looked at Charlotte as he said this. "But becoming a public figure has its advantages. I should know. Namely, it would be very hard for someone to harm you and for it to go unquestioned. But if you go off on your own, with no identities, no one to look for you, a person could get away with anything."

"He has a point." Charlotte peered at me, begging me to reconsider.

Keira and Marcus's eyes held the same hopeful glare.

"I think it's a good idea," Marcus said. Of course, he agreed with Julian.

"We should at least consider it," Keira added.

But they weren't thinking it through. This plan meant putting our lives entirely in Julian Stone's hands and ignoring a very scary repercussion.

The rest of the world thought my sister was dead. The CIA had convinced us to stay quiet, for the sake of avoiding this exact type of public scrutiny. *Girl back from the dead! Chained to a sink! Photographed in the trunk of a car! News at eleven.* Once Julian came forward with Keira's story, even an edited version, we'd become a *20/20* special that would air in perpetuity, only increasing our chances that some persistent reporter (not Julian) would eventually dig for the facts we left out—like the motive behind my sister's abduction. This would inevitably lead to our parents, which would lead to espionage, which would lead us to being the children of crime lords who might also *not* be dead. What sort of lives would we have after that? We'd publicly be known as the children of Benedict Arnold, and there would be nothing Julian Stone could do to stop that. Both of our options sucked, but at least with mine, we got to suffer without the spotlight.

"We can't." I shook my head, looking at my sister. "You know this. Even if Julian tried to protect us, and I believe you would"—I smiled at him in appreciation—"some other journalist would not. Mom and Dad's lives, their crimes, would come out. Everyone would know our names, our faces, and not in a good way. Every job you applied for, every guy you met would know who you are—or think they know who you are. We'd never be able to trust anyone."

"Like that's so different from now," Antonio quipped, as if this were funny, as if he had a right to an opinion.

Marcus and I both shot him a look.

"*Que?*" Antonio shrugged. "From what I've heard…"

"Don't," Marcus interjected, eyeing him with a warning.

Unspoken words passed between them. Marcus had talked to his brother about me. It made sense. I talked to Keira. But the way Antonio was looking at me, I felt like a girl seeing her name scrawled on a bathroom stall. These weren't romantic dreamy conversations, Marcus complained about me. Suddenly, the two sips of champagne floating in my stomach turned sour.

"I don't know," said Keira, pulling my attention. "I hear what you're saying, but going on the run, constantly looking over our shoulders, doesn't sound much better—"

"If we do what Julian's saying, we can never take it back. We can't undo a globally televised interview," I pointed out, desperate to make her see reason. "We'd have to live forever as the children of terrorists. Do you think anyone's going to want to hang out with me at school? Do you think a parent is going to trust you to care for their sick kid once they read your name on a hospital chart?"

"But we didn't do anything wrong," Keira whined.

"Like that stopped them from kidnapping you!"

"I could frame the story to present you in the most positive light, make sure everyone knows you are completely innocent, the victims in all of this," Julian offered.

"I believe you, Julian," I said, my voice filled with exasperation for having to defend my position. "But you're *one* journalist out of millions. Not to mention, what if our parents *are* alive? If we're in hiding, we can go through it together, quietly. But if we go public, the press, the whole world, will eat us alive."

"We should at least talk this out before you go anywhere," Charlotte insisted.

"No. We shouldn't." I tossed my hands in the air. "I know you all want to offer your opinions. I know you think you have our best interests at heart. I get that. But *my* gut told me that Craig was a psychopath, that Keira was alive, and that I should keep searching for her no matter what." I eyed my sister pointedly. "If I had listened to anyone else's opinion—*anyone else's*—you'd still be chained to a bathroom sink somewhere."

All eyes instantly darted away, mouths shut like the truth was a poisonous fog they refused to breathe. But they couldn't ignore it. This wasn't *their* lives. It was Keira and me. And the last time Keira asked questions about our parents and spoke out, she disappeared from a tub full of blood.

We had to go into hiding to stay safe. I believed that in my heart. It was what the CIA recommended, after all—they gave us new names, new passports, and told us to get lost. Charlotte and Julian infiltrated that plan. Without asking us. And even though I listened to them, then listened to Marcus's fear over his missing brother, I now had to listen to myself.

"Okay, we'll do it your way." Keira grabbed my hand in solidarity. Finally. "We'll leave. You're right." She smiled at me, and in that one gesture, I felt less alone.

Julian nodded once. "All right." He projected his voice like a practiced politician. "This is *your* decision to make. We all know that. So if you need to leave, please know this is not goodbye forever. It is just goodbye for now." He rested a reassuring palm on Charlotte's shoulder, and she leaned into him, physically needing the support. I was leaving her, after everything she'd done, and I knew she'd blame herself, but this wasn't about one picture. It was much more than that. Julian squeezed her arm tighter. "Department D has ruined enough lives. It will not ruin any more. We *will* expose them, I promise you that, and like you said, the choice you're making *can* be undone. You can change your minds, so…" He looked at all of us. "'Til we meet again!"

He raised his champagne flute, and there were a few

halfhearted mumbles of "Cheers," but the toast felt worthier of a wake than a sunset.

Marcus kept his eyes on the patio tiles, his expression grim. I wanted to hug him, kiss him, and take that horrible look off his face, but I'd only make it worse. This was happening.

Antonio shifted toward Keira, and she dropped my hand. They resumed their conversation, smiling and saying good-bye before they really had a chance to say hello. It was better this way, I told myself. The two of them could move on before anything started, before anyone got hurt.

Marcus and I couldn't say the same.

CHAPTER FIVE

A knock on the door at three in the morning is rarely a good thing. My eyes cracked open, my down comforter twisted around my torso as I glanced blearily about my dark hotel room. For a moment, I didn't realize where I was. I'd bounced from city to city, country to country so much in my life that all the beige, generic interiors had become indecipherable.

The knock sounded once more.

London. I'm in London.

I rolled onto my side, sitting up as my eyes swung to the bed beside me. It was empty. Keira wasn't back yet. She already seemed buzzed from champagne when we left Julian's flat, but she insisted on having "one last drink" in the hotel's lobby bar. With Antonio. His criminal past with the organization that kidnapped her didn't seem to be as much a deterrent as I thought it should, but there was no point in fighting. We were leaving London. All of our relationships would be ending soon enough, whether we wanted them to or not.

I yanked open the heavy door, expecting to find my

sister. "Seriously, you better not puke in here," I hissed, squinting as I flicked on the too-bright overhead light, my eyes momentarily blinded by the illumination.

"No. Just tired," said a familiar accented voice.

I rubbed my groggy eyes, peering through the fluorescent blaze at Marcus, who looked as exhausted as I did—eyelids half drooping as he leaned an outstretched arm against the doorjamb for support.

"Where's Keira? What happened?" I jolted, an intravenous shot of adrenaline suddenly coursing through me.

"She's fine." Marcus raised a hand in reassurance. "At least, she's having...*fun.*"

"Where?" Though I already knew the answer.

"In my hotel room. With my brother."

"Oh."

I forced myself not to judge my sister for her fantastically bad taste in men. After all, I'd spent a lot of time worried that my sister might never be her "old self" again. Maybe I could take that worry off my long list.

"Sorry." Marcus shrugged, acting amused, if not proud, of his brother's player status. I didn't feel the same. "But I can't sleep in there for obvious reasons."

"Come in," I offered, reminding myself that Antonio was Marcus's brother. And Marcus trusted him, so nothing bad was going to happen to my sister tonight. I hoped.

He followed me into my room and dropped onto the bed across from me. "Do you have any water?" he groaned, pressing his palm to his forehead.

"Hungover already? You haven't even slept yet."

"My brother ordered shots. Again." He rubbed his temples.

"How many did Keira do?" I sounded like a disapproving mom.

"Less than me. I should have stopped when she did."

My sister voluntarily stopped drinking before the party was over? That was new.

"What was she doing if she wasn't drinking?" I fetched a glass from the bathroom and filled it with cloudy, lukewarm tap water. I returned and handed it to him.

"Grilling my brother about his work at Dresden, or Department D, or wherever." He chugged the water.

I smiled—my sister interrogated Antonio, while he was drunk, or more specifically, while he was drunker than her. Maybe she wasn't her "old self." Maybe she had changed, and in ways that went beyond slumped shoulders. "What did Antonio say?"

"The same thing he told us." Marcus set the empty glass on the nightstand. "He went into more detail about exactly how much he hated his job. He sounded miserable."

"I can't believe your parents recruited him." My eyes narrowed. Why would they want to put their child in danger? "Do you think they'd try to recruit you?"

"No." Marcus shook his head, his bangs dripping into his eyes. I loved when his hair did that. "They hardly talk to me about work."

"Do they know Antonio's here?" My voice sounded casual, but really, I was pressing to learn if he was still in contact with his parents. Maybe if Marcus cut ties, forever, maybe if he broke that thread to Department D, we could possibly stay together, he could come with me, and we could see each other again.

"I sent them a text telling them Antonio's fine. But we're still not speaking."

My head fell. Of course he texted them. He didn't want them to worry. He was their son, and they were alive, and he'd love them forever. He'd choose them. I knew that, even if I didn't *want* to know it.

Our days were numbered.

"How did we get here?" I sighed.

From my parents abandoning us, to me now abandoning Marcus, my life had become a series of events I had no control over. Because if I had a choice, I'd take Marcus's hand and go off to NYU or Duke or Berkeley. We'd go to college, and Keira would go to med school. She'd live with Charlotte, and we'd have apartments next door to one another. We'd all go on double dates and hang out in a coffee shop like they did in *Friends* reruns.

A heaviness gripped my chest as I felt a faint hint of the funk mist over me. I didn't want to say goodbye to him.

My eyes welled, and Marcus noticed; he reached for my hand.

"You don't have to worry about my brother and Keira," he said, misreading my emotion, thinking I was upset because they were together. I was, but that wasn't what had my eyes burning.

"I'm not. And I know you're happy he's here. You obviously talk to him…*a lot.*" I couldn't help but remember the way Antonio joked that I didn't trust anyone, then the look he shared with his brother. I didn't want to see Marcus's face now.

I picked at a loose thread in the comforter. I was leaving, by *my* choice, but it still bothered me that Marcus said something to make Antonio react that way.

Despite the deadly espionage, I was still a girl.

Marcus squeezed my palm tighter. "I told him all about us. How you tripped Wyatt Burns in the cafeteria. How we rode off together after you were hit by a chicken wing—"

"Aw, the good old days…" I mocked. God, that felt like a lifetime ago.

"You've been fearless since the day I met you."

"You're the one who saved *me* from the chicken wing heard 'round the world," I pointed out. "And from Luis Basso in Cortona…"

"Then you saved your sister."

He sat up and tucked a lock of hair behind my ear. He had that boy smell of sweat and leather that made my cheeks burn. Then I spied the bull tattoo on his neck, resembling the ink on his brother's arms. "You told Antonio more than that…" I pulled away.

Marcus ran his hands through his messy locks, his face looking too tired (and drunk) to have this conversation. "I told him that you sometimes have…*trust issues* with new people."

"Everyone is new to me. And you. We've moved around our entire lives."

"But my brother isn't new, not to *me*." He lazily swung his head my way. "I know you think he's a spy, but I *know* him. He never wanted to work there, and he's out now. You don't have to leave because of him."

I wasn't leaving because of him. I was leaving because of *everything*. He couldn't expect me to trust this stranger with my sister's life. There wasn't another person in this world I could trust with that anymore, not even our own parents. *That* was why I was going.

Marcus read my eyes.

"When are you leaving?" he asked, sadly looking up through his lashes. He ran his fingers along my cheek like he was making a mental drawing. Pinpricks covered my skin.

"I don't know." I was lying. My suitcase was already packed. I wanted to check the train schedules for tomorrow before Marcus could use the butterflies in my stomach to change my mind. *God, I want to stay...*

He moved his fingers to my mouth, tugging my bottom lip from my bite, and it was as if every hair on my body lifted upright. I closed my eyes. What if people only got one shot in life to feel this way, and I was running away from it?

"I don't want you to leave," he whispered.

"I know." I wanted so badly to tell him how I felt about him, but the words piled on top of each other at the back of my throat. Any grand gestures now would only make things worse, and the pain was bad enough.

I opened my eyes, and he was staring at me like he wanted to look at nothing else for the rest of his life, like he wanted *me*. I reached for his face, sliding a strand of hair from his eyes, and his breath hitched, eyes darkening. I might never see him again. This could be our last night together.

I lifted my lips to his, slow at first, then his fingers slid into my hair. He groaned, squeezing me tight, and I pushed him back onto the mattress and moved on top. I was wearing an old Red Sox T-shirt and lacrosse shorts, not exactly my best look. Why couldn't I be the type of girl who slept in satin?

My hair tumbled into his face as I kissed him. His mouth tasted like stale red wine.

He moved the hem of my shirt toward my head, throwing Big Papi's number onto the floor. We'd never gotten this far. Venice and Amsterdam were too chaotic, and afterward, we were so focused on finding Antonio that we were never alone, never feeling romantic.

"I'm so glad my brother kicked me out of the room," he whispered.

"Uh huh." I nodded against his lips.

"I've wanted to be with you for *so long*."

There was such longing in his voice that an alarm went off in my head. *Be with me. He wants to be with me...* Did I want that? Could I handle that? Could I really *do* that and never see him again? My face flamed. Was I excited? Was I scared?

This was our last night together.

Our last night.

I'd never see him again.

"Wait." I pulled away, breathing heavily as I looked down at him beneath my body. His lips moved for mine once more, the look in his eyes making it very clear what he wanted to do next. "Hold on."

I sat up straighter, still straddling him as I ran my fingers through my tangled hair, doubt warring within me. I was feeling everything he was feeling, sweating like he was sweating, panting like he was panting, but I was starting to realize there was a big difference between us, one we'd never discussed. "Thing is, um... I mean, like, I've never really, you know, done..." I gave him the look of *please don't make me say it out loud.*

"Ever?" he asked, his eyes wide.

"Boyfriends haven't exactly been my priority," I admitted, staring at a crack in the ceiling. "You can say Keira and I took our parents deaths very differently." I returned my gaze to his. "If I leave, it's just...I don't know if or when I'll see you again. And I don't know how I'm going to feel about that." I lifted myself off of him, sitting beside his long frame as he covered his eyes with his forearm and sighed heavily—with annoyance or disappointment, I wasn't sure.

"Fine. Whatever," he grumbled.

"I'm sorry." I sounded as small as the child I felt like. "I just don't know if it's a good idea, if I know I have to go soon—"

"Mira." He yanked his arm down and glared at me, his eyes angrier than I expected. "You might be able to convince yourself that's the reason, but don't expect me to listen."

"Marcus—" Obviously, I knew he'd be disappointed, but I never thought he'd be mad.

"No. It's true. The reason you're stopping all of this"— he sat up, gesturing to the two of us—"is not because you're leaving or because you're a *virgin*."

An involuntary breath huffed out of me, as if even my lungs were offended. There was something about hearing that word "virgin" aloud that felt like I was being slapped with a sexist insult. Only women were virgins, guys just "haven't done it *yet*."

"You're stopping because you don't trust me." His words slurred around the edges as he spoke faster. "You say you do, but you don't. Not really. You don't trust me when I tell you I know my brother. You don't trust me when I promise not to speak to my parents about you. You don't trust your sister to offer an opinion on when you're leaving or what you should do next. You don't trust Julian to tell your story, even though we *all* think it's a good idea. You don't trust the police to help you. You don't trust the CIA to keep you safe. You don't trust the whole damn world." He pointed a finger at me. "You ran, full speed, toward an assassin in Venice. By yourself. Leaving all of us behind, everyone trying to help you. Those aren't the actions of a girl who's fighting *to live*."

His eyes were still glazed with booze, but his intention was perfectly clear. This was what Marcus had talked to his brother about, what he really thought of me, and this truth hurt more than any punch from a random spy.

My jaw dropped as I stared at him. He thought I was

so screwed up I was incapable of trusting anyone, of loving anyone.

"I'm going to sleep," he hissed, then dropped back onto his pillow and rolled over. Within moments, he was snoring, a drunk deep slumber, and I continued to sit there, gawking at him, wondering if it was true, wondering if I trusted anyone. Even myself.

CHAPTER SIX

The culinary tradition continued. Keira and I were seated in a booth at the Sun in Splendour pub in Notting Hill, which I wasn't positive was the best fish and chips in all of London but possibly the best fish and chips in a neighborhood where Julia Roberts had once filmed a movie. Keira insisted we visit the posh address, which used to be more bohemian back in the days Julia and Hugh Grant pretended to wander the streets. Now every block was so gleaming white that the townhomes didn't look lived in, and there were as many ridiculously priced fashion boutiques as there were quaint bookstores near Portobello Road. But the pubs were still pubs—scratched wooden booths mixed with tin ceilings, crystal chandeliers, and beer stickers papering the walls. In true British style, we ordered our beer-battered fish doused in vinegar with mushy peas that were mashed like potatoes, and a scotch egg that was like a deviled egg only wrapped in Stovetop stuffing. We also had warm beer.

It was the lone family tradition we could cling to. There might not have been ham on Christmas or sausage stuffing on Thanksgiving, but we'd be damned if we didn't try the famous cuisine in every destination we traveled. London would be no exception—even if we were leaving tomorrow.

I leaned back in my rustic wooden chair, staring out the large pub windows, which were so old the glass looked warped and wavy, the panes held together by black mullions. It reminded me of Boston. Of Marcus. Everything reminded me of Marcus. I couldn't stop his words from echoing in my head. I ran after Craig Bernard in Venice, alone. Yes, I could see why some might consider that a death wish, but I got my sister back at the end of it. So didn't that mean I was right? My plan worked.

But that wasn't what was bothering me. It was the other part—the annoyance in Marcus's eyes, the feeling that he'd spent the day complaining about me to his brother, and his insistence that I didn't trust him or anyone else. Of course I trusted Marcus. He was with me every step of the way through Italy—well, except for that Craig Bernard street fight, but that wasn't because I didn't trust him.

Was it? No, of course not.

I could admit to having problems connecting with people—professional psychologists diagnosed me as being "emotionally detached" after my parents "died." That was old news and, frankly, justified. I told my parents I hated them, and then their car burst into flames (or so I thought). I had issues. But Marcus was one of the few people I let in. At least, I thought I did. I was closer to him than I'd been with any guy, or friend, ever. Except for maybe Charlotte. She was right there with Marcus in my very small, but quite existent, circle of trust. How could he doubt that?

Or was he doubting me? Was this how he really felt about me? Or had Antonio put these thoughts in his head? I didn't remember Marcus questioning my feelings before his brother got here. Sure, I might have been the one who made us stop last night, but it wasn't because I *wanted* to stop. I wanted to be with Marcus, but I couldn't seem to shut down the part of my brain dedicated to protecting me at all costs — even from Marcus, even from myself.

I stabbed at my food. Like everything fried, the breading tasted better than the fish, kind of like KFC. Pubs really should just serve breading on a plate with a side of vinegar; give the people what they want. I glanced around aimlessly, my eyes landing on a gas light outside, and I found myself wondering if it was really burning gas in its old-fashioned black frame, or if the city had replaced all its antiques with LEDs. Was anything real anymore?

"Should I ask where your mind is at or just let you brood silently?" Keira questioned, as she sliced open her breaded egg.

I hadn't told her about Marcus. It was as if repeating his words would make his accusations real or more embarrassing. Especially after she'd spent the night with Antonio probably without a second thought. Despite everything that happened to her, months of captivity orchestrated by a man she thought was her boyfriend, she could still hook up with a guy who worked for Department D. It made no sense. Sometimes, I felt my sister and I understood one another in ways no one else ever possibly could, while at other times, I worried we didn't share a common thought.

"I'm going to miss everyone, that's all." My voice cracked, the force of Marcus's words trying to break out.

"You know, we don't have to go, not alone at least." Keira dug her fork into a lumpy mound of mashed peas that only tasted good if you doused it with vinegar, but at least the sour smell was appropriate for the conversation.

"Maybe we could *all* walk away from this together?"

"Their parents work there."

"They're not speaking to their parents."

"Marcus texted them yesterday." I dropped my fork, frustrated. "Keira, do you really think I want to leave Marcus? Of course I don't. But all of you ganging up on me isn't helping."

"We're not ganging up on you."

"Yes, you are. Everyone is. You're acting like I'm forcing this unreasonable decision. Marcus said it last night. He thinks that I can't trust anyone, that I don't listen to anyone. But we don't have another option!" I sat back with a huff. "Even if you put Marcus and Antonio's parents aside, think about this—what if Mom and Dad *are* alive? We could be putting everyone we know in danger just by being near them. Who knows how many enemies they have and who those enemies might try to kidnap next?"

"They had those enemies *before* the accident, and that didn't change anything," Keira retorted.

"*Didn't change anything?*" I squawked. "Mom and Dad were either killed because of those enemies or they faked their own deaths. I'd say that changed *a lot*. There are countless people trying to use us to get to them—the CIA, Department D, Randolph Urban, and who knows who else—and the only way to get all of them off our backs is to make sure they *can't find us*. We can't do that while living with two brothers whose parents play golf with the kingpin, while drinking champagne in a penthouse of a guy who wants to put our faces on the evening news."

"Do you really think Randolph Urban is ever going to stop looking for *you*?"

She didn't know about the baby picture. No one did, aside from Charlotte. I wasn't sure why I was keeping it a secret. If I spoke up, Keira might understand why I was so determined to leave right now, why I thought the danger was getting too close. But then I'd also have to talk about what that photo meant, about him possibly wanting to be a dad and how that made me feel. I'd sooner get on a train.

"He can look all he wants. He won't find us." I stared at my food.

"He's a spy. No, actually, he's like the king of the spies. And you're his..." She let her voice trail off.

Daughter. I was his daughter. That was the word she couldn't bring herself to say.

It wasn't that I was in denial. I knew I would have to face him eventually, but I was hoping that day would be far in the future when he wore an orange jumpsuit with a pane of glass between us. Not today. And not through a constant *drip, drip, drip* of memories.

"Urban has bigger problems to focus on right now than me." I kept the truth about the photo for later, when we were safe and countries away. *When our problems are over.* I tore my paper napkin in half. *We'll admit to everything.* I ripped it again. *When we're alone, away from everyone, all by ourselves.* I tore it again, and again, shredding the napkin until I had a fluffy pile on my plate.

"Look, I don't know what happened between you and Marcus last night, what he said to get you this upset." Keira stretched her hand across the table and swept the paper shreds away. "But I know you trust him and me and Charlotte. You're not broken, Anastasia, any more than I am." She hesitated, taking a deep breath before her next words came out. "But Urban *is* your father. You can't run from that."

My eyes shot up. *Did Charlotte tell her? Does she know about the photo?* I searched her gaze for some hint of the truth, but I wasn't sure. We'd become too skilled at lying to one another.

"I swear. This is about doing what's smart, for us, and that means getting as far as away from Department D as possible. Let's move on." I clapped my hands, sharp, trying to force a smile and shift the energy of the conversation. "There's an upside to all of this. Tomorrow we'll be someplace new. We'll get new jobs, make new friends, meet new people. We'll start over."

"We're always starting over." Keira sighed, wiping her greasy hands on her jeans. "Are you still thinking France?"

"Yeah, we can choose a town together, and we both speak French. The people hate Americans, so they're not going to ask too many questions. It's perfect." This was the fantasy life I'd wanted to have with my sister ever since she went missing—me and her, together, somewhere new, safe and normal.

"*Anastasia!*" The call came from behind me.

I turned toward the pub doors and spied Charlotte aglow in the amber light of a wall sconce, her golden green eyes stretched wide.

Something was wrong. Department D. Urban. They found us. Found me. I jumped to my feet, rising so fast that I nearly toppled my wooden chair to its side.

We should have left sooner. Why did I wait? Why did I listen to them?

"What happened? Where are they? What's going on?" Fear clenched my throat as my eyes darted around the pub for assassins.

Keira rose beside me, her gaze locked on me like she'd never seen me before.

"It's not them," Charlotte insisted, ringing her hands together, tears in her eyes. "It's…it's Tyson."

Tyson? My karate buddy? What does he have to do with anything? He was back in Boston, at Brookline Academy, eating lunch in the cafeteria with Regina or practicing roundhouses in our old studio. What could possibly be wrong with Tyson?

"I'm...*I'm so sorry.*" Charlotte's voice cracked, her face morphing into a familiar look of pity.

No. Absolutely not. I shook my head, hair whipping back and forth, trying to block out whatever she was going to say next.

I knew that look. I'd lived with that look for years.

I can't possibly be having this conversation again.

I closed my eyes, the acidic stench of fried fish suddenly everywhere. My whole life I'd been standing on a cliff waiting for the next push, and it always came.

Finally, I opened my eyes.

"I just heard from Regina, in Boston," Charlotte continued when I looked her way. "She called my parents and got my number here. She was trying to find you. My parents are still your legal guardians, you know, so she figured they could get in touch with you..."

She was rambling, doing her best to stall, and I understood. No one wanted to deliver this news. Only I'd sadly become an expert at receiving it.

"Just say it," I said, giving her permission to inflict the pain, my fingernails digging into my palms so hard I felt my flesh give way.

"It's...it's Tyson," she repeated, sucking her lips and tilting her head in sympathy, eyes pooling with thick puddles. When she swallowed, a visible lump traveled down her throat. "He's...he's dead."

CHAPTER SEVEN

I held it together at the pub, for the sake of Charlotte and Keira. I didn't want to worry them. Quietly, I climbed into the spacious interior of a charming British taxi, one of those black hatchbacks with a bulbous shape and rounded silver grill. All it needed was a British flag on its antenna and it would have been perfect for a postcard. That was where I was as I was hit with the details of my best friend's death — riding in a postcard.

I sat on my hands to hide the shaking. I pretended that I didn't hear my bed calling through the rainy London sky, begging me to collapse, inviting me to lay down, stay down, let go. I could hear Tyson's name mentioned again and again, by Charlotte, by Keira. I could picture his face.

We got back to the hotel, and I sprinted to my room, shouting promises that I was okay and that I'd meet them in the lobby for breakfast in the morning. We needed to discuss next steps, they said. We needed to decide what to do. I kept nodding, saying I agreed, saying we'd all sleep on it and discuss it in morning. Then I closed my hotel room door and clicked the heavy deadbolt. That was when the first tear dropped. They didn't stop. I stumbled to my bed, collapsing, soaking my pillow, my entire body convulsing. *Tyson's gone. Tyson's dead. Tyson. The boy with the huge smile, the kid I sparred with in karate, the boy who let me sit with him and his girlfriend in the cafeteria, the kid whose father was dead and who could actually relate to what I was feeling. He was my first friend in Boston, my first real friend* ever. *Now he's dead. Everyone I love is dead. Why does this keep happening?*

Several knocks pounded on my door. I didn't answer, not when it was Marcus or Charlotte or Keira. Tomorrow, I would pull myself together; I would do all the things they needed me to do. I'd talk strategy and make decisions. But tonight, I stayed in bed. I wasn't strong or brave or rational. I was a seventeen-year-old girl whose best friend was dead, and I wanted to be alone.

When the sun came up, I climbed out of bed without a blink of sleep and turned the shower all the way to cold. I stepped behind the ivory plastic curtain, eyes wide from the shock of ice pelting my skin as I washed off the funk, freezing any remaining tears inside of me, jolting my system awake. I stepped out shivering, not using a towel, letting the goose bumps take over. Then I tied my wet hair in a bun, got dressed, and went downstairs to meet my friends.

We argued for hours. Everyone had ideas, theories. Tyson's death was a homicide, a mugging gone wrong. It was in all the Boston newspapers. Charlotte had articles on her tablet. The demented part? I wanted this to be true—I wanted my best friend's murder to be a senseless act of violence, another crime statistic, just like his father. Because if it wasn't arbitrary, that meant he may have died because of *me*, because he was connected to my family. We couldn't ignore the alarming coincidence.

Only that possibility made me want to willingly wave the funk in like an old friend, so we instead focused on the immediate issue—Tyson's funeral.

I wanted to go, and practically everyone down to our waiter had an opinion. None of them mattered. Tyson was my best friend, and I was not going to ignore his death. I would say goodbye, and I would make sure my absence didn't cause Regina any more pain. I may have abandoned them with a text message, but at one point we were the three outcast musketeers; now her first love was gone. I could only imagine how lonely Regina felt, and I was going to be there to support her, to honor the last friendship, the last tie I had to my old life, my normal life. Because the truth was, I missed being the person I was when I was their friend. I had to say goodbye to that. Not to mention, if Charlotte and I didn't leave our supposed European finding-ourselves expedition for a friend's funeral, we'd not only look heartless, but suspicious. That led to us deciding to attend the funeral together.

Keira freaked. She wanted to come, obviously, but the entire world thought she was dead—Charlotte's parents included. She couldn't pop up at a funeral with an "I'm alive!" banner and a Welcome Back to Life party. So Marcus insisted *he* come. He'd attended Brookline Academy, his presence at the funeral wouldn't seem out of place, and he'd add an extra layer of protection in case any mysterious enemy was lurking in the wings. On the surface, the idea was solid, and I desperately wanted his hand to hold through this, but ultimately, we decided that placing me, Charlotte, and Marcus in the same building, steps away from Dresden's headquarters (from Department D's headquarters), was dangerous, not only for us but for everyone paying their respects. Even Julian agreed.

Besides, my greatest fear wasn't a spy jumping out of a church pew and attacking me in front of an open casket; it was Keira being kidnapped (or harmed in any way) while she and I were separated. I had a hard enough time being away from her for one night while at the Guy Fawkes festival. So I pleaded with Marcus to stay behind and protect my sister. If Tyson's death wasn't accidental, if it was some horrific Department D plan meant to separate us, then Keira couldn't be left alone.

Eventually, everyone agreed, and Charlotte and I boarded a plane for Boston. We landed at Logan Airport, and we went straight to her parents' house. It only took minutes for me to realize I didn't have the Academy Award acting prowess to deal with the Conners. They thought my parents, my sister, and my best friend were all dead, and they were gawking at me like I was a leper missing a foot who'd just been diagnosed with AIDS. I couldn't tell them the truth, so I bolted out of the house to meet Regina. The funeral was tomorrow, and I needed to hear everything in person—exactly what happened and how. Then I wanted to hug her before all of the fake hugs she was about to receive. I wanted her to know that I understood, *really* understood, more than most. More than anyone. I wanted her to know I was still me.

I sipped my cinnamon cappuccino, my eyes on the café's entrance as I waited for Regina in a coffee shop. A flash of daylight shone as the glass doors opened, illuminating the rustic brick-walled café as my friend walked in. Her shiny, stick-straight black hair was unexpectedly short, cropped from her waist all the way to the nape of her neck, angling down toward her chin. And she had bangs. She looked completely different, cute but different. Had I walked past her on a street, I might not have recognized her.

I stood from my cushy rust-colored chair and waved halfheartedly. When she saw me, her eyes widened, as if she were surprised I'd actually shown.

"You look different," she said, approaching the wood table, stealing my words. I instantly hugged her, but she didn't hug back. Her arms hung limply.

"I was going to say the same to you." I pulled away, awkwardly creating space between us. Mentally, I understood why she didn't want to be held, but it still made the air around us colder. "I like the bangs." I tried to smile.

"Thanks. So did Tyson." She brushed them to the side.

"Regina, I'm *so* sorry."

We both plopped into wingback velvet chairs, befitting an urban hipster café, surrounded by BU students absorbed in their laptops. It was nearly Thanksgiving break, and the large college campus had the buzz of midterms, the feeling that everything was rushed, stressed, and vital. We were the only patrons in the coffeehouse without schoolwork on our table.

"How did this happen?" I asked when she didn't speak.

Regina closed her eyes, wincing like the act of inhaling oxygen caused her pain. *Ugh.* I had never been on this side of the conversation, watching someone relive the anguish. Usually it was me, my tragedy, my agony. And while I felt the hollow ache of Tyson's death, he wasn't my first love.

"I was there," she started. "I watched him die. I held him…to the end."

The audible sound that escaped my chest caught her attention. I hadn't known. Not for sure. The news articles said that Tyson was mugged downtown with "a friend," but there was no mention of a name because the "friend" was a minor. Since Regina hadn't said anything to Charlotte's parents, nor to me when I called to set up the coffee date,

I'd hoped it wasn't her.

I reached for her hand across the table, but she pulled away, crossing her arms as she leaned back on her burnt orange cushion. I remembered not letting Marcus touch me after Keira's disappearance, and for the first time, I realized what that rejection felt like, how hard it was to want to be there for someone who didn't want you to be there.

"Things got bad after you left. Tyson's mom fell apart. I don't know what started it, but she was drinking all the time, like vodka for breakfast. Tyson would run around the apartment throwing out bottles, but she'd always find a new spot—lampshades, toilet tanks." She shook her head, anger creasing her face. "Obviously, she got fired from work. They had no money. Their electricity was turned off, then their water. Tyson was working at the store as much as he could, skipping school to work extra shifts, trying to make ends meet. His grades tanked, of course. He was put on academic probation. Still, they didn't have enough money. They were getting evicted."

She glared, eyebrow cocked as if daring me to say I cared. In a way, she was right—I wasn't around. I'd been consumed with the horror that was my life, and I never stopped to think about the friends I'd left behind. But it wasn't because I was heartless; it was because I was a little busy saving my sister's life.

"You have to understand, every penny Tyson made meant food on the table, time spent out of school, and rent to keep them from living *in a car*." She spat the words with a hatred I didn't know she was capable of, then she squeezed her dainty hands into fists and tucked them below her armpits. She looked like she was barely containing the urge to throw punches at everyone within reach. "We had gone to a free concert at Government Center, and when we were walking back to the T, this guy came out of nowhere. He asked us to hand over our money, just like that. But he didn't have a gun or anything. He thought we would simply give him our wallets, because he asked in a scary voice. Obviously, we should have. I know that. Everyone knows that. But Tyson refused." She closed her eyes, and I knew she wanted to erase that memory like an Etch-a-Sketch, shake and start all over with a fresh picture. Unfortunately, it didn't work that way.

"The guy reached for Tyson, like he was going to grab his arm or find his wallet himself, I don't know." She looked up at the funky lights hanging from the ceiling, crafted out of old car parts, her brain clearly replaying the scene. "Tyson reacted, like on autopilot. Suddenly, there were kicks and fists everywhere. It was crazy." I could picture it. Tyson and I both had double black belts in karate, only he was over six feet tall and built like a wide receiver. His size and reflexes were impressive. "Everything happened so fast, and at first, I thought he was winning. Tyson looked so strong, so in control, and I stood there watching in awe. I didn't move. I didn't scream. I didn't call 911. I didn't take a video. *I. Did. Nothing.*"

"You froze. That's normal," I offered sympathetically, but her eyes turned deadly, and I instantly regretted my words.

"What do you know about it?" she spat.

I suddenly felt sympathy for every person who said the wrong thing to me after my parents died, after Keira disappeared. Nothing about this was *normal*. I hated seeing Regina living through the torturous drip of what-ifs. I wanted to lift some of the agony off of her.

I exhaled slowly, not wanting to make things worse. "You're right. I wasn't there. But I also wasn't there for my sister when she was attacked, so I know what it feels like to be helpless and full of regret."

Regina met my eyes, her teeth gritted, tears clinging to her lashes, and her gaze harsh. For the first time, I realized she wasn't merely angry at the world, she was angry at *me*. She was wondering what would have happened if I had been there. Because a year ago, I would have gone with them to that concert, I would have been on that walk back to the T, and it would have been two black belts against one mugger.

Finally, she grunted and glanced away. "I had never seen Tyson fight before, not like that, not for real. And I thought it would be over quickly. I thought he would win. I mean, I understood why he didn't want to hand over his wallet. He couldn't. It was all he had. His life was shit. He was so stressed out, and at one point, I was worried Tyson was going to kill *him*. I never saw the knife. I guess Tyson didn't, either. One second, he was throwing an elbow at the guy's jaw, and the next Tyson was dropping to the ground, real slowly, like he'd just decided to sit down. I didn't see the blood at first, and his face looked so confused." She paused, her big brown eyes clearly still seeing the image that haunted her. "The guy ran away, and I went to Tyson and saw the knife sticking out of his stomach. He never had a chance to say anything, not a word, but his eyes were open all the way to the end. I held him until he stopped breathing…"

Her voice trailed off, and I involuntarily reached for her hand again, my mind reliving the moments I spent diving into a tub of my sister's boiling hot blood. It was a pain I'd wish on no one, yet here I was witnessing that same anguish on the face of one of my best friends. Only her pain was final. Tyson really was gone.

"People are gonna try to come up with the right words to say tomorrow, but there are none," I said as she finally let me hold her palm. Her nails were painted black. I never remembered her painting her nails before. "What you went through, what you're going through, defies words. No amount of flowers or 'I'm sorrys' is gonna change that."

She nodded, saying nothing.

"Are the cops helping? Are there any leads?"

I'd read online that no arrest had been made, and the prospect of finding my sister's attacker had been the only thing that snapped me out of my funk. Regina needed that.

Rage returned to her face. "They said the knife to Tyson's abdomen was so precise it severed a major artery. If it had been a few millimeters either way, he probably would have lived. But he bled out before the ambulance arrived. It was like the guy knew exactly where to stab him."

She held my stare, and I could sense an undercurrent in her words, like the wound was too surgically exact, like she didn't think a random street thug could get so lucky. Fear cut through me, and I shivered, imagining assassins.

"Do they have any suspects?" my voice shook. The thought that I could be connected to this made my stomach feel wrung out to dry. *Please don't let this have anything to do with me...*

"There were no cameras in the alley. They got prints off the knife, but they're not in any database. I tried to give them a description, but it was so dark and everything happened so fast... I'm pathetic." Her forehead crinkled with frustration. "You see all these shows, all those what-would-you-do type things, and I did *nothing* to help him."

"This isn't your fault," I insisted.

"No," she snipped, her eyes ice-cold. "But it was definitely *someone's* fault. Why am I even here right now?"

I'd expected the grief, I felt that myself, but the resentment and rage steaming off of Regina like body heat had me worried about what she might be capable of, what she might do next.

"Regina, are you talking to someone?" I asked, despite how much I despised when people asked me this exact question. I was a hypocrite, but I knew I'd hate myself more if Regina hurt herself.

"You mean a shrink?" she scoffed.

"I know it sounds ridiculous, believe me *I know*, but if you think it might help…"

"That is definitely *not* what will help me." She cleared her voice and straightened her posture like she was ready to move on. "So how was your trip?" The look in her eyes suggested she didn't really want to hear about my adventures in Europe, like the fact that I might be having fun offended her. *If she only knew…*

"It's been hard," I admitted, trying to squash the conversation.

"You still grieving?"

"Of course," I lied, sipping my cappuccino to hide my fake expression. My sister was currently in a hotel room in London, and my parents were rumored to be hiding in an evil lair somewhere, but I couldn't exactly say that.

"So it's just you and Charlotte over there, traveling around?" Her voice sounded suspicious, and I wasn't sure how to react. Was I being paranoid? Was I too accustomed to hidden sinister meanings?

I tried to stick to the facts, my mind flicking through the honest tidbits I could share. "Yeah, I've been taking online courses. Art History and stuff. I should be able to get an online diploma. Charlotte's parents have been really understanding."

"Uh huh." She nodded, glaring like she didn't believe me. "Well, then, tell me a story, get my mind off everything. What's something cool you've done over there?"

Saved my sister from crime lords. Fought assassins. Researched my criminal family. Learned my parents might be alive. Oh, and my dad's not my dad...

"We spent a lot of time in Italy. Lately, we've been in London," I replied.

"Wow, that sounds awesome—traveling the world, not caring about anyone. Maybe I should do that."

"It wasn't *awesome*, believe me." My eyes stretched to emphasize exactly how legit that statement was. She might have been sensing guilt oozing off of me, but it wasn't because of how much partying I was doing. "Regina, what you have here, your family, it's rare. They love you, all three million of your Filipino relatives. I'm guessing they're already at your house, fighting over who gets to be there for you the most." She was the only person I knew whose parents had been married for more than thirty years, she was drowning in loving siblings, and her entire extended family lived within a thirty-minute drive. Sunday dinners were all-you-can-eat buffets, so I could only imagine how many wagons had circled at the Villanueva residence.

"They don't know *how* to help me. They're just making themselves feel better, saying rosaries 'round the clock and dedicating Catholic masses. It means nothing—to me or Tyson—and it's definitely not gonna change anything." Her jaw twitched.

I sat back in my velvet chair and yanked out the only tactic I had left, the one I'd planned with Charlotte on the plane, the best advice I could give a grieving person who didn't believe in Heaven or anything beyond a big dark void.

"Did you know it's scientifically proven that after you die, your energy remains?" I recited the atheist grief blog Charlotte had found. "It's called the Law of Conservation of Energy, and it says energy can neither be created nor destroyed. So Tyson's body heat, his actual vibrations, and particle waves, haven't gone anywhere. It's been measured by physicists, before and after someone dies. It means all of the energy that made up Tyson, every bit of it, is still here, on Earth, all around you. You can feel him. Literally. It's proven by science."

Regina looked at me, her big brown eyes softening for the first time, her jaw relaxing as she considered my words. Everything about her seemed to ease. "Thank you for that."

I exhaled with relief as I finally caught a glimpse of my old friend. She was in there somewhere, but she needed time to find her way out of the funk.

We were burying our friend tomorrow.

CHAPTER EIGHT

There were as many eyes staring at me at the funeral as there were staring at the red oak casket in front of the altar. It seemed every student at Brookline Academy attended, even most of the teachers and administrators. It was like my high school reunion, only I was still in high school. Technically.

The service was being held in a massive, historic Episcopal church on Tremont Street. The sweeping gilded altar was surrounded by so many colorful frescos and stained-glass windows that I felt I'd been magically transported back to European soil. Maybe they weren't as ancient, but it seemed American cathedrals could still be impressive.

I sat in a carved walnut pew in the rear of the church. Regina and her enormous Filipino Catholic family encompassed several rows in front. Tyson's mother was in the first pew. It was painful to watch her hobble down the aisle, doubled over and sobbing, her somber black dress wrinkled and sagging like a child playing dress up. She appeared to be hemorrhaging weight; her cheeks

were too sharp and her eyes sunken as if her chocolate
skin had dissolved into a thin layer of tissue that was now
slipping from her bones. A man, who I recognized to be her
brother, Tyson's Uncle Donovan, was physically supporting
her weight. She was the grieving mother, the surviving
member who warranted sympathy, yet I had to wonder if
she was sober right now. I had to wonder if she felt guilty.
Responsible.

Charlotte sat beside me. The scene was all too reminiscent of Keira's memorial, my parents' memorial. We were
doing this again. Beside Charlotte were her parents—my
legal family. Recently, they'd helped me sell my family's
brownstone. They even worked with a contractor to demol-
ish the master bathroom and the ominous claw-foot tub
before it went on the market. The last place I lived with my
family sold in less than a week. I told them the money would
be used to pay for college. Really, I planned to use it to run
away with Keira. I wasn't sure what our plans were now.

The pastor finished his remarks, commenting on Tyson's
"love of life," his "courage" after the loss of his father, his
"unyielding dedication to his mother," and his "bravery"
as he protected Regina from a violent mugger. While this
was all true, it was also oversimplified. Tyson wasn't given
a choice in forming those characteristics. His father was
murdered, much like his son, on a street in Boston. His
mother fell apart and never put the pieces back together.
Tyson became the head of his household at the age of
ten, and by seventeen, he was caring for an alcoholic
parent and financially supporting her by working at a
convenience store. Given a choice, he would have been a
reckless, carefree teenager playing too many video games
and worrying if he could afford a tux for prom. But that
wasn't an option for him.

Or me.

Regina stepped up to the podium, her hands visibly shaking as she held a tablet.

"I can't believe she's speaking," Charlotte whispered in my ear.

Neither could I. Regina hadn't mentioned giving a eulogy when we'd met yesterday, and she didn't look to be in an emotional place to comfort anyone. But she was his closest friend and his biggest love, and Tyson would want to hear what she had to say. Maybe this would help her.

"Thank you for coming," Regina said into the microphone at the podium, her voice a whisper, yet still amplified beneath the sloping arched ceilings. "It's so remarkable to look out and see all of these faces. Principal Jaworski, teachers, classmates. You all came...*for Tyson Westbrook's funeral.*" The tone of her voice made me uncomfortable. I could almost feel the rage from last night simmering under the surface. "Not many of you knew Tyson, not many of you spoke to him. Not even his teachers. Not really. No one asked why he was missing so much school lately. No one asked what was wrong at home." She looked at his mother, who sluggishly lifted her head, as if Regina's words were just now cutting through her inebriated fog.

"Tyson was another black kid failing out of school, failing to make friends, failing at life. But you all showed up today to *pay your respects.* If only that respect had been there for him while he was alive." A murmur started to grow among the crowd, collective whispers of, *"Did she just say that?"*

"Make no mistake, Tyson's death is a tragedy, but it was a *preventable* tragedy. The failure here wasn't from the kid who worked forty hours a week to keep a roof over his head on top of going to high school, yet who still got put on probation when he couldn't miraculously get all of his homework done fast enough. The failure wasn't from the son who took care of his mother, who cleaned up her puke every day since his father died, every day since he was ten years old, completely ignoring his own grief. The failure wasn't from the friend who desperately worried about the girl cloaked in tragedy, the one who ran away and who we probably never really knew." I stiffened in my pew, blinking in shock as her words reached in and pulled a chunk out of my soul. My hands quivered. I knew she was angry with me for leaving, I could sense it last night, but to hear her announce her rage from a podium at a funeral for our friend added a new layer of humiliation and grief. Charlotte gripped my thigh, squeezing in consolation.

"The failure was from a bunch of people, an entire community, a school administration, his own family, who didn't care enough to ask 'what can we do to help *you,* a kid, get through the day? How can we put *your* needs first for once? How can we make sure you don't become so desperate, so alone, that you'd die for the thirty-seven dollars in your wallet?'" She spat out the words as she glared heatedly at his mother, who appeared so stunned she'd actually stopped sobbing. "I don't believe in God. I don't believe in Heaven. I don't believe Tyson is floating on a cloud somewhere in a 'better place.' But I do believe the love he and I shared was real. It may be the only real thing in this room. And if that's true, then at least I was able to give him that during his way-too-short time on this Earth. I was able to give Tyson something real. And I hope it was enough for him. But it definitely wasn't enough for me."

Regina looked up from her tablet, observing the sea of open mouths in the chapel, and her face stayed blank. She turned to Tyson's casket, rested her hand briefly on the shiny wood, then marched out a side exit near the altar. She didn't look back.

"Can't say I've ever seen someone drop a mike at a funeral before," Charlotte said as we stood outside of the church. Its towering exterior with pitched roof turrets and rows of slender stained-glass windows almost looked reminiscent of Notre Dame Cathedral in Paris. In a different life, I was in France right now with my sister, starting over. In this one, I was burying another person I loved.

I shivered in the shadow of the structure. It felt like such a massive place to mark the end of such a short life. Cars honked on the busy street as city buses whizzed by, only not loud enough to submerge the nearby conversations.

How could she say that? At a funeral? His poor mother. She's in bad shape. And to accuse us! *Who the hell does Regina think she is?*

Sadly, I knew the answer from experience: She was someone who loved that boy so deeply and then had to put his body in the ground. There's only one way to feel about that.

"She's pissed," I said in her defense.

"You think? If someone recorded that In Memorium screw you, it would go viral," said Charlotte.

"Let's hope cell phone usage at a funeral would exceed anyone's standard of bad taste."

"In this group? Who knows?" Charlotte glanced around at my classmates as I squeezed the tense muscles in my neck. Regina blamed me. She knew I was lying. I wasn't sure how much she knew, but I could see it in her eyes yesterday, and I could hear her accusations ringing in my head with the church bells. *You never cared about us!* Bong!

You never looked back! Bong! *You're a liar!* Bong! *We never knew you!* Bong, bong, bong!

"You okay?" Charlotte peered at me, her tone sounding more nervous than sympathetic.

"I deserved it," I said.

"No. You absolutely did not." She grabbed my forearm like she could squeeze her point of view into me.

"I ran away. I left them with a two-line text message."

"Because your sister was, you know…" Charlotte didn't want to finish her sentence in a crowd of gossipers or Keira's survival would be trending online within minutes.

"I know, but still. It's true. They don't know me. And I *am* lying to her. She can feel it."

"All she feels is grief."

"Tyson died for thirty-seven dollars." That reality blackened the last minuscule piece inside of me that still wanted to believe in hope and kittens. How could his life be worth so little?

"It's horrible. It's unfair. It's completely messed up, but so is what happened to you and Keira." Charlotte's voice was thick with sadness. "You can't save everybody. And if Regina knew what really happened, what you've been going through, she never would have said those things. Besides, I don't remember her or Tyson banging down your door when Keira disappeared."

This was true. Tyson and Regina both avoided me after my sister's memorial, as if my tragedy was not only devastating but awkward. They didn't know what to say, how to be there for me, so they simply weren't. I understood that better now that I was on the other side, and it made me appreciate the people who were there for me—like Charlotte.

I stared at the white puffy clouds overhead. It would

be nice to believe Tyson was floating around up there somewhere, but unfortunately, I agreed with Regina. Endings were never that clean and sparkly. I turned my head and spied Tyson's uncle guiding Mrs. Westbrook into a black stretch limo. She was blamed for her son's death in front of a church full of people. If she wasn't on the brink of an overdose before, she might be now.

"I hope someone's staying with her." I imagined how worried Tyson would be. "She shouldn't be left alone."

"It's hard to feel sorry for her given everything," Charlotte whispered in my ear so low even the pigeons couldn't hear. "It's terrible to say, but it's true."

"I know. When it comes to parents, Tyson and I pulled some shitty cards."

Being in Boston had me thinking of my mom and dad a lot. It had me thinking of Randolph Urban. It had me imagining all of those unwitting "family" get-togethers now warped by funhouse mirrors—twisted and stretched in ways that were hard to look at or even recognize.

"We should head home. I don't think the post-funeral brunch will be highly attended." Charlotte nodded to her parents, who were waiting in the car to avoid the cold November air of New England. After insisting I "didn't deserve that" and asking several times if I was okay, Charlotte's parents released a diatribe on why Catholics rarely give eulogies. Instead, their people stuck to a historic script, and maybe this was why. Grieving people shouldn't be given microphones.

"Sorry, I don't think I can go back to your house yet." I gave her a *don't hate me* look. I didn't want to insult her family, but her home required us to maintain a constant stream of lies that was not only exhausting but very guilt-inducing. Regina had already seen through me, seen something. How long before Charlotte's parents did, too?

"Okay, but I wouldn't stand around here too long. You're turning into a sideshow." Charlotte gestured to my former classmates huddled and whispering in the granite courtyard, their eyes on me. I was "the girl cloaked in tragedy," as Regina said, and it was so true I might as well have it tattooed on my lower back.

"I still can't believe they came," I grumbled, agreeing with Regina. She, Tyson, and I had been exiled by these peers years ago, too poor, too brown, and too depressing to be worthy of their time. Now, they showed up acting all grief-stricken and concerned. It was as fake as a reality show.

"The funeral details were posted online."

"Of course they were. This is probably the social event of the fall season."

Charlotte's green eyes pulled wide as a cough rose up from behind me.

"*Ahem.*"

I shifted to see Julianna Gold, a girl from my ninth grade English class. A pack of her fellow field hockey players, and their equally athletic boyfriends, stood beside her. Among them was Wyatt Burns, the boy who gave me a wonderful send off to Europe by way of a chicken wing to the forehead after my sister disappeared. It was so nice to catch up.

"I just wanted to say I'm sorry." Julianna tilted her head in sympathy as she looked at me, her blond hair dripping to her elbows, perfectly straightened. "I know Tyson was a good friend of yours."

I glanced at our classmates, all listening, and waited for the punch line. None came.

"Um, thanks," I said in a hesitant tone.

"And I'm sorry about your sister. I never had a chance to tell you that. You know, before you left." Julianna's freckled nose continued to scrunch with empathy.

Is she being sincere? Ironic?

I blinked in response. Julianna and I had completed an English project together on Miss Havisham's ill-fated wedding during a *Great Expectations* unit in ninth grade. We made a two-tiered vanilla cake, which wasn't fully cooked in the middle, and a playlist for the imaginary wedding reception. Julianna was nice. We got an A, and then she never spoke to me again.

"Are you coming back to school?" she asked. Everyone stepped closer, as if not wanting to miss a syllable of my answer. I was surprised their thumbs weren't poised over their cell phones ready to blast out my reply like social media stenographers.

"I don't think so." I eyed them curiously.

"Are you staying in Boston?"

"No, um, we're going back to Europe in a couple days." I nodded to Charlotte.

"You know, that's, like, *so* cool," Julianna said. "I think it's awesome you're taking time off, traveling."

"Yeah, I guess."

"Have you been to Paris?" blurted a girl from behind her, Darlene Sproles. Her dark hair was pulled into a bun, accenting her high cheekbones, and she wore a fitted black dress with a tight string of pearls around her neck, like she was styled for the funeral by the *Condolences* line at Nordstrom.

"No, not recently," I said, thinking of how Keira and I had recently missed our chance to go to France. "We were in Italy, London, and Amsterdam…"

"Did you smoke pot?" asked Wyatt Burns, like the

question made him cool.

My lip curled, not wanting to acknowledge his stupidity, but also not wanting to cause a scene by saying what I really thought of him. "That wasn't why we were there."

"How about London? Did you go to the theater?" asked Chris Wentz.

"Um, not yet." I didn't know how to respond to these questions, or why they were asking them, or why they were speaking to me at all.

"You totally should. I hear the shows are even better than in New York," he continued, his dream of seeing his name in a Playbill practically blinking above his head.

"Yeah, I'll do that." I nodded awkwardly.

Then the lightning round began:

"What's the beer like?"

"Did you go to a bar?"

"Do they card over there?"

"How's the shopping?"

"What are people wearing?"

Charlotte leaned toward my ear. "Looks like you're finally popular."

"I guess tragedy is *in* this season," I whispered back.

"Well, don't let the press conference go on too long," she retorted. "My parents will freak if you get back late."

"Don't worry." I nodded.

But the questions kept flying as I stood there, puzzled:

"Did you go to a beach?"

"I hear they go topless."

"Did you see Big Ben?"

"Or William and Kate?"

I'd spent my whole life as a freak—either as the new girl who wasn't staying long enough to bother fitting in or as the orphan with the dead parents. Never in all that time did my freak status lend itself to popularity. Only now, I was a girl traveling without a chaperone, on a seemingly endless backpacking adventure. Or so they thought.

I watched Charlotte climb into a sedan with her parents as I lied through a series of questions desperate for a way out.

Then I heard the heavy thud of footsteps thundering from behind me.

Before even turning around, I knew it was her.

CHAPTER NINE

Regina marched my way, the rubber soles of her knee-high boots skidding in the granite courtyard. "Having fun?" she shouted. "Enjoying your little reunion?"

She flicked her gaze at each of our classmates, like if she were granted an X-Men power, she'd choose to shoot them with beams of energy from her corneas. Everyone recoiled.

"I'm so glad you didn't leave," I said, and I really was. I didn't know where she ran off to after her eulogy, and my next step was to track her down, make sure she was all right.

"Yeah, this is so much fun. Glad I could bring you all together," she snapped. "No, make that—*Tyson* is so glad. He just needed to get stabbed in an alley for you to become homecoming queen."

I reached for Regina's arm, but she jumped back like my hand was on fire. "Don't touch me! Don't you *ever* touch me!"

I raised my palms in defense. "You're right. I won't. But maybe it's time to go home. Are your parents still here?"

"What? I'm not a baby. I don't need my mommy," she

spat, spit actually landed on my cheek. I pretended not to notice. "What I need is to talk to *you*. Alone."

"Fine. Great. Let's do that." I nodded and turned to our group of classmates, but they were already backing away, making a slow exit for the street and the T station down the block. Thankfully, it didn't look like anyone was recording this, because I doubted Regina wanted to go back to school to watch her meltdown circulate on social media. "Where do you want to talk? Do you want me to take you home?"

I immediately scanned the street for a cab.

"I'm not going anywhere with you. Besides, this isn't going to take long." She grabbed my arm hard, like she wanted to hurt me, then dragged me to the side of the church. There was a little alley that linked the ornate building to a small parking lot. It was empty, aside from a dumpster, and it reminded me of the alley in Cortona, before I met Luis Basso, before I learned the truth.

I yanked my arm free and forced Regina to stop walking. "What is it? How can I help?" I asked, trying hard to keep my voice calm as I fixed the sleeve on my black wool coat, now awkwardly bunched from Regina's grip.

"*Help?* You think you can *help?*" Regina yelped. "You've done enough. You're the reason we're here. You're the reason he's *dead!*"

I took a deep breath. Her eulogy made her opinions about my sudden "vacation" very clear, and I could tell last night she doubted every word that I said, but Charlotte was right—there was only so much blame I could accept, and being responsible for the death of my friend when I wasn't even in the country was beyond even my self-loathing standards.

"Regina, I'm *so* sorry about Tyson, more than you know, more than I can put into words. And I'm sorry I ran off, and

I wasn't there when you needed me, but you know what happened to my sister—"

"Do I?" She cocked her head, her face suggesting that I wasn't going to like what came next. She reached into the pocket of her long, black dress coat and pulled out a folded sheet of computer paper. "You and Charlotte, you've been traveling around the globe, all depressed with grief?" Her voice held an accusatory tone.

"Yes," I lied, though my gut told me I shouldn't. Regina knew something, and I was about to get caught, but what exactly could I do? The list of things I was keeping from her was too vast for me to guess what she might have uncovered. I stared at the paper in her hand, knowing deep inside that it was about to burn our friendship to the ground. "I get that things were horrible for Tyson after I left. I wish I could have been there, I wish I could have helped, but things have been horrible for me, too."

"Yeah, I guess, hanging out at vineyards, making out with boys, that's *so horrible*." She unfolded the 8.5 x 11 sheet of paper and shoved it in my direction—it was a photo of me kissing Marcus at the train station in Cortona. The same one that had been shown to Keira during her captivity.

I stumbled back, reacting like a vampire confronted with a cross. "Wait. What? How?"

"How did I get this?" She shook the paper so it rattled in the air like a poster at a pep rally. "*How?* From the man who killed my boyfriend."

My jaw fell toward the gritty concrete as the hate radiating from my friend notched up to a nuclear level. "What are you talking about? *What?*" I spoke four languages, yet I suddenly felt like I no longer understood what she was saying.

She exhaled, preparing herself for what came next. I did the same.

"It all happened as I said—the mugging, the fight, the knife. Only before I could get to Tyson, as he lay bleeding in a dirty street, dying, his murderer gave me this." She extended her arm to shove the picture closer to my face. I flinched at the sight of myself wrapped around Marcus. "And that's not all! It came with a message. Want to hear it?" She was smiling like the Joker in *Batman*, her eyes crazy and her tone wild. "The message is for you, after all."

I didn't move. My mind was so full of questions, my brain shut down, overloaded, short-circuited. I could practically smell the burning ozone; nothing computed.

Regina went on, her voice taking on a hollow monotone. "He said, 'Tell Anastasia this isn't over, and if she thinks she can hide from us, she's kidding herself. We can get to anyone, and we will. Unless she gives us what we want.'" She eyed me pointedly. "Did I say that right? He made me practice it a few times to make sure I remembered it all, before he *spit* on Tyson's body."

I thought back to how Regina said she froze as she watched her boyfriend fight for his life. When faced with assassins—Craig Bernard, Luis Basso—my body reacted. I had innate instincts. I was brave. But facing my best friend right now—or the girl who used to be my best friend—had me stunned motionless.

"Regina," my voice was barely a whisper, "I don't know what to say…"

"You don't know what to *say*?" she shrieked. "How about telling me what the hell is going on?"

"I…I can't." I blinked rapidly.

"Are you kidding me? Tyson died for you!" she shouted,

crumpling the photo in her hands, squeezing it into a ball like she wished it were my head. "While you were running off kissing some boy, Tyson was bleeding to *death*!"

"It's not like that."

"Yes it is! What have you gotten yourself mixed up in? What did you get *us* mixed up in?" She stomped toward me like she wanted to hit me, like she wanted me to stand as still as a punching bag and let her take her revenge. I almost did. I deserved it, but I needed to find the words to explain.

"It's Keira..."

"She's not dead, is she?" Regina interrupted, the accusation written in every crease of her face.

I didn't know what the right thing to do was. If I told her the truth, I'd be putting her in more danger; I'd be giving her information about people who apparently were willing to kill for a lot less. But could I actually stand there and lie to her after what she'd been through?

"After Keira disappeared, everything went to shit," I admitted, trying to find any words I could offer. "I've been trying to get out of this, figure out what's going on and end it, but if I tell you any more, I'll be dragging you into it—"

"Tyson's dead! Because of *you*! You already dragged us into this. Don't you get that?" Her hands swung, willing me to get within striking distance even though we both knew she couldn't fight. Not that she needed to. She was hurting me enough with the truth. "Did you once think of us? Maybe think to give us a heads up? Maybe a phone call to let us know you were in trouble, that *we* might be in trouble?"

"I never thought anyone would involve you," I defended honestly. Sure, I worried they'd go after Marcus's brother, maybe Charlotte or even Julian. But kids from my high school who no longer had any contact with me, why would they do that? How evil was this organization? And was this how Department D acted when my parents were around? Were Mom and Dad like this?

"Obviously, you were wrong about everything," Regina hissed. "So who are these people? Drug dealers? Mobsters? Do you owe someone money? Somebody killed Tyson to send a message *to you*! What's next?"

I have no idea.

I dropped my chin, suddenly feeling sweaty in the cold Boston air. My face was flushed, my vision blurring like I'd stood up too fast. Regina was right to blame me in her eulogy; I just didn't realize how much so. Everything was my fault. Why didn't I warn them? Who was next?

Keira. I have to call Keira.

They knew I'd be at this funeral. What if they killed Tyson to make that happen? What if this was a set up? What if they were going after her now?

My head shot up. "Regina, I have to go."

"What?" She looked as though I'd gone from evil to mental case.

"I have to go. I'm sorry." Slowly, I felt my brain start to reboot, my senses returning. I thought of Craig Bernard. "The man who attacked you, did he have a scar on his lip? Dirty blond hair?"

"No." She shook her head, confused.

"An Italian accent? Short and stocky?" I continued, picturing Luis Basso.

"No." She sounded even more perplexed. "He had red hair. Freckles. Skinny. He looked like a wuss until he started fighting…"

"Did you tell the police about all of this?" I had to know everything if I was going to protect us. I had to know how bad this was.

"I gave them the guy's description but not the message. He said if I told anyone other than you, especially the cops...*he...he said...he said he'd kill me. He'd kill my parents*," her voice croaked, tears flooding her eyes. The fear she'd buried so deep below her rage exploded, on her face, in her breathing. She hyperventilated, bending over. No wonder she looked so conflicted; her grief was thrown into a pot of a fear so thick I wasn't sure the two would ever separate.

"Oh, Regina!" I wanted to hug her but knew she'd sooner beat me senseless. "God, I'm so sorry! That's not going to happen." I reached for her, guilt cutting me so deep I felt physical pain in my chest, but she slapped my palm away.

"How do you know? You're the one who did this to us! This is your fault! I should just turn you in, tell the cops everything, maybe they can—"

"No!" I snapped, fingers flared. "You can't. And I'm not saying this to protect me; I'm saying this because we have no idea who we can trust. And I'm talking about the cops." I thought back to my sister's disappearance, to how unhelpful the Boston PD had been, how they were giving updates to Randolph Urban, how Department D was headquartered in their city. "I can't get into it. It'll only make things more dangerous for you, but believe me, I'm going to do something."

"Like what?" she asked, disbelieving, already knowing I couldn't possibly have an answer.

And I didn't.

But I had a place to start.

• • •

Keira was safe. I spoke to her myself, told her everything in a flustered conversation as I darted down Boston sidewalks through bursts of welcomed, icy air gusting off the Charles River. Julian assured me he'd hire security that would be there within hours, and once again, I was appreciative of our British friend's willingness to expend cash to keep us safe, to keep my sister safe. Both he and Marcus swore they wouldn't let Keira out of their sights, let alone out of Julian's apartment.

Then I called Charlotte at her parents' house, and before we hung up, she moved up our flights to Europe to tomorrow. It wasn't safe for us to be separated and exposed. We needed a new plan. Tyson's death, that message, changed everything.

My brain pulsed with the echo of Regina's morbidly flat voice: *Tell Anastasia this isn't over, and if she thinks she can hide from us, she's kidding herself. We can get to anyone, and we will. Unless she gives us what we want.*

The last line was everything: "Give us what we want."

My parents. They wanted my parents, and they thought Keira and I had the ability to "give" them. We didn't. At least, we didn't think we did. After three and a half years of abandoning us to fend for ourselves, our parents potentially came out of hiding in Venice when my sister was kidnapped—if you were to believe Keira's drugged recollections of hearing their voices. I wasn't sure I did. Keira was desperate and high on sedatives; her brain could have been playing tricks. But if it wasn't, if she was right, if Craig Bernard was telling the truth and our parents were alive, then every enemy they ever made now thought that hurting us was the key to drawing them out.

Tyson was the first casualty.

And the message was sent to me. Whoever did this

knew me well enough to know that Tyson and Regina were my best friends in Boston. They knew how much Tyson's death would affect me, and they also had possession of a photo of Marcus and me kissing in Cortona. A photo that was shown to Keira, in captivity, while she was being held by Department D agents. That made Randolph Urban an obvious suspect. Only he had just sent a baby picture to Charlotte via email, knowing it would reach me. And it did. He clearly had ways of sending me a message that didn't involve killing anyone, so why would he do this?

But if it wasn't him, then who was it? Who else wanted my parents? How long was that list?

I didn't know, but I did know two people who might, and they worked in a skyscraper in the middle of Boston.

Marcus's parents.

I'd called ahead. They were in the office.

My black boots skidded to a halt on the pavement, almost careening into a man in a suit talking into a cell phone and staring into space. He cursed and shoved past me as I stood motionless on a busy city sidewalk staring up at the soaring building. Compared to its neighbors, the blue glass skyscraper was unremarkable in the Boston skyline. It didn't have a famous antenna like the Prudential Building, and it didn't glow in neon like the Citgo sign. It could be plopped into any city, American or otherwise, and no one would notice it.

Yet it was home to everything that was wrong in my life.

I stepped inside the lobby, its slick black marble floor gleaming as a giant digital wall advertised the accomplishments of the Dresden Chemical Corporation. I knew from experience that behind the wall was a massive pit of employees with blood-red desk chairs, frantically dashing about while executives looked down from exposed hallways that led to their closed office doors. I'd never been to the NY Stock Exchange, but from what I'd seen on TV, stockbrokers held a similar frenzied activity. Now I wondered if every single one of Dresden's employees was a criminal or if any really did think they were working for a high-tech chemical corporation as the wall of digital images suggested. My eyes glazed over the smiling, multicultural stock photography faces posed in front of hospitals and power plants, as the enormous screens skipped from one exotic locale to the next. Names of chemical inventions flashed, some used every day by ordinary people in their kitchens and some used to protect our armed forces. Biomedical advancements were touted along with the number of lives they reportedly saved or helped each year.

This was a great company, an important company. And it was all a lie or, more specifically, a front. But I guessed even the Italian restaurants laundering money for the mob still had to make meatballs.

I bit my thumbnail as I waited for the Reys to descend from their corner offices. I didn't have to announce who I was when I arrived, the security guard welcomed me by name and assured me that the Reys would be down momentarily. It seemed my phone call to the operator asking for their whereabouts was easy to track. Or maybe they'd been tracking me for months.

"Anastasia, welcome!" greeted a very cheery voice with a thick Madrileño accent. *"Ay, familia!"*

I turned to see a middle-aged woman gliding my way. She was probably only five foot two, but she was wearing sky-high heels that lifted her to my height. The crimson soles of her shoes matched her ruby suit, its jacket flaring slightly and its skirt clinging to her curves in a way that suggested a very expensive tailor. But what stood out more than her power suit was her demeanor: she was moving so confidently that guys half her age turned to look in appreciation. Beside her, about a foot taller, was Marcus's doppelganger, only aged a few decades and with Antonio's facial hair—he had a salt and pepper beard and matching mustache. He wore rimless glasses in front of his distinctive dark eyes, and his round rosy cheeks smiled to reveal two dimples that matched his boys'.

"*Aanastaaasthia*," cooed Marcus's mother, drawing out the sound of my name with Spanish flare, much like her son. "It's such a pleasure to finally meet you!" She hugged me like we were old friends, and I stiffened in her embrace, my arms at my sides. Then she kissed both my cheeks and let go only so her husband could do the same. Suddenly, I had a new understanding for my sister's aversion to displays of affection.

"We've heard so much about you!" Marcus's dad greeted, pressing his lips to the sides of my face in a way that would have been creepy even if I didn't suspect him as working for the enemy. He was Marcus's dad. Yuck. "I'm Carlos Rey, and this is my wife Rosario."

"Rosa, please!" she corrected him. "We're all family here."

We are? My brow furrowed. That was news to me. I was under the impression we just met.

"Um, hi," I muttered, not sure what to make of the overly familiar introduction from two people who might have killed my best friend and might be trying to kill my entire family, myself included.

"*Por favor*, tell us, how is Marcus?" asked Carlos, his grin impossibly wide.

"Okay, I guess."

I wasn't sure what I expected when I walked into the

building. At best, I was hoping for answers, some hint as to whether they knew anything about what happened to Tyson or Keira. At worst, I'd considered armed guards rappelling from the ceiling with machine guns ready to whisk me away to a secret bunker while they forced me to tell them where my parents were hiding. But in all the scenarios I'd mentally considered, hugs and kisses weren't on the list.

"And how's Antonio? He's with you now, no?" Rosario questioned.

"Yes, he and Marcus are together." I chose my words carefully. "Seems Antonio is happy not to be working *here* anymore."

If my dig bothered them, they didn't show it. Their smiles stayed firm, like my parents' would have. "*Ay, sí.* I wish he would have told us how he was feeling," Rosario offered.

"We just want him to straighten up, *entiendes?* Stop the partying," said his dad, then he eyed me with a devilish smirk. "Not that a few drinks is so bad…" he teased.

"Oh, Carlos!" Rosario playfully patted his arm.

Who are these people?

"We heard about your sister, *Keeirra*. She's okay, yes?" Rosario continued, her tone suddenly somber and her face full of concern. She reminded me of a news anchor asking a question of a bereaved family member, her face oozing sympathy on camera while she secretly checked her lipstick and fluffed her hair between breaks.

"Yes. Thankfully, I was able to rescue my sister from her violent kidnapping." My tone was intentionally hostile as I attempted to squash their charm, jostle out the real them. My best friend was killed to send a message to me, their boss was sending me baby pictures, and my parents might not be dead. I was done playing mind games. "Antonio tells me that news of Keira's survival made its way around Dresden, or should I say *Department D*?"

Rosario's eyes flexed only slightly as she placed a palm on her heart, the red tips of her fingers looking like fiery daggers on her porcelain skin. "*Ay, gracias a Dios.* I'm so glad she's safe."

"I'm sure you are." My sarcasm was thick.

Carlos leaned toward me. "I can imagine what you must be thinking, what Marcus must be thinking. Please tell our son our dealings with Department D are nonexistent. Our work is focused on Dresden."

"So you wouldn't have forced Marcus to do Department D's bidding, like you did Antonio?" I stared him straight in the eyes.

My parents started this awful organization, so I had no intention of giving anyone else's parents the benefit of the doubt. These people worked here. They knew of Department D's criminal activities which, in my book, made them at least partially guilty for what happened to Keira and Tyson (if not entirely guilty).

"Antonio has issues with responsibility. If he spent as much time studying and working, as he did drinking and partying, we would have recommended him for a job at Dresden. But he has no discipline, no ambition. He wants everything *easy, easy, easy*." Rosario flicked her manicured hand in the air, sounding exasperated, as if not realizing she was mocking her own son. "We thought he could start at Department D, prove himself a little bit, and then maybe we could move him to Dresden or, even better, get him to go back to college."

"*Marcus* is our good boy," Carlos went on, nakedly displaying favoritism for his younger son. "We would have never let him touch Department D. He's too good for that."

"Well, I'm sure *Antonio* will be happy to hear it." Oddly, I felt offended on Antonio's behalf, and I barely liked the guy. No wonder he didn't want to talk to his parents.

"So how are you and Marcus doing, with everything?" asked Rosario, her voice low like she didn't want to be overheard. There were only a couple of other people in the lobby, and none within earshot, but still, I doubted Department D was a discussion they wanted to have in the lobby of their legitimate enterprise. "It must be a shock to learn about all of this. We want to explain it to Marcus, but ever since he found Antonio, he doesn't want to talk to us. Antonio's poisoned him." She looked disgusted by the "bad" son, as if this were *his* fault. When really, they recruited him. They chose this.

Maybe Antonio was telling the truth when he said he's been desperate for a reason to run from here?

"Well, Marcus has some good reasons for staying away from you. We all do." I looked at them pointedly. "I just came from Tyson Westbrook's funeral, and I had an interesting conversation with his girlfriend, who was there when he died."

"*Ay!* The young man in the news!" Rosario cried, dramatically tossing her hands toward the heavens before making the sign of the cross. "He was from your school! He was a friend?"

"My best friend."

"*Pobrecita.*" She held out her arms for an embrace, and I took two steps back. I was not letting these people touch me again.

"*Lo siento,*" said Carlos, his face expressing the perfect amount of sympathy, as if he were an actor given a stage direction.

The fake condolences were getting ridiculous. I may not have been there to defend Tyson at the end of his life, but I would be there for him now.

"Are you kidding me?" I yelped. "I know everything. *You* know I know everything. Someone killed my best friend and then left me a message!"

They stared at me, unblinking, looking completely confused.

"A message?" Rosario's perfect brow didn't furrow, but it looked like it wanted to—Botox. "Are you okay? Is everything all right?"

"Of course I'm not okay!" I shouted, my voice bouncing off the marble.

"Please, lower your voice," Carlos insisted, eyeing me carefully.

"Why? You don't want me to shout it, right here in the lobby?" I saw a micro-twitch in each of their dark eyes as a few people in the lobby began looking our way. Maybe everyone in this place worked for Department D, or maybe they were oblivious. Either way, I was not going to stay silent anymore. Someone from this organization sent me a very violent message. Well, now it was their turn to hear what *I* had to say. "We all know what's going on, we all know about my parents. If they're alive, I have no idea where they are. And I have no intention of finding them or *giving them* to anyone. So stop killing my friends."

"What? We would never!" Rosario gasped, as if truly appalled.

I almost believed her. That was the problem in dealing with spies: they lied with such sincerity you'd think you were getting the truth straight from the Pope. It was starting to make me crazy, like I couldn't trust my own eyes, my own gut. These people worked for Department D. I knew that for a fact.

"Well, then, pass the message along to Randolph Urban." I stepped toward them, my voice low and threatening as my heart crashed against my chest. "Baby pictures will not manipulate me. Neither will pictures of Marcus and me at a train station. I know that photo was taken in Cortona by a Department D agent. So whoever sent it to Regina wanted me to know it came from this company, right here." I pointed to the big corporate digital screen. "They want me to know you killed my friend, one of you. What I don't get is *why*. Why Tyson? Why now?"

It didn't make sense. Keira and I had been safely reunited for more than a month. We hadn't stirred any trouble, aside from locating Antonio, who was already one of them. So why kill an innocent kid? There were other ways to find my parents, if they were even out there.

Regina's words replayed in my head, repeating and repeating, until my mind grabbed hold of a phrase I'd previously overlooked: *If she thinks she can hide from us, she's kidding herself.*

I thought back to the timing of events. Charlotte told us about Tyson's death while Keira and I were eating fish and chips, the day after we had decided to go into *hiding*. Was that it? Did they somehow know about our plan? Was Julian's flat, his terrace, bugged? Maybe they heard our entire conversation as we toasted champagne; maybe they were trying to force Keira and I to keep searching for our parents, to keeping drawing them out? It was what we feared, after all—that Department D would keep coming after us as long as we played their game. It was why we wanted to walk away.

Maybe, somehow, Department D knew that.

"I don't know what Antonio told you, but we have

no involvement with that side of the business," Rosario insisted. "What's happened to you and your sister, it's horrible. But that has nothing to do with us."

Carlos stepped toward me, his dark eyes taking on an authoritative look quite different from the cheery disposition he'd expressed earlier. "I know you don't trust us. You think Department D had something to do with what happened to Keira, to your friend, but if it did, that has nothing to do with our engineering firm."

"Or us," Rosario interjected.

"In fact, my wife and I are working to ensure that Dresden will thrive regardless of what happens to Department D. We know the FBI is building a case. It's only a matter of time, and we want to make sure Dresden does not go down, too," Carlos explained.

"We do good work," Rosario went on, her eyes pleading with me to understand, as if my opinion mattered. It didn't, not on this, but it was clear that their sons' opinions mattered very much. "We save lives. We've even started a foundation to donate our technological advancements to impoverished communities worldwide. The Dresden Chemical Corporation is worth protecting."

"But if you want to bring down Department D, and whoever is running things there, we won't stop you," Carlos offered, a bit too easily, like he was daring me to continue the fight, like he wanted me to light the match and watch the spies burn.

Wrinkles spread across my brow. If he were involved with Department D, he wouldn't present me with a challenge to destroy it, would he? Maybe he was telling the truth and he was an engineer hoping to unlink his firm from criminal ties. But if so, then why didn't he work someplace else? There had to be hundreds, if not thousands, of successful engineering firms. Why stay here unless he approved of their underhanded dealings? Or maybe he'd had a change of heart? The offer to go after "whoever is running things" could signify a break with Randolph Urban, and it could explain why Urban was in hiding. Maybe there was a mutiny on the corporate pirate ship.

"Where's Urban?" I asked, hedging my bets.

Carlos and Rosario exchanged a look. "We shouldn't have this conversation here," she replied before her brown eyes shifted around the lobby and landed briefly on a security guard. He nodded her way, then she abruptly looked at her diamond watch. "You know, I didn't notice the time. Why don't we have lunch?" she suddenly suggested. "I'm free for at least forty minutes."

"Splendid." Carlos clapped once in agreement. "*Aanastaaasthia*, do you like sushi?"

"What?" My face twisted like they were performing some sort of improv show.

"No, how about steak?" Rosario offered, her hand on my back as she ushered me toward the sliding glass doors. The security guard stepped alongside her, as if he had been waiting for a signal, and all three of them casually led me toward the exit.

"I'm not having lunch with you! I'm not going anywhere with you."

"Well, there's this great farm-to-table place—"

"Are you delusional?" I shouted as I was guided through the doors into a circular drive where a black car was idling, the driver looking directly at me. My heart seized.

They were throwing me into a car, they were kidnapping me, and they were taking me to an undisclosed location. Everything they'd said was bullshit; they were stalling, killing time until they could put their plan into action and drag me away. Every fear I'd had when I walked into the lobby was true. They killed Tyson, they wanted to kill my parents, and they'd do anything to make that happen.

I skidded to a halt and frantically glanced in every direction, eyes pleading for a place to run, when I heard the squeal of tires ripping into the covered portico. I shifted toward the sound as a midnight blue sedan screeched to a stop and its driver's door swung open.

I didn't know who I was expecting—a spy? An ax murderer? The police?

My parents?

When the figure stepped out, I sighed with relief. I recognized his face. And the bow tie.

It was Allen Cross.

CHAPTER TEN

Allen Cross was the professor who gave me answers in Rome, who told me about Department D, and who helped me find my sister. He had been friends with my parents, he was a fellow spy, and now he was here.

"Thank God." I shook Rosario's hand from my back and put distance between us.

"What are you doing here, Allen?" Carlos asked, as if they had run into each other at the country club.

"What do you think?" Cross sounded like the question was dumb.

"We were just about to take *Aanastaaasthia* to lunch," Carlos explained.

"Sure you were."

"She's been through quite an ordeal," Rosario added.

"Yes, her friend's funeral." Cross looked at me. "That's why I'm here."

"I don't care why you're here, I'm just glad you are." I moved away from the Reys, prepared to march to Cross's car, but their hulking security guard reached out a thick fist.

"Let her go," Cross demanded, his voice menacing for

a man with a bald head and liver spots.

"Of course." Rosario smiled cheerily. "*Aanastaaasthia's* free to go wherever she likes. We were merely hoping to hear more about how our boys are doing."

Cross pursed his thin lips like he expected a better lie. I didn't. The Reys might be engineers, or they might be evil spy overlords, but one thing was certain—they did love their sons, or Marcus at least, and they did care what they thought of them. Their questions about their kids were the only part of our interaction I didn't doubt, which meant if they did kill Tyson, if they did inflict this pain on me, on Regina, I was in possession of a surefire way to hurt them. Marcus would never forgive them.

I turned to his parents, my voice steady. "I saw Marcus's face, when Antonio told him that you know about Department D, when his brother admitted he worked for the spies who kidnapped my sister, when he said you recruited him, *made him* work here. Marcus was broken. So how do you think he's gonna look when I tell him you work for the people who killed my best friend?" Neither parent said anything, but their jaws stiffened, reality sinking in. "You see, I know how he's going to look, how he's going to feel. It's the exact same way I felt when I learned the truth about *my* parents. And you know what I feel toward my parents now? Hate. Nothing but pure hate." I ground my teeth, and Carlos and Rosario could see that I meant it. Their perky poker faces folded as they considered being loathed, beyond redemption, by their children.

Then I summoned my inner Phoenix, every lesson I learned from watching my parents control their tempers yet be dangerously threatening at the same time. "If you work for the people who sent me that *message,* if you *are* the people who sent that message, trust me, you will get a response. From me. And I will make sure it hurts you just as much. In every way I can."

With that, I marched to Cross's car, opened the passenger door, and sat down. No one stopped me. No one said anything.

Until Cross began to drive.

For someone who spent the last three years with a crippling fear of vehicular transportation, I tended to spend a lot of time in speeding cars. I sat rigid, one hand gripping the car-door handle, the other gripping my seat, while my mind spun faster than the tires. Usually, when a girl met the parents of a boy she liked, she worried about making a good impression—wearing the right dress or trying to look intelligent and well mannered. I, however, threatened the Reys and accused them of murder while trying not to be kidnapped.

Marcus's parents killed Tyson, or they knew who killed him, or they worked with whoever killed him. How was I going to tell him that? *OMG, your parents are so adorable! And they kill people! We had such a great time!*

Or maybe they didn't kill people. Hopefully, they didn't. And hopefully neither did the guy sitting next to me.

"How did you know where I was?" I asked as Cross raced into a tunnel of Boston's infamous Big Dig. Apparently, long before I lived in the city, the traffic was so clogged that they spent billions (and billions and billions) to build highways underground. Now we were left with a series of human-sized rat tunnels lit by rows of fluorescent lights that gave the feeling of a spaceship switching to hyper speed. I'd had numerous nightmares about stumbling in these dark channels unable to escape as flaming cars whizzed at me. I wasn't a dream expert, but I imagined there was some symbolism in there.

"I heard about the death of Tyson Westbrook, and I had a feeling you'd turn up. I do not believe events transpired the way the police claim," Cross said.

"No kidding." I huffed.

I filled him in on my conversation with Regina and the deadly message she received while standing over her boyfriend's lifeless body.

"Well, that communication was rather overt." His face was flat, void of sympathy, as if the news were a memo from corporate.

I scrunched my nose at his reaction. "Tyson had nothing to do with anything. He was completely innocent. Doesn't that bother you?"

"I've been in this business a long time. What do you expect me to say?"

I expected him to treat this as more than another bad day at the office. Tyson was a normal teenager. No, actually, he was an extraordinary teenager, one who faced more challenges than any kid his age should and who managed to handle them all, before someone Cross knew, someone he might have had dinner with, ended Tyson's chance to rise above the circumstance he was born into.

"You're as bad as the rest of them," I spat.

"I probably am." His eyes stayed on the road. "But would you prefer me to fill you with a bunch of *I'm sorrys*?"

"I don't need a bunch, but one wouldn't hurt. 'Hi, Anastasia, I'm sorry your best friend died *because of you…*'"

"Fine. Hello, Anastasia, my condolences on the loss of your friend. I believe you were recently speaking with the two people who killed him."

"What? *No!*" I yelped, feeling a pang so sharp, I grabbed my gut.

No, no, no! Not Marcus's parents. Sure, I'd let my mind go there, I even threatened them, but I was really hoping it was some random Bob from Dresden Accounting, who had gone off his psychedelic meds in a rogue murderous rampage unaffiliated with anyone my friends or I had ever met. Not our parents, not any of our parents. My skull thudded against the passenger headrest. "It can't be them. They couldn't do that to Tyson, to *Marcus*. Are you sure?"

Cross glanced my way. "As soon as I heard of your friend's death, I knew it wasn't an arbitrary homicide. It never is." He adjusted the grip of his hunter green bow tie, aggressively tugging it loose as if our conversation were suddenly choking him. Good. It should bother him.

"Department D wants your parents, and they are going to draw them out—for vengeance, for a public shaming, for the fun of watching their loved ones twist in agony." He was spitting as he spoke, cracks showing in his perfect spy facade, which was oddly concerning and comforting at the same time. "They're not going to stop. We already know Department D kidnapped your sister, and then led you on a wild chase to find her. Why? To get mummy and daddy's attention. But what good did it do them? What did they achieve?"

"Nothing. It didn't work," I pointed out.

"Exactly. They didn't get your parents. At least, as far as I know," he continued. He started removing his black overcoat, while he was driving, at least twenty miles per hour over the speed limit, in a narrow city tunnel. I clenched the door handle tighter and noticed his cornflower blue button-down was blotted with sweat stains. "Every Department D plan has layers. And this one is meant to systematically destroy you, your sister, and everyone you love, bit by bit, until your parents either swoop out of the dark to help, or they accept that their revenge will be taken out on the next generation through a soul-crushing, never-ending cycle of pain."

"Well, mission accomplished," I quipped. "My soul is officially crushed."

"I wouldn't say that yet. Things can always get worse. Trust me, methods for inflicting pain are pulled from a fathomless abyss…" His voice faded, hazel eyes twitching. This man didn't flex a micro muscle of emotion in Italy, but now his face was growing openly upset.

"Are you okay?" I asked, unsure I wanted the answer.

"Of course." He adjusted his posture, shaking off his heavy mood and clearing his throat. "I'm just an old man tired of old games."

I chose to believe him, mostly because I preferred his stoic disposition and wasn't sure I wanted to know what had him so rattled.

"This isn't a game," I pointed out. "My friend's dead."

Somewhere outside of this windshield, in a windy Massachusetts cemetery, Tyson's body was being lowered into a pile of dirt. Forever. He'd have no college memories, no career, no first apartment, no dog, no piece of crap car, no kids, no life. Because he had the audacity to befriend me.

Cross sighed. "There will be more casualties. You need to prepare yourself, because they won't stop until they get what they want."

"Who is *they*? And why do you think Marcus's parents are involved?"

While everything Cross had told us to date was accurate, I was not going to return to London and induct Marcus into the Evil Parent Club without proof.

"The Reys are highly intelligent, next-level geniuses. Don't get me wrong, we've all got our gifts. Urban dreamed up all of this." He said it like a compliment, the way you'd refer to Steve Jobs or Walt Disney. "Your parents, they were the ones in the field. They got their hands dirty, oversaw every mission, every agent, every win. But the Reys, they were behind the scenes, working in labs, sitting at computers, no one knowing what they were doing. Don't be fooled by their charm. They're vicious, manipulative snakes."

"So they're not nice people. None of you are." Even I suspected Rosario and Carlos's cheery personalities were about as authentic as a beauty queen during the interview segment, but that didn't prove they were murderers. "How do you know they killed Tyson?"

"Because I know the Reys, the *real* Reys. They're two of the brightest minds in the field of science worldwide, and they think that makes them invincible, that no one will suspect them. But I *see* them. And trust me, I know from experience that they are not above killing people to send a message." His jaw was clenched so tight his lips barely moved as he spoke, beads of sweat forming on his bald head. He hated these people, passionately, but that didn't prove they killed Tyson.

"The Reys have a teenager. Marcus went to school with Tyson. They were the same year. Why would they kill a kid just to send *me* a message? Their sons are literally traveling with me in London. They could have texted."

"Because the message isn't for *you*!" he snapped, raising his voice for the first time and glaring at me like I was an irksome child who couldn't keep up with the conversation. "That's only the surface layer, and I told you, every Department D plan goes deeper." Cross suddenly cut in front of a white SUV, the car jerking so much my seatbelt locked. You weren't supposed to change lanes in a tunnel; even I knew that, and I didn't drive. I glanced at my rearview mirror. He was driving like we were being followed, but I didn't see any cars moving erratically behind us. Maybe he always drove like this? Maybe in his mind, he was always being chased? "Whoever killed your friend is making it clear that they're *not* above killing children. Don't you get that? They're making it clear that they're not above killing *you*."

The word plopped like a stone in my gut. "But...but they didn't kill me in Italy...me or Keira," I stuttered. "They didn't want to hurt us. You said so yourself." My mouth suddenly grew dry.

"And *you* said that plan didn't work. So the game has changed."

"But my parents worked for the company, all of them, *including* Urban. I thought that meant they wouldn't kill me?" Not that I was feeling warm and fuzzy toward my bio-dad, or any of my parents, but I was willing to grasp at that genetic link if it meant I stayed alive.

"It means *Randolph Urban* won't kill you. And he won't. But your genetics mean nothing to the Reys. If anything, it's added leverage, a weakness they can exploit."

I strained to see holes in this darkness, some hint that he was wrong. "There are other people who would see me as a weakness. It doesn't have to be the Reys. What about other enemies? Other spies?"

Was that really my best-case scenario? That yes, people were threatening to kill Keira and me, and already murdered my best friend, but at least it wasn't my boyfriend's mom and dad?

"This is personal. This is coming from within the

organization, from someone who knows you. And only someone very high in the organization could order a hit like this, could go after *you,* the child of the kingpins— *all* of the kingpins. So if you take away your parents and Urban, that only leaves the Reys. They're the only ones with enough power to make this play."

"So everything they said was crap? They're not trying to save the engineering firm from Department D and the FBI?"

"Oh no, they *are* scientists, and I'm sure they do want to preserve Dresden Chemical. But they also want to save themselves. Your parents being alive changes everything."

"But we don't even know if they *are* alive!" I yelled through my teeth. "They can't be, they just can't. Because if they didn't care about our grief, or Keira's kidnapping, or me being orphaned *again*, then they're not going to care about some kid from my high school or anything else that happens to us *ever*."

Cross slowly turned my way, his expression completely open, and for the first time, I could see it in every wrinkle of his face, like a fortuneteller reading a palm. *Don't say it.*

"Anastasia, your parents *are* alive. You must know that by now."

I shook my head, the car flicking to flame broil and my cheeks filling with heat, black spots swirling with the blinding light at the end of the traffic tunnel. *No, no, no.* I really wanted my parents to be dead. I wanted them to be in the ground. I wanted to believe they loved us.

I started rocking, my body unsure if I needed to puke, pee, or faint. Then we burst out of the tunnel, the gray sky glaring so brightly it seemed paper white compared to the darkness in the car.

"How long have you known?"

"A long time."

"How. Long," I growled.

"I helped them fake their deaths."

Fire.

Wrath. I'd heard the word before; it was a biblical term, one of the seven deadly sins. But I never knew exactly how wrath differed from anger until that moment. It was when rage turned into something primal, something uncontrollable, something that caused a physical flame to burn in my chest while a waterfall roared in my ears, something that could make a good person kill.

"Let. Me. Out." I unbuckled my seat belt.

"No."

"Let me out!" I screamed, my face whipping toward him.

"No."

I reached for the door handle, yanking so hard I could have ripped it off. "You can't keep me here! What, are you going to kidnap me, too?" I was prepared to dive into traffic, but the door was locked, and the controls were on the driver's side. I was trapped. He'd planned this.

"I'm not holding you hostage. I only ask that you listen." All the stoicism of his earlier demeanor had returned, and now he sounded like a CEO explaining an earnings report. *"There's no need to panic. We have a plan to turn things around. Just hear me out..."*

"You asshole. Why would I listen to *you*? You've been lying to me since the day we met!"

"I have. But not for the reasons that you think."

"I don't give a sh—"

He abruptly held up his hand in protest, and I quieted. Partly because he displayed a lot of power in that one gesture, and partly because I was violently angry yet also desperate to hear his answers. Even if they were coming from a pathological liar.

He pulled over to the curb and parked in front of a rack of city rental bikes. I found myself oddly wondering how many places I'd walked by in my lifetime where others had suffered their most agonizing moments. Because I was about to have one of mine beside a row of sky blue bicycles that hipsters rode to work in an effort to be environmentally friendly.

"Things were getting tense in the organization. There was a difference of opinion on the types of clients we were taking, how jobs were being handled. Your parents were planning a takeover, of the hostile variety. They had a lot of people on their side. Like I said, their work was on the ground, so the staff was with *them*. And their plan would have worked. Only Urban found out, and he ordered a hit. Without going into detail, I'll say that I helped your parents get out, and I helped make Urban think his hit was successful."

"No, you don't get to do that. More," I hissed. "I want to know everything."

"I'm guessing you didn't tell your friend Regina everything, did you? After she delivered that message." He eyed me like he knew my answer, like he was throwing it in my face. "She must have had a lot of questions. Did you answer them? Or did you keep things to yourself to protect her?"

"This isn't the same thing. I'm already in this," I insisted, my nails digging into the passenger cushion, threatening to break off.

"And your friend isn't? She watched her boyfriend die." He raised a hairy gray eyebrow. "Sometimes things are safer left unsaid."

"How could you keep this from me? *How?*" My voice

cracked, and without warning, tears slid down my cheeks. I had no idea which emotion was causing them. I'd hated my parents, I'd grieved them, I'd loved them, and now I was betrayed by them. How could I resent two people so much for abandoning me, yet still want to see them? Just that thought added another heavy bucket of guilt onto my already tired shoulders; I slumped forward, my head in my lap.

"Because Department D wants you to lead them to your parents. You know that. That's why they led you to me in the first place. Once they found out your parents were alive, they suspected I was the one who helped them fake their deaths. So they showed you that picture of Aldo Moro knowing it would lead you on a path to me and hoping that I'd tell you where your parents were hiding. Then all they'd need to do was follow you to your parents' front door."

"*Do* you know where they're hiding?" I looked up.

"I did," he admitted. "I don't anymore."

"Did you know where they were when I was searching for Keira?"

"I lost track of them not long before she was taken."

"And you didn't tell me any of this?" I screamed, arms hugging my chest. I had been close. Cross knew where they were, and I could have found them, and that knowledge cut something deep inside that I didn't want to admit existed.

"I couldn't," he explained. "Everything Department D has done lately has been in service of either drawing your parents to you or you to them. If you went looking for them, if they came out of hiding, Urban and the Reys would get exactly what they want. They'll kill them, or torture them, or nail them to a billboard in Vegas. Everything I've done has been to protect your parents from that, to protect *you* from that. But things have changed."

"How?"

"While you were searching for Keira, I lost contact with your parents. I haven't heard from them in weeks. I don't even know if they're aware that you and your sister are okay. They've disappeared."

"From where?" My voice was small. "Where were they living?"

"Cuba."

Cuba. A country ninety miles from the coast of Florida. I could have taken a dingy to find them, not that they wanted to be found.

My parents are alive. Really alive... How could they do this to us?

"I checked Havana. They're not there. They haven't been in a while."

Stop it. Stop caring about them. I squeezed my eyes tight and tried to summon every ounce of strength I had to force away the grief and let the anger return to my soul like a lifelong friend. I was not going to let these people control me, hurt me, or break me. Ever. Again. "Why should it matter to me if they took off?" I bit off the words. "They obviously don't want to see me."

"Because Department D is after them, and the message from your friend's murderer suggests they haven't found them yet."

"Well, good for them! They obviously excel at disappearing." My hand flung in the air. "Though I'm not really sure who I'm rooting for. Maybe my parents deserve to be kidnapped. Better them than us, right? But the Reys did just try to shove me into the back of a car. You know, they seriously need some new material." I almost laughed, maniacally, hysterically, my mind crazed. "I mean, you're an evil spy. What do you think they should do? Tie me to a stake in Boston Common? Dangle me from the Eiffel Tower? Throw me in a tank of sharks in Bora Bora? Really, please, tell me what I should expect. Because it's pretty clear my parents aren't coming to my rescue, or if they did show up to save Keira in Venice, they sucked pretty bad at it. So come on, what's their next play?"

"You're right, Venice was a disaster," he said, as if my outburst were entirely logical and deserved a response. "But don't think your parents were being noble trying to save your sister. They were trying to save *themselves*."

I wasn't hurt by his words, I wasn't even shocked. Turned out my capacity to be disappointed in my parents had an infinite capacity. "Of course. That's all any of you care about, right? Yourselves?"

Cross reached for my arm, his touch surprisingly gentle. "I can imagine what this all sounds like, and I wish I could sugarcoat it, but the truth is, if your parents come out of hiding again, Department D won't waste the opportunity. They'll kill them. Or worse, they'll kill you."

"God forbid you sugarcoat," I quipped, yanking my arm from his. I had a double black belt in karate and spoke four languages, yet somehow, I'd become the helpless damsel tied to the train tracks by a villain in a top hat. And those villains were my parents. "So let me get this straight: if my parents stay in hiding, Department D will likely kidnap Keira and me, torture us, kill our friends, then us, in order to draw them out. But if my parents emerge, then Department D will kill them, and likely us, just to make them watch. Do I have this right?"

I squeezed my hands into fists, wanting to punch him, the car, the world, the pope. I couldn't stay in this vehicle anymore; it was too hot. I reached for the handle, tugging, again and again, harder and harder. I slammed my fist on the window, pounding a staccato rhythm. It wouldn't open. Nothing would open. I had to get out.

"Breathe." He put his hand on my back. I shrugged him off. "Breathe," he said again.

Reluctantly, I did as I was told. I didn't have much choice. He held the keys, literally. I breathed down to my belly, and slowly my mind began to calm.

"You're angry, and you want out. I get that. I've been there. Believe me." He looked at me with gold hazel eyes that had long ago accepted that life wasn't fair, and I briefly wondered how long it would be before my own eyes took on that melancholy glint. I imagined it would be much sooner than I'd like.

"I don't have any children," he confessed. "Back when you were younger, I bought you and your sister gifts because I knew you were the closest I'd ever get to having my own. My life, this life, it's not good for kids. It's why my ex-wife and I split up. I wanted her to have a chance at a normal life and a normal family…" He quieted as a cloak of sadness covered his eyes, then abruptly, he cleared his throat and shrugged it off. "When your parents left, when they faked their deaths, they too thought they were giving you a chance at normal lives."

"Well, we didn't end up normal now, did we?" I cocked my head.

"No, you didn't." He placed his wrinkled hand on mine. "But back in Italy, when your sister was missing, I thought there was a *chance* you could return to normalcy. It's why I didn't tell you that your parents are alive. It would have only put you in more danger, and I should know, I've been carrying this secret for years. But, despite all my efforts, I wasn't able to stop it, stop anything really." He sighed heavily, his mouth turning down in a way that suddenly made me want to comfort *him*. I was used to this man delivering dire news like it was a weather pattern, but watching his neck muscles strain, his jaw fight to maintain his crusty composure was like seeing a surgeon sobbing in the break room. I hadn't known he was capable of feeling emotion. "All that work and we all still ended up here. This isn't going to end. You're not simply going to walk away. Your parents are out there, and Department D wants them found. As long as that's the case, they're going to come at you again, and again, and again in every way conceivable, using everyone possible."

"So what do I do?" I asked.

"What do you want?"

I stared at him, the question illogical.

"What do you *want*, Anastasia?" He said it like he expected an answer, like it somehow mattered.

A few months ago, I was flirting with Marcus in a grocery store in Boston, I was going to movies with Tyson and Regina, I was winning karate tournaments, and I was taking T trains full of giggly college students snapping selfies on their phones. That was what I wanted, to turn back the clock. But what good would those dreams do me now?

"Do you have a magic wand? Are you granting wishes? I'm seventeen years old! What do you think I want? I want to go to college. I want to hang out with Marcus and Keira and not get shot. I want my sister to become a doctor. I want to live wherever I want and never have to look over my shoulder. I want to forget any of this ever happened. And I don't want anyone else I know to get hurt. Can you make that happen, oh magic genie?"

"Maybe." He nodded. "But there's only one way to do it."

He paused, dramatically, as if hoping I'd fill in the blank.

When I didn't, when I couldn't, he finally dropped the uranium-filled reason he had tracked me down, why he really intercepted me in front of Randolph Urban's office:

"Anastasia, you need to bring down Department D. Forever."

CHAPTER ELEVEN

Allen Cross had a plan, and it didn't involve me toppling a global espionage ring by myself. He practically had a PowerPoint demonstrating how we could do it, step by step. Eventually, I left him, head spinning, and sprinted to the smartest person I knew—Charlotte. If Cross's plan had holes, she would pick at them like snags on a sweater.

Only she didn't find many snags.

In fact, she thought his plan could work.

We'd talked nonstop, huddled under the flannel sheets in her childhood bedroom, and then continued the conversation on the plane back to London in voices so hushed we could barely hear one another in our narrow coach seats. Charlotte agreed that we couldn't live the rest of our lives waiting for a sniper bullet to hit us or someone we loved, and the only way to prevent that inevitability was to dismantle the organization that taped the "Shoot Me!" signs on our backs. Hiding in anonymity wasn't an option when people we cared about were still dangerously (and often obliviously) living out in the open.

So we arranged to meet our band of misfits in Hyde

Park, a large green expanse of bike paths, ponds, gardens, and shivering ducks. Being November in London, the air was as damp as a rainforest only with a temperature just above its capacity to freeze. People carried umbrellas like they carried their cell phones, because you never knew when the steel wool clouds might decide to open. But Charlotte insisted we meet outside. Department D could be following my every move in the hopes I'd lead them to my parents, meaning we couldn't trust a waiter or a shop clerk. We already suspected Julian's flat might be bugged, and despite him hiring a high-tech security team to regularly sweep the place, we didn't want to risk it. Our paranoia had grown.

We tugged our wheelie bags through the Grand Entrance to Hyde Park. The urban oasis had an actual gate a few stories high with marble arches and pillars, because that's how they did things in Europe. I was surprised there wasn't a moat with alligators. Thankfully, it was within walking distance to the train station. We'd traveled straight from Heathrow Airport—we didn't pass Go, we didn't collect $200. This talk couldn't wait another second.

Sienna leaves fluttered by as we crossed the crunchy grass. It was fall in England, and while the country did enjoy the changing of seasons, the trees didn't enjoy the same foliage as *New* England back home. There were no shades of ruby, amber, or canary, no hint of cherry or wine or lemon-lime. Just hunter green turned to dull orange or flat brown with some overgrown end-of-season gardens mixed in. Overall, the scene made me miss the city I left. No matter how many bad memories Boston held, it was still my last actual home, the last place I was *me*.

"Omigod, you're okay!" Keira greeted, jumping from a park bench as soon as she saw us. "I can't believe Tyson's funeral and Regina! I'm so glad you're back."

I smiled at the sight of her, a perverse piece of me feeling relieved—Department D hadn't killed her; they hadn't killed *my* person. They'd killed Regina's. It was a thought so dark, I tried not to let my mind float there longer than a flicker for fear the funk was lurking in the abyss.

Marcus, Antonio, and Julian stood at her side, all with varying degrees of welcoming smiles.

"Hola." Marcus stepped toward me. No hug. Instead, he rubbed my arm in a friendly gesture that was not romantic, and I couldn't help but notice that Antonio didn't take his eyes off his brother, like he was studying our interaction. I wondered what they'd discussed while I was away, while the bitter girlfriend inside me whispered that I didn't want to know. In all fairness, I had been talking about them, too—with Allen Cross, and I was betting our conversation was much more disturbing.

"So what's with the outdoor meeting?" Keira asked. "What's next, coded messages in parking garages?"

"Don't laugh. It's possible," Charlotte warned, none of them realizing how serious she was.

"I assure you they didn't find a single listening device in my flat," Julian insisted, his navy cashmere scarf tucked into the neckline of his wool coat in a way that made him look like a millennial catalog model.

"I know. I believe you. It's just…" Charlotte peered at me, then back at the group. "This is *big*."

They all turned their attention my way, and I felt the urge to stand on an apple crate, except this ominous speech required a whisper.

"Okay." I wrung my freezing hands together. "As I said on the phone, Tyson wasn't mugged, he was murdered by Department D. And that message to Regina, it wasn't just to us." My stomach cramped so badly I worried I'd have to run to the bathroom if I didn't spit this out soon. "Cross thinks they were sending a message to Mom and Dad." I looked at my sister, eyes soft. I hadn't wanted to say this over the phone. "Keira...they're alive. He confirmed it. It was them you heard in Venice."

Keira stumbled back a step, and Antonio caught her wrist, steadying her. She gazed at him, and he rubbed his fingers against her arm, comforting her in a way that brought me back to surveillance footage of Boston, to images of Keira with Craig Bernard, consoling her about our parents, right before he kidnapped her. Antonio looked exactly the same.

"This involves you, too," I said sharply, watching him touch her, his lips whispering so closely, the teal green '80s hoop earring she was wearing jiggled. Then he kissed her ear. Gross. I wanted to rip every follicle from his hipster beard and make him eat them one by one.

"Cross thinks your parents killed Tyson," I blurted.

The painful gasp that expelled from Marcus made me instantly regret my words. This wasn't what I'd planned to say or how I planned to say it, but seeing his brother touch my sister so soon after their parents tried to shove me into a car triggered an involuntary reaction.

I dropped my head toward my scarf. "I should have said that differently," I muttered, wishing I had stopped for a second to consider Marcus's feelings. He wasn't Antonio. He wasn't his parents.

"So you didn't mean it?" he asked.

I peered at him. He and Keira wore matching expressions—mouths open, eyes wide, waiting for me to make this better, to take it away. I couldn't. But I could tell my story. So I did, from the baby picture I received from Randolph

Urban, to my confrontation with Regina, to the photo of Marcus and me, to my clash with the Reys at their corporate headquarters, to Allen Cross's theories about Tyson's death.

"To be clear." Antonio cocked his head, brow furrowed. "You think *our* parents are evil people who slaughter children for financial gain?"

"If it makes you feel better, I also think *my* parents were evil," I rebutted.

"*Are*," Keira corrected. "Present tense. They're alive."

"It seems that way."

"I can't believe it." She stared at a fountain, as though the large-mouthed fish with water trickling out of its flared nostrils was now somehow very interesting and not at all disgusting. But it was better than looking at one another. "They weren't abducted. They weren't held hostage. They left us. By choice."

"Yes." I refused to plead our parents' case or offer hypotheticals that might make our abandonment seem justifiable. The only thing that got me out of bed this morning was not a Buddha-like understanding of their actions, but a burning need to avenge Tyson and any connection his death might have to me. I owed my parents nothing.

"Unfortunately, I have a passing familiarity with profound parental disappointment," Julian interjected, the epitome of manners. "My condolences."

"You really saw my parents?" Marcus rubbed the back of his neck, his voice sounding bewildered. Then he looked to his brother, dark eyes begging for answers, for behind-the-scenes Dresden information. "You worked there. Do you think they could have had something to do with this?"

"No." Antonio barked like Marcus was stupid for asking

the question. Then his nose wrinkled. "Are you really going to listen to *her*? I hear no proof, just opinions from Allen Cross, who is a liar. Do not believe *them*."

Seriously? Them? I was a "them." With a few sentences, Antonio placed me on the opposing side, as if I were a bad guy, as if I wanted to say any of these things. Of course, I didn't. It hurt me too, but that didn't stop my sister and Marcus from shifting away from me, inching closer to Antonio, the soggy grass between us growing more expansive by the second.

"I'm sorry I have to tell you this. It's awful. I know that," I apologized helplessly.

Marcus tugged harder on his neck, and I could practically see the knots growing; I felt them in my own shoulders, a headache brewing.

"Antonio's right," Marcus replied. "Cross has been lying since day one. He didn't tell you that your parents are alive. He didn't tell you that Urban is your father. Now he's claiming *my parents* are murderers. I don't believe him."

I probably wouldn't, either. But they weren't in that car. They didn't see Cross's demeanor, how different he seemed from our encounters in Rome. He was no longer the stoic spy relaying half-truths. He was emotional. He cared. It wasn't like before.

"Cross swears that whoever ordered Tyson's hit had to be very high up in the organization, because his death was designed to hurt *me*, and whether I like it or not, I'm the child of the three Department D founders." The words brought a bitter taste to my mouth. "Going after their kid would require someone with a lot of power, and he says your mom and dad are the only ones with enough influence to do that."

"Our parents are engineers!" Antonio sounded

exasperated. "They have nothing to do with Department D!"

"Yes, that's what they said to me, too. But Cross says—"

"*Cross says, Cross says…*" Antonio whined, mimicking my voice. "We don't believe him!"

Marcus nodded, agreeing with his brother. I had become the person who was accusing his parents of murder. How hard did I really want to argue this position?

"I get it." I stepped toward Marcus, closing the gap between us and growing a newfound sympathy for every messenger who had ever come before me in all of history. "You're right, we don't know anything for sure, and no one has to take anyone's word for anything."

A middle-aged man on a bike peddled past, wearing shorts and a tank top in November, a little terrier trotting beside him off leash. I fell silent, afraid the dog might be bugged. That was my life now. Even inappropriately dressed cyclists were suspects. I lowered my voice. "I'm done being crash-test dummies waiting for the next disaster to slam into us. This has to end. So I agree with you. It's time to get proof."

"How?" Keira asked, her face looking like I'd suggested we swim home to Boston.

"We have a plan."

We walked toward Kensington Gardens, fountains spraying unnecessarily as ripples of rainwater dotted their surfaces. The front of my jeans was soaked, my legs chilled in a way that only hot chocolate and a fireplace could help. It wasn't that the rain was coming down hard, it was that it was misting in every direction to the point that an umbrella was useless. Like the rest of London, we eventually relied solely on our hoods, with my every step sloshing puddles onto my weatherproof boots.

Marcus and Keira trudged beside me. Charlotte, Antonio, and Julian were a few paces behind. We were relaying our plan to mini groups—it felt safer than shouting it loud enough for a crowd of six to hear.

"The whole thing revolves around the Dresden Kids," I began, my breath making little frozen clouds in the air. "Think about it. They've thrown us together our entire lives. They made us each other's only friends. They forced us on each other at every company party, after every move. Why? Because we have one thing in common—we are all the children of Dresden employees. Which likely means we're all the children of *Department D* employees."

"So how does that help?" Marcus asked, his black leather jacket making a wet squeaking noise as he gestured between the three of us. "*We're* Dresden Kids, and we didn't know anything about Department D until a few months ago."

"Yeah, and supposedly our parents ran the thing," Keira added, her feet dragging through the puddles, her shoulders returning to their slumped position. She knew Tyson, and now he was dead because of us. Who was next? Keira had a lot more friends in Boston than I did. She socialized with half the hospital. Would Department D really hunt all of them for sport?

"That's just it. Our parents, *all* of our parents"—I looked at Marcus, eyes pleading for him to see we were in this together—"are on the upper rungs of this ugly ladder. They weren't personally destroyed by it."

"Urban put a hit out on Mom and Dad, and then they faked their deaths. Is that destruction?"

"Yes, it is, and now we're seeking revenge for that, which

is exactly my point." I flicked my finger her way. "Think of Dresden Kids like people on the Internet. Most only write reviews for things they hate, right? Well, the Dresden Kids are like that, like *us*. The ones who will talk to us are the ones who *hate* Department D. Remember Luis Basso's uncle?" I grabbed Marcus's arm, hoping to squeeze understanding into him. "The one my parents screwed over?"

"You mean the reason Luis wanted to cut you open on the top of a mountain in Cortona? *Sí. Recuerdo.*"

"Well, Cross says there are a lot more people like him. Tons of former employees, former allies, and regular people who were set up as patsies, locked in prisons, or had family members killed because of Department D. He thinks they'll want revenge, just like I do for Tyson. He's going to name names." I shivered, from the air or the conversation I wasn't sure. Nearby, empty rowboats rocked in the middle of a pond with fat swans swimming about. I'd imagine in a different season this place was idyllic and bursting with flowers and romance. Today, it was full of wet cement.

"What are we supposed to do with these names?" Keira asked, digging her hands into her pockets.

"We track them down and gather evidence."

"That's the plan? Are you kidding me?" She rolled her eyes.

Did she have a better idea? I didn't hear anyone else offering suggestions, and I was done waiting for the next assassin. I was done being the victim running up the stairs and tripping clumsily on a sneaker. It was time to fight back, however we could.

"What type of evidence are you talking about?" Marcus asked, sounding almost as leery as my sister.

"Like Aldo Moro. We have that photo proving my parents

were deleted from a historic crime scene, but that's only *one* case, and we don't have the original. We need more." My speech accelerated. "We need to prove how widespread and lethal this corruption is. We need to tie crimes to all those world leaders Randolph Urban has hanging in his office, because Cross says they're displayed as threats, not accomplishments. We need evidence, and Cross doesn't have access to Department D files anymore, but he swears it's out there, and he can help us find it."

"Oh, how kind of him to let us do all the work for him," Keira griped.

"Really, if these kids have evidence, why haven't they used it yet?" Marcus asked.

"Because it's them against the world," I said. "And we know how that feels."

Or maybe we didn't. Marcus wouldn't even look at me. Back in Italy, it felt like he was the only person in the world who understood me. Now, I missed him and he was standing right in front of me. It was starting to feel like not only me against the world, but me against all of them.

"Why would they trust us?" Marcus ran his hands through his messy black hair, dampened in a way that made me want to touch it. Touch him.

"Because we'll offer revenge," I said simply. "Alone, they know they'd accomplish nothing. Maybe some low-level flunky would be arrested. But together, with our help, we can burn that place to the ground."

"*Sí.* With my parents still in it."

I splashed to a halt. Kensington Palace loomed in the rainy distance, the windows of the first floor glowing with ocher light, its scale seemingly not much larger than Randolph Urban's mansion. A statue of a queen stood before it. Low reflecting pools with fountains sprayed like starbursts at our sides. And the boy I'd come to care about more than any boy, ever, stood in front of me, scowling like I *wanted* to hurt his family.

I was done being a "them."

I reached for his hands. We weren't wearing gloves. I could feel his skin, cold and rough. I rubbed my palms against his, hoping to warm him as I stared into his near-black eyes, desperate to reconnect. When he finally met my gaze, he seemed so different from the carefree guy chugging beers with his brother. I wanted to be the one who put the dimples in his cheeks.

"Marcus, I've thought about this a lot. I spent a good chunk of a transatlantic flight mulling this over with Charlotte. And we came to a conclusion—we have absolutely no idea who's lying," I stated plainly, willing him to feel me, feel how much I was on his side, *our* side. "Your parents claim that they're engineers hoping to preserve a legitimate corporation in the event that Urban goes to jail. Cross claims they were almost as high up in Department D as Urban himself. My parents were dead; now they're alive. Urban was a family friend; now he's a bio-dad sending me baby pictures while trying to kill my parents. For a *second* time. Until we have evidence, it's all theories, rumors, and somebody else's version of events. That's why we need to do this. These Dresden Kids might know who screwed over their families. They might be able to point the finger at someone *specific*. This won't be information coming from Allen Cross or Craig Bernard. This will be eyewitness testimony from kids like us. Why would they lie?"

Marcus closed his eyes, wincing like it hurt to think of his parents in this awful group. I closed the gap between us, and he leaned toward me, pressing his forehead to mine. It felt so good, so familiar. It felt like trust. We stood there, calm, breathing, as if silently praying our proximity to each other might ease all the chaos that put us at odds. I squeezed his fingers tighter. I wanted to bury my face in his chest, close the door, pull the drapes, and pretend none of this was happening. But I didn't think there were drapes thick enough. You couldn't black out truths that were coming from inside your head.

"What if they aren't innocent?" His voice broke. "What if my parents really are involved?"

"Then we'll deal with it. Right now, we don't know," I said, my forehead still resting on his, eyes closed, rain misting on our cheeks, our lashes. I could smell the wet leather from his jacket. I could feel the heat rising up from his skin.

I didn't want to hurt him, but I believed Allen Cross. I believed his parents weren't simple scientists with toothy smiles and perfectly coiffed heads. But Marcus had the right to cling to hope until proven otherwise. I wouldn't take that away from him.

"So Cross is just going to give us a list of names?" Keira blurted, interrupting our moment. Achingly, I pulled back from Marcus, from the first time in days I'd felt connected to him.

"Then what?" she continued, kicking a puddle, water spraying from her boot. "We're going to run around the world tracking down random people? Hope they have shoeboxes under their beds labeled 'Department D Evidence?' Hope they don't try to kill us, too?"

I opened my mouth to respond, but Keira kept speaking.

"Have you noticed that ever since Italy, you think you can do anything, that no one will question you. Especially me. Because I'm the victim, right?" Keira spat. "Did you ever think you found me because Urban *wanted* you to find me? These are spies, Anastasia, assassins. They're playing us. Playing *you*. Do the rest of us even get a say in all this?"

I shifted back on my heels. *Gee, tell me how you really feel.*

Keira glared at me—head shaking, molars chewing her cheek—like we were back in Boston and I was in trouble for ditching school. She looked like the guardian she was, like she called the shots, and I realized somewhere along the way maybe that had changed.

"Marcus, could I have a minute with my sister?" I asked.

Keira squinted her eyes, recognizing my tone; it was the we're-about-to-have-a-fight tone. Only I didn't want to argue. I wanted a long overdue discussion.

I walked down a footpath, away from the palace, away from the home that raised many queens, many leaders.

I waited for my sister to follow me.

I knew she would.

CHAPTER TWELVE

Keira and I sat on a damp wooden bench beside a pond littered with golden leaves. A royal blue plastic bag was tied to the metal railing beside us, full of birdseed, and my sister was feigning interest in a flock of black ducks with snowy white stripes down their foreheads. Despite the persistent rain, the ducks kept swimming in the icy water, quacking away.

I yanked the hood of my raincoat tightly around my face as I stared at the Peter Pan statue across the footpath. It was famous, marking the spot Pan stood in one of J.M. Barrie's legendary stories. I knew this because there was a cell phone tour offering the explanation, which I listened to, because it was preferable to talking with my sister. We sat silently, neither of us wanting to start the argument.

In what felt like a bad omen, there was a bouquet of long-stemmed pink roses abandoned at the foot of the soaring bronze statue. Blush petals were scattered about Peter Pan's mountainous base, the clear plastic flower wrapping haphazardly torn open, and its hot pink tissue soaked. I could almost envision a woman furiously slamming the gift to the ground and storming off—a peace offering gone wrong.

Keira finally slapped her hands on her thighs, wiping the remnants of birdseed on her wet jeans, and sighed heavily. "What are we gonna do?" she asked, kicking the heaps of mushy brownish leaves under our boots.

"We're going to find some Dresden Kids," I replied.

"That's not what I meant." She cut me a look.

"I don't think I'm some spy or assassin." I echoed her words as I pulled at my scarf, covering half my face.

"You think you're invincible. You think you're smarter than the rest of us. I'm not ungrateful. I know I wouldn't be here if it weren't for you." Her head leaned toward me as her gaudy teal polka dot hoop earrings clanked against her hood. "But I can't sit silently forever, doing everything you say, without question, just because you rescued me."

"I never said that you have to do everything I say or that I'm smarter than anyone else. But Keira, this plan makes sense, and if I had listened to *anyone else* before, you wouldn't be here."

"That's just it!" She pointed a finger at me. "There's nothing I can say to that. End of argument. You saved me, so I have to shut up and ignore every instinct in *my* head saying your plan is crazy."

"It's not *my* plan. Allen Cross, a professional spy, came up with it. And I am listening to what you think of it right now, which is a lot more than you did for me, when you ran a DNA test on Mom and Dad. You told *Craig Bernard* and not me. You trusted *him.*" The words spilled from my lips faster than my brain could warn me to hold them in.

Every day since Venice, I forced myself to swallow any feelings I had about my sister's decision to chase our parents' secret pasts. It was over. It couldn't be undone.

But the truth was, she lied to me. She never told me what she was doing, and instead she confided in a psychopath. That hurt.

"I know." Her forearms collapsed onto her thighs, her body hunching, wet hair falling into her lap. "I started all of this. I brought Craig Bernard into our lives. I *slept* with him. I *know*. Trust me, I live with that every day."

"I'm sorry. I shouldn't have said that." I rested a hand on her back.

"Don't be. We need to say this stuff. We're holding too much in. We're lying to each other." She swung her head my way. "Randolph Urban sent you a baby photo, and you didn't tell me? You *know* what that means, and you acted like you suddenly wanted us to move to France, like that picture thing had nothing to do with it?"

"It didn't." Though I really wasn't sure. I wrapped my arms around my chest. "I don't know, maybe it did. But going into hiding was a good plan. I wish we had done it. I wish we were there now."

"It wouldn't change anything. Tyson would still be dead."

"You don't know that."

"You are not the center of the universe," Keira said, only she didn't mean it as an insult. "Bad things happen, and they're not your fault. You can't control everyone."

"I'm not trying to control you." I shook my head, jaw tight as I clenched my arms more firmly around my body.

"Maybe you don't realize you're doing it. But look at you—you're so different now. Every muscle in your body is tense, all the time. You're always angry and scowling."

"And you think you're the same?" I tossed back.

Keira was kidnapped; that crime forever changed us both. Maybe I did have a hard time smiling, but she had a hard time sitting up straight. Was that so hard to understand? My best friend was murdered. His killer left me a message. Marcus's parents might be involved, and a spy told me my dead parents were alive right after a funeral. *I'm sorry if my shoulders are a little knotted up.*

Keira dug her hand into the plastic bag of birdseed and threw a handful at the ducks, a little too aggressively this time. "I know this is my fault, I get that, but I don't want to feel like your problem for the rest of my life. *Somebody deal with Keira, stupid Keira, helpless Keira.*"

"I do *not* act like that."

"When you got that message from Regina, the first thing you thought was that I would be kidnapped."

"Because you were recently kidnapped!"

"Yes, I was. I made a *huge* mistake, but that doesn't mean you need to lock me in a tower and exclude me from every decision."

"Do you have any idea what it was like to sit at Tyson's funeral? To see his casket? We put Mom and Dad in the ground." I gave her a knowing look, one only she could fully understand. "Now they're coming back from the dead, and I'm supposed to be okay with that? Meanwhile, my best friend was stabbed on the street in front of his girlfriend. Because of them. Because of *me*."

"*I am so sorry.*" Now it was her turn to rest her hand on my back. "I wish I could have been there for the service. I know what that must have been like for you. But I couldn't go, because the world thinks I'm dead. Do you have any idea how *that* feels for *me*?"

"No," I admitted, my voice defeated. It was starting to feel like we were living in the same house, the same reality, but not really seeing each other.

"I have no friends. I can't contact anyone. People I care about are still mourning me. I lost my job. You guys are my whole world, my only world, and you all either think I'm a screwup or a child."

"We do not!"

"Are you kidding me? You're the worst—you don't trust me, and you're clearly pissed at me," Keira said, her gaze steady. I could see that she meant it. *How could she mean it?* "You planned this whole Dresden Kid thing with *Charlotte* and then *told* me this was how it was going to be. You told me we were moving to France. You lied about the baby picture. You don't care what I have to say about anything. And just now, you put all this effort into making Marcus feel better, about *his* parents, but when you told me Mom and Dad are alive, you just said it. Not when you first found out, not as soon as you got out of the car with Cross. No, you told Charlotte first. Why? So you could break it to me in person? Well, thanks for that. You didn't even give me a hug."

My mouth snapped shut.

Is she right? Am I mad at her? No, I'm not. I would know if I was.

I thought about Keira's safety, her feelings, more than I thought about anything else in my life. I was going to tell her about the baby picture eventually. And I didn't hug her, because she didn't like to be touched. That was her choice. Wasn't it?

"I mean, Keira, you know—"

"I don't feel the same way you do," she cut in, not letting up. "Not about Mom and Dad. Cross says they left because of us, so we could have normal lives, so we could be free of Department D. I believe him. I know it didn't work out that way, but I believe they were trying to save us."

Her voice was so soft, but for the first time, I really heard her. My twenty-four-year-old sister was asking for permission, from me, to have her own feelings about our parents. I blinked at the realization.

"You're right." My tone was sincere. "We don't know why they did what they did, and you have a right to feel however you want about them. But so do I. People have been hurt and killed, because of them, including you. And I don't think I will ever be able to forgive them for that. But that's how *I* feel. I can't force you to feel the same."

"I am so sorry about Tyson." She squeezed my leg. "It is wrong on so many levels, but this plan, I think we need to at least consider other options."

"Like what?" I cocked my head in my hood. It had stopped raining, but we didn't adjust our jackets, as if we needed the barrier surrounding us.

"Like we let the CIA handle it."

"You know the CIA is not on our side. Cross said so himself. They want to track us back to Mom and Dad and send them to death row, if not worse. Is that really what you want?"

"No, but the CIA is a lot more equipped to destroy Department D than we are."

"Yeah, but they haven't done so yet, and there's probably a reason for that. They could be in on it," I pointed out. "These are Dresden Kids we're talking about. They'll trust *us*. They'll talk to *us*. I believe that."

I looked at the Peter Pan statue looming across the way and wondered briefly if Peter's origin story included parents who'd abandoned him. Maybe Peter hated them; maybe he resented them so much that he never wanted to grow up to be like them. Maybe the Lost Boys weren't all that different from the Dresden Kids—we had Randolph Urban, and they had Captain Hook. Now, if we could only find a crocodile.

"Okay, say these kids do want to help us, say they even have evidence—which is a big if—*then* what? Will you go to the CIA, or any form of law enforcement, and let *them* deal with the spies?"

I looked her square in the eyes; it was a compromise I could make. I nodded. "Yes. We'll turn the information over. We'll let the CIA, or whoever, bring down Department D. We won't have any direct contact with them, I promise."

Keira paused, assessing me, then smacked her lips, seemingly satisfied. "All right. But I don't really think that's a promise you can keep. You know, at some point, we *will* see Mom and Dad again, whether you want to or not, whether we choose to or not." She pulled back her hood so she could really see me. "There are too many forces at work here, and you need to be ready for that. They're not some evil strangers hiding in the shadows. They're our parents. And I don't think it's going to be as easy for you to hate them when you see them face to face."

"Trust me, it's very easy to hate them." I kept my hood up.

"Your feelings might change."

I bit my lip to keep from listing my resentments in alphabetical order. (A is for Assholes, Abandonment, Assassins, Archenemies; B is for Bastards, Boat chase, Blood, Bruises...) I could go on and on, but I didn't want to fight with Keira anymore. We were finally on the same team again. This plan would work.

We were going to end Department D one Dresden Kid at a time.

We just needed Allen Cross to send us the first name.

CHAPTER THIRTEEN

We were holding a meeting to conspire against an international ring of criminal spies on a giant Ferris wheel. Admittedly, before I knew anything about espionage, I would have pictured these types of meetings to occur in obscure passageways or the rare books sections of Gothic libraries. But no, Julian rented a private capsule on the London Eye. There was champagne on ice and an array of imported chocolates. We officially had two rotations on the wheel to plot exactly how we might save our lives.

"Look at this view!" Julian pointed as we dangled forty stories above London in a tourist trap sponsored by Coca-Cola (there were red logos everywhere). "I would have been remiss to let you miss this experience."

I leaned against a curved glass panel. We were hovering in a futuristic bubble above the River Thames, its water so russet it reminded me of the muddy Charles back in Boston. The day was clear, a forecast so unusual that Julian broke nearly every speed limit to get here to ensure the unobstructed streaks of sun didn't suddenly disappear.

I gazed at Big Ben on the opposite bank, the iconic

structure glowing in the salmon light. A fuzzy reflection of the clock tower, and its adjacent Parliament buildings, shone in the water. Red double-decker buses whizzed on top of bridges as ferries shuttled underneath. For a moment, I was reminded of Venice, of Craig Bernard diving onto a ferry and tumbling into the current. His body was never recovered, and I knew he was still out there. It was one of the reasons we needed this plan to work.

"It's pretty amazing," said Charlotte as she bit into a strawberry smothered in dark chocolate.

"Are we sure this is safe?" I rested my forehead against the curved glass, hands gripping a metal railing as we ascended. Below us, I could see another glass pod full of tourists snapping pictures. On the ground, people were scurrying along, buzzing between a hot dog vendor and a McDonald's restaurant, from the aquarium to the movies. It looked so peaceful from up here.

"I assure you there has never been an accident on the Eye," Julian replied as he adjusted his designer shades. The setting sun was bouncing off the river so intensely it created a glare I didn't know London could muster. It made me squint. "There's no need to worry."

"I'm not worried about the Ferris wheel falling apart. I'm wondering if it's safe to talk here?" Somehow an assassin in Boston knew Keira and I were planning to run and hide, a decision we'd made an ocean away only a day before Tyson's death.

"I made the reservation under a fake name," Julian reassured me. "And I had my security team sweep for bugs."

"We still haven't found anything at his flat," Charlotte interjected.

"If Department D knew you and your sister were going into hiding, if that was what prompted the message to your friend, I don't know how they uncovered the information."

"But it's definitely safe to talk here today," said Charlotte.

They were finishing each other's sentences. Last night, I watched Charlotte order Julian's favorite Indian as he taught her how to pair the perfect wine with her chicken tikka masala. (He recommended pinot noir.) Earlier today, he made her coffee without her even asking—milk and two Splendas. I wanted Charlotte to be happy (God knew, she deserved it), but it felt like I was losing her or like I was losing every connection I had to my old life—starting with Charlotte and ending with Tyson and Regina.

"I promise we will have no breaches in communication today, at least not electronically," Julian insisted. "Feel free to speak your mind."

I think Keira already got the ball rolling there. I stayed up half the night repeating every word she'd said to me, and I'd come to one conclusion—she wasn't being fair. Everything I did was for *her.* I gave up high school. I sold our brownstone. I moved to Europe. I fought assassins. All for her. Now she was complaining that I didn't listen to her enough. Yes, I trusted my gut more than I trusted hers, but that was because her choices got us here, and her choices currently had her flirting with a guy who worked for the enemy.

I looked toward Keira as she huddled near Antonio. I knew he was Marcus's brother, and Marcus loved him and trusted him. But I had reasons to be suspicious, only instead of understanding my very logical reservations, I found myself standing alone on the opposite end of a capsule watching Marcus, Antonio, and Keira share a laugh. A surfboard-shaped bench separated us; it was only a few feet long, but it felt like miles.

"Trust me, I'm an expert," Antonio bellowed, lifting a

full bottle of champagne in one hand and a triangular cake knife in the other. *"Mira esto!"*

"I don't think you use a knife to open champagne." Keira sounded like this was a very bad idea.

"Yeah, don't you wrap it in a towel first?" Marcus offered.

"*Sí*, if you suck," Antonio mocked.

"Seriously, I think you use your thumb." Keira looked to Julian for confirmation, her eyes begging for help.

"Yes. Please, allow me." Julian approached the group, hands outstretched, prepared to show his wealth of experience with high-end beverages.

Antonio snarled as though he'd fling the bottle at Julian's head if he took another step. "I got it," he insisted. Julian stopped.

"Okay, *hermano*." Marcus clapped with encouragement. "Let's see you do this." He was smiling with deep dimples, eyes so full of awe, it looked like he was about to watch his brother throw the opening pitch at Fenway, not open a bottle of wine.

Antonio exhaled in a puff, pumping his broad shoulders and bouncing on his toes to rev himself up. Then he raised the thick bottle, his tattooed arm outstretched and nearly touching the pod's ceiling. The heavy silver knife was clutched in his opposite fist, poised to smack the cork into the air.

Suspense sizzled through the capsule.

"Omigod, omigod, omigod…" Keira wriggled, wrinkling her eyes like she was afraid he'd chop off his hand (which was a possibility I wasn't entirely rooting against).

"*Uno, dos, tres!*" Antonio counted.

Then in one massive swoop, he swung the knife in a hard upward slice toward the cork, only instead of sending the bulbous top flying, a loud crash echoed off the walls. We all watched, in slow motion, as the bottle shattered in two and a wave of white fizz exploded.

"Aaah!" Keira yelled as foam spouted from Antonio's hand like a fountain, hitting himself, the white ceiling, and everything around him. The top half of the green bottle clattered to the floor while the bottom half stayed clutched in his thick fist. Antonio's dark jeans and white T-shirt were soaked, dripping with bubbles, and everyone erupted in laughter.

Including me.

"I should have recorded that!" Charlotte cried, snorting.

"Bravo!" Julian clapped.

Antonio hung his head, chest shaking with hysterics, as Marcus patted his back. "That was awesome!" he congratulated his brother, and even I couldn't help but smile wider.

"I swear I have done it before," Antonio defended, still laughing, dimples in full force, matching his brother's.

"I completely believe you!" Marcus cheered.

"And I can't say I hate the wet T-shirt," Keira teased.

"I did it all for you," Antonio offered, blowing her a flirty kiss. Then he grabbed my sister in a champagne-soaked hug, and she pretended to flinch from his sticky embrace, squirming as he squeezed her tighter, rubbing his sopping beard in her hair. I knew she was loving it, which was why it froze the grin on my face. She was falling for him.

"It's okay to laugh." Charlotte nudged me. "Antonio just made a complete ass of himself."

"I know," I replied, my expression melting to a frown.

Keira molded her body into Antonio's, kissing him sweetly.

"Or you could ignore them and enjoy Buckingham

Palace!" Charlotte darted to an interactive touch screen that labeled every building in view. Julian instantly rushed to her side, displaying the techno gadget. They were completely in their element.

And I was completely alone, a "them" once again.

A body pressed behind me, a hand on my hip. I knew his smell; even through the fog of champagne on his now-damp clothes, I could have closed my eyes and known it was Marcus—that unique mix of leather and sweat. I gazed at the tangerine sunset creating a black silhouette of the historic British skyline. It was a romantic moment, a honeymoon moment. I knew this in my head, but I couldn't feel it. Not like my sister. Not like Antonio.

"Deep in thought?" Marcus whispered in my ear.

"Aren't I always?"

"*Sí.* Want some champagne?"

"No." I continued staring at the sky as it shifted to a dusty rose.

"I'm sorry about Tyson. I wish I could have gone with you."

I nodded, the back of my head brushing against his chest.

"I know you miss him. I know you cared about him, but you don't have to be miserable all the time just to honor his memory."

What?

I pushed off the window, spinning around to glare at Marcus. *He's going to tell me how to feel about my dead best friend? He's going to explain* grief *to me?* The look on my face made his eyes widen.

"I didn't mean to offend." Marcus backed away. "But death can also remind us we're alive."

"So it's a good thing?" I snapped.

"No, of course not."

Where was this coming from? Antonio? I didn't remember Marcus wearing YOLO T-shirts before. Sure, maybe I'd go bungee jumping and hang gliding when this was all done, but before then, I was busy not being killed by spies.

I walked toward Charlotte, toward the only person left who still understood me. "Can we discuss the plan?" I asked.

"Sure." She nodded, her eyes flicking toward Marcus and seeming to read our mood. She gave me a concerned look, and so did Julian. Then they both pulled tablets from their shoulder bags.

"Okay guys, we have some names," she announced.

"Cross sent over a list of five," added Julian.

"Now we need to figure out who's going where and how." Charlotte plopped onto the wooden bench, pulling her feet crossed legged, exposing a stringy hole in the knee of her jeans. Julian sat beside her.

Antonio quickly stepped forward, leaving Keira behind as he tried to read off Charlotte's screen, almost a bit too eager.

"We're still doing research on the families," Charlotte explained.

"The list is diverse." Julian swiped at his screen. "Of the names Mr. Cross provided, three are related to Dresden employees, but two have no familial connections to the company. Instead, they were clients whose families were destroyed by Department D—even worse than *mine*." He sounded oddly impressed.

"*Bueno.* Let's hear them. Where are we going?" Antonio smacked his lips.

So now he's on board? Yesterday, he acted like I was

an evil traitor trash talking his benevolent parents. He said
my plan was ridiculous and unnecessary. Since when did
he become my champion?

An uneasiness moved through me as I eyed him. "Um,
maybe we don't need the names right now."

Our pod hit the apex of our climb, a weightless feeling
rushing over me. It lifted my stomach.

"*Porque?*" He looked my way.

"Charlotte said they're still working on the details. We
should wait," I lied. For some reason, I now didn't want
him to know too much.

And he knew it.

Antonio thudded toward me. "Do you think I still work
there?"

"No. I mean, I don't know. It's just—" My stomach
continued floating in space.

"Anastasia, he quit." Marcus said it like it was simple,
like he was offended that I didn't miraculously trust his
brother. His own parents badmouthed him (which was
rather messed up), and yesterday he did nothing but
criticize Cross's plan. Now Antonio was suddenly first in
line to get to work?

"I'm sorry." I shrugged, though I wasn't sure I meant it.
"But you used to work for these people. You're connected
to them."

"Aren't we all?" Marcus eyed me with a look that
seemed as confused as it did hurt. "Will you *ever* trust me?"

Of course I trusted him; it was his brother I didn't trust.
How many different ways could I say that? This wasn't
about him or us.

"Anastasia, I get why you're nervous," Keira conceded.
"But his past gives us some inside information."

I dug my hands into my hair, wanting to shout, *What*

if he's their *inside man?* "Your parents still work there."

"Do you really want to talk about parents?" Antonio shot me a look.

"Yes! My parents suck, and if they were here, I wouldn't trust them, either."

"You don't trust anyone," Antonio spat, then he looked at Marcus. "I don't know how you deal with her…"

What did he just say?

"Pause!" Charlotte hopped up, jumping between us before I could take that comment and shove it down Antonio's throat. "If we even want to attempt this plan, we need to stick together. There are six people in this pod. Six. That's it! We need to add to that number, not subtract from it."

"Tell *her* that." Antonio pointed to me, then knocked back a glass of champagne in one gulp.

I guess they figured out how to open a bottle when I wasn't looking.

"What do you want to do?" Charlotte asked me, and I heard Antonio grunt like she was giving the rookie the ball on the final play.

I was tired of defending myself; it was my life, Keira's life, on the line.

I turned to Julian. "Look, let's be honest. When we first met, I knew you had your own motives, your own reasons for being here, and you understood why I held back, didn't you?" Julian nodded, his turquoise eyes full of more kindness than anyone else in the pod right then. My gaze shifted to Marcus. "Everyone here proved themselves in Italy."

"So it's *my* fault I wasn't there?" Antonio gawked at his brother. "Are you really going to let her blame me because *you* chose to let me keep working for that organization even after you found out it kidnapped family members?"

"No one is blaming you," Marcus said, his eyes screaming apologies, on *my* behalf, like I was so embarrassing. "And I tried to contact you. You never called back."

"I told you the truth about my job the second you found me," he hissed.

"I know you did. But you didn't see what *she* went through."

Finally, Marcus was defending me. At least someone understood, at least someone had my back.

"Are you seriously taking *your girlfriend's* side over mine?"

"She's not my girlfriend," Marcus retorted.

My heart slammed into my throat. *What?* Only I knew what he said. I could see the words floating around him in dark little clouds. *She's not my girlfriend, she's not my girlfriend, she's not my girlfriend...*

The insult hollowed me out, scooping everything I felt for him, everything I thought we felt for one another. I shifted to the window, hiding the tears that were building inside. *Do not cry. Do not cry in front of him.* A sour taste filled my mouth, heat rising in my cheeks. Sure, Marcus and I hadn't made any "official" pronouncements. We hadn't had *that* talk, but I didn't realize it had to be said. I'd assumed we meant something to one another. *After everything we've been through...*

"It's not like that." Marcus stepped to me, hands outstretched. I jerked away. "I didn't mean it that way. It came out wrong."

I felt our pod slowly moving back toward Earth, our ride ending.

"He's my brother," he added.

I guess I knew where I stood, what he really thought of me. I wasn't going to argue my way out of rejection. I wasn't going to beg him to care about me. If he didn't want to be my boyfriend, fine. I'd gone my entire life without one; I could do it again.

Tears pushed at my lashes as I wrapped my arms around myself, squeezing the ache in my chest. I'd never meant anything to him. It was all in my head. How could I have been so wrong? Did he care about me in Italy? He had to have. It felt real.

I cleared my throat. "Keira and I will go together to find the first kid." I looked only at Charlotte. "Antonio stays here. He can keep you and Julian safe while you continue researching the other names. I don't want to leave you unprotected."

All politeness was gone. He worked for Department D, maybe he still did. Or maybe he would scare off a bunch of kids whose families were destroyed by the organization. I didn't know. That was the point.

"What about me?" Marcus asked, reaching for me, sounding almost as pained as I felt.

Oh, don't act hurt now.

"One of the names that Cross sent over is a kid in the UK," I explained, and Charlotte nodded in confirmation, her eyes dripping with sympathy, with pity. I gritted my teeth. "You can get him on your own."

"You're sending my brother alone?" Antonio yelled like he wanted to shake me.

"I've seen your brother in action. He can handle himself." My tone was as cold as I felt.

"Anastasia." Keira looked like a disapproving mom. "You're my sister. I love you, and I know you've been through a lot." She eyed Marcus like she wanted to toss him off the Ferris wheel. *That*, I appreciated. "But you know this isn't right. Maybe you and Marcus could go together, and Antonio and I..."

"No," I cut her off.

"I guess she tells you all what to do. Great girlfriend you got here!" Antonio quipped, nodding to his brother and knocking back another swig, bubbles dripping down his hand. Then he looked my way. "Oh, I forgot, she's *not* your girlfriend."

I wanted to punch him, and I was pretty sure he wanted to punch me, too. Then Marcus cut between us.

"It's okay. I'll go," Marcus said. "She's right. I can handle it on my own."

"The Dresden Kid we're sending you after is only fifteen years old, and he's a short train ride from London," said Julian, sounding afraid to enter the conversation. "I could go with you if you want."

"No, Anastasia's right." Marcus looked at me, his eyes full of apologies I didn't want to hear. "You need to stay with Charlotte and find out everything you can about these families so there are no surprises."

"Yeah, like someone attacking my brother while he's off alone." Antonio glared at me.

I hugged my chest tighter. I was sending Marcus to meet a potential member of a criminal family, with no backup, all because he hurt my feelings. I couldn't do this. I shouldn't do this.

"It's okay. I'll be fine," Marcus said as if reading my mind. "*Lo siento*. I don't know why—"

"Don't." I held up my hand.

He stopped talking, and our pod returned to ground level. We all moved toward the exit and stepped off of the still-moving tourist attraction.

The Ferris wheel never stopped turning.

CHAPTER FOURTEEN

Saint Paul de Vence was much like Tuscany, only the people spoke French and everything smelled of lavender. It was a medieval mountain town, a day trip from the beaches of the French Riviera, and it was lined with ancient stone streets featuring shops selling everything from tablecloths to modern art to local herbs. Chalice-shaped fountains gurgled almost lyrically as photo-worthy alleys peeked behind every corner. Roads were so narrow cars couldn't drive, making it a walking city, much like Venice. Ah, memories. I was haunted by them.

I spent the entire high-speed train to France reliving the London Eye, not the views, not the sunset, but the last five minutes, especially four specific words — "She's not my girlfriend." I wouldn't let Marcus take them back. Not in the pod when we descended back to Earth. Not in Julian's car when he tried to hold my hand. And not later that night when he knocked on my hotel room door. Taking it back, trying to offer some retroactive explanation wouldn't change the fact that he said it, that he meant it, at least in that moment. The thought was in his head. He would never be able to suck the tears back up from my cheeks, the ones that fell the moment I got back to my room and slammed the door.

I'd never had a boyfriend. I knew I was doing everything wrong. I didn't flip my hair. I didn't sit on his lap. I didn't let us go all the way the night after Antonio arrived. Maybe that was a mistake, or maybe I got lucky. I didn't know. There was no advice column or horoscope to offer insight on how to talk to your boyfriend while your friends were being murdered and your parents were implicated in their deaths. We were complicated. *I* was complicated. But that was what made us work; at least that was what *I* thought. Except it seemed we only worked when it was *my* parents who were the bad guys. The second his brother entered the mix, the second I mentioned his parents might be corrupt, Marcus pulled away. I felt it the moment Antonio insisted his family wasn't "that bad." Sure, they knew about Department D, they worked for the organization, but they didn't *really* do bad things. Marcus jumped on that, and any suggestion I made to the contrary, any theory, pushed him further away. He told his brother I didn't trust him. He probably told his brother much worse than that. What else did he really think of me? And he wondered why I stopped us that night?

"Who needs a StairMaster when you can live in Europe?" Keira grunted as we climbed the steep hills of Provence. Even wearing sneakers, our ankles twisted on rounded rocks that were probably set in concrete sometime during the reign of Louis XIV. And we thought Boston was old.

"Seriously. There is no excuse for anyone living here not to have a butt like J.Lo."

Keira and I didn't chat much on the train, but in a good way. We watched a Sandra Bullock movie on her tablet and shared a bag of Gummy Bears while Marcus's words echoed in my head. All she said was, "Let's see how this goes, and we'll take it from there." There was no sense fighting about a plan that we hadn't yet tried. If this kid slammed the door in our faces and refused to utter a word, then the entire strategy would need to be rethought.

So a lot rested at the top of this hill—our first Dresden Kid, Dani Zamen. He was a Turkish teen whose mother spent two years in prison for reporting on a fake military coup. Department D orchestrated evidence related to the false coup and arranged for the imprisonment of any journalist who didn't report the "facts" the way they wanted. His mother was one of those journalists.

"This kid could hate us," Keira pointed out. "What if it was Mom and Dad who did it? What if he pulls out a gun or something?"

"I've handled worse," I said, remembering Italy.

"That doesn't make me feel better." She sounded winded. Our climb was a mix of curving roads and deep wide steps. We'd developed a pattern—*step, step, up; step, step, up.* It was exhausting, yet rustically beautiful, but we had the determination of tourists chugging to the crown of the Statue of Liberty: we were only doing this once, and the payoff was worth it.

"Are you worried about Marcus?" she asked, as though it were a casual question. *Hey, look at that cloudless blue sky! The French country buildings! Doesn't the air smell like flowers? By the way, do you think you sent your non-boyfriend off to his death?*

"Of course I am," I admitted.

Not that I wanted Antonio to go with him, there was something too eager about the way he suddenly wanted to help with the plan, but I should have at least told Julian to go. Only that would have left Charlotte alone with Antonio.

They were right—I didn't trust him. Antonio hadn't provided any inside information on Department D. He claimed he wasn't high enough to know any, and maybe that was true, but he needed to bring something to the table other than his ability to chug alcohol and hit on women. Now Marcus was alone somewhere in the English countryside meeting a family that was destroyed by my parents' organization, by *our* parents' organization (though I doubt he saw it that way).

"I know Marcus made a dick comment. But if it helps, I don't think he meant it. He feels really bad," Keira defended, giving me a look like she knew she was diving into choppy water.

After the Ferris wheel, they'd all gone to the hotel restaurant. Instead, I chose room service. I didn't answer my door when they knocked. I was humiliated in a pod on the London Eye in front of all of them, and more than that, I was pretty sure I was dumped for the first time in my life. I didn't have any experience with this sort of thing, and maybe since I "wasn't his girlfriend" in the first place, this didn't count. But it felt like a dumping. And it hurt, on top of all the other hurt I was already feeling about Tyson, my parents, and my sister. There was only so much a person could take before she pulled up the sheets to her chin and turned off the light.

"All I'm gonna say is Marcus loves his brother," Keira went on. "How would you feel if he tried to convince *you* not to trust *me*?"

I hung my head. *Did she have to put it that way?* My chest already felt like Marcus slipped a serrated knife inside it. Now my sister gave it a good whack.

I stared at the rounded stones beneath my Converse.

"It's too late to do anything now. Let's just focus on Dani."

"Okay, I see the sign." Keira pointed ahead.

A Turkish import shop sat nestled between a French clothing boutique and a high-end stationery store. According to Charlotte's research, Dani Zamen and his mother fled to the French countryside for a fresh start. His mom's journalism days were behind her, as was her imprisonment. Now, based on their kaleidoscope-like window display, they spent their time selling Turkish bowls, lamps, tiles, vases, and jewelry in colors that seemed to explode against the ancient beige stone exterior.

"So we just walk in and ambush him?" asked Keira.

"That's the plan."

"Well, at least we've got a plan."

A bell jingled as we stepped into the densely packed shop. Every surface was filled with stacks of dishes featuring patterns so elaborately painted you'd never eat off of the surfaces, let alone wash them. Bulbous brass lamps looked like they held magical genies. Chandeliers dangled with glass mosaic globes. Cases were lined with sterling silver jewelry.

Next to the register was the face we'd memorized from pictures—Dani Zaman.

I looked at my sister. No turning back.

"Excuse me, do you speak English?" I asked, stepping toward the counter. Turkish was not one of my languages, but Keira and I could both speak in French if needed.

"Of course," he answered. "How can I help you?"

"Well, Dani, we're hoping *we* can help *you*." I cut to the point.

His face instantly changed, a hardness falling over his

maple syrup eyes. This was not the gaze of a teenager who spent his days watching cat videos on the Internet. This was a kid who'd seen tragedy. I should know; I wore that look myself.

"What do you want?" He sounded defensive.

"I realize this is unexpected." I kept my voice calm. "But my name is Anastasia Phoenix, and this is my sister, Keira." I looked for a hint of recognition when I said our names, but there was none. "Our parents used to work for Dresden, for Department D."

Embers lit in his eyes at the mention of the organization's name.

"Then you'll understand when I tell you to get the hell out." Dani marched around the counter.

"I know. I get it." I raised my palms.

"You *get it*? Are you kidding me?" His thick black brows crumpled like caterpillars as he halted a few paces away. "Do you have any idea what they put me through, put my *mother* through—"

"Yes, I do," I interrupted. "Because they did the same to us. Our parents are dead."

He rolled back on his heels, sizing us up, suddenly not sure how to react.

Technically, I was lying. My parents were alive, but we hadn't seen them with our own eyes, so that gave us deniability. Besides, what Keira and I knew for sure was what we actually went through these past three years as orphans, and that was the story the Dresden Kids could relate to, that was how we'd get them to identify with us.

"We thought our parents were engineers up until the day they died in a car crash, their bodies burned beyond recognition. We've spent the last three years on our own," I said, reciting the carefully edited speech we'd rehearsed.

"I'm sorry to hear that," Dani offered. He still sounded suspicious, but I could tell we'd quelled his anger. "But I thought you said they worked for Department D?"

"They did, but we didn't know that, not until I started questioning their deaths, who they were. Then I was kidnapped," Keira explained. The kindness in her voice and the softness in her body—the way her shoulders rolled forward and her lashes fluttered—made Dani's whole chest relax. He was listening to her. "My sister and I could have died, because of the work our parents did, because of enemies we never met." When she turned to me, any frustration she expressed regarding Antonio or my bossiness was wiped from her hazel eyes. Keira was on my side. We were the Phoenix sisters. United.

"What do you want from me?" he asked.

"We want you to help us get back at the people who put your mother in prison," I explained. "We want you to help us get revenge on Department D."

He tilted his tan face to the side like he hadn't heard us correctly. "Your parents worked for them. So did my stepfather, before he got my mother locked up in a Turkish prison and left me to live on the streets. How do I know you're not working for them too?"

"Because my best friend was recently murdered by Department D, and they promised to pick off every person I've ever met unless we pick them off first." My tone was harsh, completely unlike my sister's gentle demeanor, but it was all I could offer. I couldn't pretend not to be livid. Hollywood was not in my future. "You want revenge for what they did to your mother? You are never going to meet two people more motivated to give it to you than my sister and me."

Dani stood silently, assessing us, and I waited patiently

for my words to sink in, for him to read my face and see how much I meant it.

Only the response I got wasn't from him.

"Let's hear them out," said a feminine voice with a thick Turkish accent.

I turned toward a back wall, and in a darkened doorway stood a woman with flowing black hair, a full oval face, and big chocolate eyes lined heavily with pencil.

It was Dani's mother, Selen.

CHAPTER FIFTEEN

We sat in regal Turkish chairs with tufted crimson upholstery and curved cushy armrests as we listened to Dani and his mom talk. The blinds to the store were drawn. His mother had closed the shop. It was as if she had been waiting for us to arrive—ever since she'd been released from prison.

"Our door was broken down by police at five o'clock in the morning," Selen said, her hands folded in her lap. "Our home was raided, and I was arrested in my night clothes by shouting men armed with machine guns. I had never been questioned by the police before that day." Selen tucked her thick black hair behind her ear, a silver earring with a white and blue stone that looked like an evil eye hung toward her jawline. "They searched our house—"

"Searched?" Dani interrupted. "They *destroyed* our house."

Selen nodded. "They took everything—my laptop, my books. Every thought I ever wrote in a notebook, on a scrap of paper, was submitted as 'evidence' of my crimes."

"The crime of being a journalist and telling the truth," Dani continued.

Selen was looking at Keira and me, but her gaze was lifeless, as though she were telling the story about someone else, someone she hardly knew. "I didn't know why I was arrested, *for months*. I sat in jail, unable to defend myself, because I had no idea what evidence they had against me. Any attempt my lawyer made to obtain this information was ignored, and eventually *he* was accused of being a criminal just for defending me. The media, journalists I considered my friends, called me guilty—all of us—because of stories we wrote, because we did our jobs."

"Hundreds of people were arrested on the same day," Dani added. "Military officers, politicians, journalists, anyone the current regime saw as a threat. The whole thing about a potential coup was a ploy, an excuse to give the government a reason to get rid of people it didn't like, that it couldn't control."

"I know." I nodded. I'd read the information provided by Allen Cross and confirmed by Charlotte's research. So far, our intel on Dani and Selen was accurate, but it was missing the details that twisted something from being a news story into being someone's life.

"My own newspaper reported I was guilty. They published evidence that supposedly proved I was a traitor, all given to them by the police but that was never given to *me*," Selen continued.

"It was a blatant conspiracy between the news and the cops. They weren't even shy about it. No one bothered to check if the supposed evidence was true. It was like they didn't care." Dani shook his head in disgust, his wavy black bangs swishing on his forehead.

I thought about Department D, their specialty in spreading false information through the media. It was so obvious that they did this. The criminal organization started by my parents was responsible for the pain this family went through. How many more families would there be? I peered at my sister, and I could tell she was thinking the same thing. We felt guilty for something we hadn't done.

"They called me a terrorist." Despite the ugly word, her voice continued to hold the numbness of someone completely desensitized. "Because I dared to investigate the case, because I didn't believe those fake coup documents. And if I didn't believe them, then I must have been in on it. They acted like *I* was the one planning to overthrow the government—me, a journalist with a young son, who had never been in trouble, not once, before." She wrung her bronzed hands in her lap. She was wearing black wide leg pants and a black button-down shirt with her hair loose, not what I expected of a Muslim woman. "The people who did this—to me, to everyone—they're still in power. No one was arrested for framing us. No one apologized for putting us in jail. I spent two years in prison. *Two years.* I shared a single toilet with sixty women. There were one thousand of us in a prison meant to hold half that number. Some women slept three to a bed. It was so crowded, we couldn't breathe—no air, no windows, flies bit us while we slept. I was kept in solitary confinement for three weeks in a cell barely as wide as my reach." She held out her slender arms. "*And Dani…*" She hung her head and released the emotion she was holding in, the tears of a broken mother.

Dani wrapped his arm around her. "My uncle took me in, he tried to get my mom out, he hired a lawyer, but then he was harassed. He was brought in by the police, and they held him for more than a week. For nothing. After that, things got bad…*for me*." He looked down at his Nikes, black Air Jordans in the middle of a village in France. He rubbed at his forehead, and for the first time, I noticed a scar that stretched into his dark wavy hairline. When he met my eyes, he didn't need to say more. The abuse was obvious.

"Now we're here." Dani clutched his mom's hand, a silver gemstone ring on every finger. He squeezed with love. "And we must move forward."

Selen nodded, but in a way that suggested she wanted to believe that more than she really did. I imagined every time she closed her eyes, she was back in that prison, back in that cell the width of her arms, back reliving that fear. I knew what that was like. Only my private prison looked more like a bloody bathroom.

My sister and I exchanged a look and nodded—it was time to say what we'd come here to say. "What if you could get back at the people who did this to you?"

"How? What happened to us goes all the way to the top, to the prime minister of Turkey. How are you going to take him down? Plan your own coup?" Dani asked. "Because I wouldn't suggest it. It doesn't end well, even fake ones."

"No, not the Turkish prime minister. We can't help you there," I said, though honestly I wasn't sure. Once we blew the whistle on Department D, who knew how far the winds of justice would fan? Maybe Department D was hired by Turkey's top official; maybe there was proof of that somewhere. It could happen, but I couldn't promise it.

"We're talking about your ex-husband and Department D," said Keira, looking intently at Selen. "We're talking about the people who really did this, who really framed you. What if you could bring *them* down?"

"How? Your parents worked there, too."

"Actually, they started the organization," I said plainly. There was really no way to get around our uncomfortable family connection but the truth. "Then Department D killed them, kidnapped my sister, sent assassins after me, and murdered my best friend. They left me a message promising things were going to get worse. So we have to stop them, and you can help us do that."

Selen sat back in her chair, the wrinkles in her face, the set of her shoulders showed her years in a Turkish prison. She was used to the world being against her.

"My mother was locked up for *not* breaking any laws," Dani pointed out. "Now you want us to *actually* conspire with you?"

It was like I was asking for the blood in their veins, and maybe I was. My sister had been held for a few months, not two years, and her conditions included queen beds and newly purchased comforters. It was nothing like the horror Selen described. *So would I really agree to help a complete stranger after just getting Keira back?*

"People are dying. We could be next." I leaned forward, elbows on my knees. If we couldn't convince them, we couldn't convince anyone. "If you have any evidence against them, anything that could help us, please…"

Selen reached for her son's arm, squeezing it as she sat up straighter. "My ex-husband's name is Faruk Onart, though you probably already know that. I'm sure his name was a lie and he wasn't really Turkish. I think he was born near Russia and spent time in America."

"Anne, yapma," Dani said to his mother in Turkish, but she shook her head. They began to argue in their native tongue, and it seemed as though Dani rebuffed his mother's decision to help, but it was hard to say for certain given that I didn't understand the language.

My hope lied in Selen's need for revenge. She was an educated, strong, modern Muslim woman who was hideously betrayed and humiliated by a man who claimed to love her. He married her to control the reporting in her newspaper, and when she didn't assist his criminal needs, he turned her into not only an accused terrorist but a fool. He took everything: her job, her friends, her home, and most importantly, her son's safety. I had to have faith that she wanted to strip away her ex-con label and slap it on the back of the man who did this to her.

A lull finally fell on their conversation.

"We have information," Selen offered, giving her son a *do as I say* look.

Dani winced, clearly hating the idea, but obeyed his mother. "The day after my mom was arrested, I followed Faruk, my stepfather—though I despise calling him that—and I saw him meet with a man in a suit, not Turkish. Money exchange hands. They were speaking English." He looked me dead in the eyes, and I caught a sense of hatred as he remembered this scene. "I have it on video."

My eyes stretched as I fought a smile that wanted to creep across my face. It was exactly what we needed—evidence, real hard evidence. I turned to Keira, whose eyes were just as wide.

"If we give this to you, how do we know our door isn't going to be kicked in at five in the morning, only this time by the assassins who came after you?" Selen asked, expecting promises I couldn't make.

"How do you know that won't happen even if you don't help us?" It was the depressing truth. "My sister and I already have come to the conclusion that we're never going to be safe as long as this organization exists. They will keep coming after us. And you will probably always be looking over your shoulder. Unless we bring them down for good." It was the best I could offer.

Selen nodded. "I'm all right with whatever happens

to me. *I* did this. I chose to write those stories. But what happened to *you*." She looked at her son. "I can't live through that again."

"And I can't live through you spending another day in that hell," Dani replied.

"You can't expect us to just hand over our evidence to you." Selen looked at me. "It's our only protection, our only proof. It's why we've hung on to it."

"How do we know you won't destroy it?" Dani asked.

"I understand, and I would probably feel the same way," said Keira as she reached into her pocket, four inches of Madonna-style jelly bracelets sliding down her wrist as she pulled out her burner phone. We all watched as she swiped at the screen and turned it to face Dani and his mother. On it was the photo of Keira shoved into the back of a classic car in Rome. She swiped to the next image and displayed the picture of her in captivity, skinny and malnourished, holding a church bulletin in Venice—her proof of life. I didn't know how often she looked at those pictures, but I imagined it was more often then I would have liked.

"It may not have been a Turkish prison," Keira went on, staring as Selen, "and it may not have been two years, but I know what these people are capable of. We are not lying to you."

Selen gripped Dani's hand for support, as if there was only one thing left to do. "We will give you our evidence."

"But I want to come with you," Dani interjected. "I want to see what you're dragging us into." His tone turned deadly. "I will not let you hurt my mother."

He wants to come with us? That was unexpected.

"Sure." I nodded. "Whatever makes you comfortable."

"Then our choice is made." Selen released her grip on her son's hand, and for the first time, I noticed an expensive gold watch on her wrist. For a boy who was living on the streets a couple of years ago and a woman who recently got out of a prison hellhole, it seemed like an unlikely fashion accessory. Selen noticed my gaze. "It was a gift from my lawyer, when he finally got me out," she muttered quickly, pushing the watch back under the sleeve of her black blouse.

"We think it's fake," Dani added, abruptly rising from his upholstered chair.

It didn't look fake. But what did I know about fashion?

"You'll put Faruk behind bars." He said it like it wasn't a question.

I stood to meet him. "We will do everything we can to destroy him and everyone he works for."

Dani nodded, but when he turned to his mother, I saw the doubt in his eyes. He dropped to his knees, clasping her delicate hands like he was at the foot of a queen. "Will you be okay here? We can change our minds. I can stay."

"I'll be fine. It's up to you now to be the strong one, to end this for us. Go with them, and you will get back at the people who did this. Don't forget that."

I knew, right then, that she'd said the right thing.

Dani was coming to England.

CHAPTER SIXTEEN

Since Keira had been taken, I'd spent a lot of time on European trains, and I rarely got to enjoy the view. Cyprus trees, stone cottages, and rolling vineyards were often overlooked as my mind focused on death threats and conspiracy theories. Dani, however, seemed to have no problem mentally diagramming every twig outside our rumbling train window; it was much more preferable to looking us in the eye as we told him all the horrible details we knew about Department D.

"So your parents were my stepfather's boss, and now I'm sitting here with you. You realize how strange that is." His gaze stayed out the window.

"We don't know if our parents had anything to do with what happened to your mother," I reasoned, resting my arms on the gray plastic table that separated us as I picked at an airplane-quality croissant that was wrapped in plastic like a Twinkie.

"But they ran the company," he said.

"We used to be proud of that."

"Proud of criminals?" His lips pursed to the side.

"They weren't criminals back then, not to us," Keira added.

We hadn't yet told Dani we thought our parents were alive. His anger was already so palpable it was getting hard to breathe in the dining car, and we didn't want to give him any more reason to dive off the speeding train.

"You have to remember, for our whole lives, they were just our parents. We thought they were these super important engineers," said Keira as the train rocked over the country tracks. "Remember that carnival Urban had in his backyard?"

I nodded, unsure why she was bringing it up.

"I was probably twelve at the time, and you were, what, five?" She peered at me, and again I nodded hesitantly. *Was now really the best time to get nostalgic?* "Randolph Urban, the CEO, hosted this huge carnival with clowns, a carousel, pony rides, acrobats..."

I could practically feel the sun on my cheeks as she spoke, my body spinning round and round as the carousel played, wind blowing my hair. I could see my parents moving through the crowd, everyone stopping to greet them, fighting for their attention.

"When it got dark," Keira went on, "we all huddled around a fire pit. The kids roasted marshmallows, and the adults smoked cigars and drank." Keira's eyes looked distant, and it was as if we were both picturing the scene so vividly we could smell the smoke. "Everyone was thanking Urban and our parents. I thought they were thanking them for the party, but eventually I realized it was something more..." I suddenly knew what she was getting at. "I remember Mom and Dad sitting at Urban's side and everyone looking at them like they were so important, like they were kings. Everyone wanted to please them—

tell the funniest joke or offer the best compliment. I felt so proud. Those were *my* parents. Everyone worked for *them*. I remember looking at the other Dresden Kids and thinking I was more important than them, because my parents were so high up in the company, higher than theirs."

I'd felt the same way. It was the pride of a kid on career day whose parent had the coolest job. What I would do to have *those* people back. But it was never real. "Now we realize it only meant they were worse than everyone else."

Keira rubbed my arm. "Who our parents are, what they did"—she looked at Dani—"is just as confusing to *us* as it is to you."

"How could they do this to kids, to families, and not care?" It was as if Dani were asking the meaning of life.

"I don't know." I shook my head. "But if you're looking for an apology, if that's what you want at the end of this, from Faruk, from anyone, I wouldn't get your hopes up." I thought of Allen Cross, and how he had a hard time offering condolences after my best friend's funeral. He didn't even apologize for faking my parents' deaths and not telling me they were alive as I ran around Italy after professional killers. I sensed a career in crime forced you to amputate many bits of your humanity, most notably the parts that feel empathy and remorse.

"Don't worry, I'm realistic about what will happen at the end of this," Dani answered, gazing at the blackened windows as our train entered the tunnel beneath the English Channel. Ochre lights flickered on the ceiling as we plunged farther below the massive body of water, zooming back to London. When he looked back our way, the glint in his eyes seemed harsher, or maybe it was the lighting. "I know you want revenge for your kidnapping, and your friend's death, but have you considered that some of these

Dresden Kids might want revenge against *you*? Against your parents?"

Actually, we'd discussed this possibility at length since Allen Cross proposed this plan, and our only hope was that Keira and I could get through to them, prove we were serious about destroying Department D, and that despite our different experiences, we wanted the same thing.

I leaned toward Dani. "The one thing we all have in common is this—we *aren't* our parents. I promise you, if the evidence points to our mom and dad, I will not be protecting them any more than they protected us. I'm offering *revenge*. Why wouldn't you want that?"

Dani looked at me, and I wished I could hear the million thoughts I saw screaming behind his dark eyes, but he stayed silent, for almost too long, before he finally nodded. "Well, I guess we have that in common—vengeance."

Slowly, our train emerged from the pitch-black tunnel, and as soon as we chugged into the English countryside, my phone vibrated in my pocket. It was a message from Charlotte. Marcus was back. And he wasn't alone.

They were all at an Irish pub near Charlotte's flat, which apparently, she still paid for despite the fact that she spent most of her time at Julian's penthouse. I'd never been to this part of London. They called it Zone 2, which essentially meant it was outside of the touristy epicenter. We could feel it the moment we stepped out of the Tube. Gone were the pristine townhomes, gaslights, historical palaces and cathedrals. Instead, Charlotte's neighborhood was bustling with women commuting in sneakers with their suits, men yelling about work into cell phones, dogs being walked, babies being strolled, and children squealing in playgrounds.

This was where Londoners actually *lived*. I couldn't believe I had never been to Charlotte's place before.

"I like it," Keira noted as we trudged alongside Dani past a boutique displaying handmade soaps with fresh flowers for sale on the sidewalk. "It's homey."

"Getting tired of glass penthouses and room service?" I asked, an eyebrow raised.

"Getting tired of living out of a suitcase," she replied.

Wasn't that the truth.

The bar was tiny, nestled on a corner with gold Celtic lettering that read, "The Auld Shillelagh," above an exterior painted the color of merlot, though I doubted people ordered anything other than beer. According to Charlotte, "it served the best pint of Guinness in London," and Julian swore it was the most authentic Irish pub outside of Dublin, as if that meant anything to me.

"Just make sure no one slips anything into my drink," Dani cautioned as he opened the door. Trust issues ran deep in our group, but before I could reassure him further, I was stopped in my tracks.

There, past a handful of tiny round tables, directly next to a wood-paneled bar cluttered with taps, sat Marcus. He was playing acoustic guitar. With Antonio.

And they were good.

I stood glued to the entry, jaw dropping as Marcus and his brother plucked at strings so quickly it was as if their fingers were dancing. It was a Spanish medley, and they weren't singing, but they didn't need to—the rhythm was so intoxicating every patron in the long, narrow pub was enthralled. There was no stage. They were sitting on low stools in front of round tables full of half drunk pints. Behind them were framed pictures of soccer teams, musicians like David Bowie and Frank Sinatra, and a blue and gold flag I didn't recognize. Marcus started leading, his whole leg bopping to keep beat as Antonio batted his hands in tempo on his guitar. Then they switched. It was clearly a routine they'd practiced before. A lot.

Keira turned to me, equally stunned. "Did you know he played?"

"No." I shook my head.

"You know those guys?" Dani asked as he stood between us, studying our reactions.

"Yeah," I choked. "It's who we're here to meet."

"Great. Let's get a beer. I know I need one." Dani stepped toward the bar, every stool occupied by patrons.

"Anastasia! Keira!" Charlotte yelled across the narrow establishment, jumping up from a table in back and waving wildly.

Marcus instantly looked my way and smiled, dimples as deep as I'd ever seen them, hands still moving rhythmically. Then he and Antonio ran their fingers back and forth across all the strings at warp speed, staring at each other, their chests leaning forward as they strained to hit the final crescendo, and then suddenly, the music stopped.

Everyone cheered. People stood. There were wolf whistles. And before they even set the guitars down for the next person, a stranger placed a dark frothy pint in their hands.

"Holy shit," I muttered.

"Yeah," Keira agreed. "That was hot."

"Come on! Meet everyone!" Charlotte beckoned.

We had to walk by Marcus and Antonio to get to their table, which was situated near a fireplace actively burning wood and filling the bar with the scent of ski lodges at Christmas.

"I'll wait for Dani. Go." Keira practically shoved me

toward Marcus. Subtle.

I stepped toward him, feeling shier than I'd ever had in my life. I hadn't spoken to him since the London Eye, since the comment that was stuck on repeat in my brain. I'd spent a lot of time traveling to and from Provence imagining what it would be like when we faced one another again, practicing all of these clever lines I'd say, how perfectly cool I would act. But I never expected an acoustic guitar. It wasn't fair.

"Hey." I nodded.

Marcus ran his hand through his messy black hair, his black T-shirt lifting to expose a toned strip of his belly. This *seriously* wasn't fair.

"I'm glad you're back safe," he greeted, and I felt an instant thrill all the way to my belly.

No. Don't. You're not his girlfriend.

"You, too," I replied coolly. "I didn't know you played." I gestured to the guitar.

"*Sí*, Antonio and I have always messed around. We're self taught."

Perfect. He was a musical genius. And he was smiling at me like there was no one else in the world he wanted to see. It made no sense. *He* dumped *me*.

"Well, you're good." I was trying to sound detached, but really my heart was crashing against my ribs so hard I swore he could hear it over the conversations buzzing in the bar. "How did you end up playing tonight?"

"It's open mic. Or open guitar." He chuckled, hand in his hair once more. He had to stop doing that. "We haven't played together in years."

"It sounded like you practiced that."

"A *long* time ago." He nodded toward his brother, the admiration so clear in his dark eyes I felt even guiltier. I had a right to be suspicious of Antonio, but I didn't want to argue about that now. After the seemingly endless conversations with Dani, I was emotionally exhausted. Now it seemed Dani wasn't the only newcomer. Seated at Charlotte's table was the teenage boy Marcus was sent off to meet in the British countryside.

"I see you brought back Ben." I pointed with my chin.

"*Sí*, you, too." Marcus's eyes followed our Turkish companion as he, Keira, and Antonio headed toward our table of friends.

Hauling the Dresden Kids back to London was not part of our plan, so it was an interesting coincidence.

"Ben insisted," Marcus explained, as if hearing my mental questions. Sometimes it felt like Marcus could read my mind, and other times, it felt like we hardly knew one another. "He's got some solid evidence, but it's complicated."

"Same with Dani." I grunted.

"They're helping, at least." Then his dark eyes turned intense. "I think in time we'll all learn to trust each other."

I could tell there was another layer of meaning to his comment, but I wasn't ready to talk about it, or us. Maybe that was a benefit to ending our romance; I could be more focused on our mission. We obviously needed it.

"Introduce me to Ben," I suggested, swiftly turning away before any more butterflies could flap through my belly.

"*Claro.*" Marcus strolled beside me.

Our group took up two round tables full of Guinness, and as soon as we approached, Charlotte and Julian started clapping.

"Bravo!" Julian cheered. "You and your brother are impressive performers."

"We're a little rusty." Marcus smiled at Antonio, whose

hand was already on Keira's knee, his eyes on me as if daring me to object. I had no desire to resume our fight, and definitely not before the hellos were even finished. I sat down next to Marcus.

"Anastasia, have you met Ben?" Charlotte gestured to the English teen across from me, whose skin was so pale I could see blue veins on his temples and in his hands. He was fifteen, but he looked twelve with long scrawny legs and a baby face that wouldn't scare a Chihuahua.

"Thank you for helping us," I greeted.

"You should thank my grandfather. He was the one who refused to drop the matter." Ben looked up at the heavens. "At least now we will get some retribution for Aunt Hilda."

Benjamin's great aunt, Hilda Murell, was sexually assaulted and murdered in the English countryside in 1984. The government convicted a teenager for the crime, only Ben's grandfather disagreed. His aunt was an outspoken anti-nuclear activist who died days before she was set to give a high-profile speech against Margaret Thatcher's nuclear power policies. According to Allen Cross, the crime had been committed by an off-the-rails pro-nuclear activist, and Department D was hired to cover up any hint of a "nuclear motive," so as not to falsely implicate the British government.

"Charlotte says you have DNA evidence?" I asked skeptically. The crime was thirty years old; how could that possibly exist?

"Not me personally," Ben said. "The police have the evidence boxed up. All I know is what my grandfather told me before he died—there were four sets of DNA found at the scene, one was the teenager they convicted, one was my aunt, and the other two have never been identified. So if it was a lone crazy teenager who killed her, why the other sets of DNA?"

"I'm gonna try to work with law enforcement," Charlotte interjected as she sipped her frothy pint. "See what we can do."

"I'm telling you, my family's tried everything," Ben warned.

"They haven't tried me." Charlotte smiled at the challenge.

She and Julian had taken charge of all technical matters, responsibilities I was happy to delegate. See, I could trust people.

"From what I've been told, your mum and dad were very...*high up*." Ben looked at me.

It appeared I'd be having this conversation with every kid who joined our group, and I caught Antonio glaring at me from across the table, eyes practically shouting, *How does it feel not to be trusted for something you didn't do? How does it feel to have to prove you mean what you say?* Our situations weren't the same, but I had to admit there were parallels. And it sucked.

"It's not a secret that my parents weren't good people. We're not covering that up," I recited the familiar lines. I used to hate talking about my parents, now it was all I ever did. "My sister and I have been hurt as much as anyone else. Believe me, we want the same revenge you do."

Ben's eyes narrowed, like he either didn't believe I could hate my parents or he pitied me for hating my parents. Both options were pretty miserable.

"It's okay. I had a nice long talk with *Ben-ha-meen*." Marcus said his name with Spanish flare. I loved when he did that. "He knows we're *all* on the same side." Then he nudged my shoulder like he wanted me to hear how much he meant it, like he wasn't just talking about Ben.

"Could I talk to you?" Marcus whispered in my ear, so close his breath sent a buzz through my body. "Not here?" He gestured to the front door.

"Sure." I nodded. I'd spent so much time envisioning this conversation that I needed to get it over with for the sake of my sanity.

Marcus extended his hand, and I clasped it. Then I followed him outside.

CHAPTER SEVENTEEN

A couple years ago, Charlotte, Keira, and I watched *The Blair Witch Project*. It was our way of celebrating Halloween—we didn't get many trick or treaters in a city condo. Now I was walking through an urban cemetery with tombstones that were hundreds of years old, engulfed by so much overgrown brush, you could barely see the names etched due to the dense ivy covering the stones. I was wearing a gray knit hat, pulled low over my ears. And my nose was running from the cold. All I needed was a close-up monologue.

"Antonio and I found it earlier today, before we got to the bar," Marcus said as he led me down what at one point was a path, though it was now smothered in mushy leaves with trees arching overhead until they met like a canopy, making the already grey sky of twilight in London even darker. "It's romantic, no?"

"I guess, in a *Wuthering Heights* kind of way," I mumbled, stepping over a fallen tree branch.

The cemetery was across the street from the pub, surrounded by a bustling neighborhood and honking city traffic. But as we walked down the unkempt paths, it was eerily quiet. Cockeyed headstones loomed in all directions, obscured by shrubs and twining vines, along with statues of winged angels, pillars dangerously leaning to the side, and stone crosses stained lime green with mold. It was as if the bodies were buried centuries ago, then an earthquake hit and no one bothered to clean up, letting nature take its course.

I had to admit, it did have a creepy Gothic charm, like I should be wearing a long white nightgown and floating ethereally over a layer of dew.

Marcus stopped at a wooden bench below what used to be a tree. Now the thick, hollowed stump soared a few dozen feet in the shape of a "V," its two massive branches amputated at the elbows. The rotten wood was almost black, and the crack down its middle suggested it might have been hit by lightning. Or it simply died, much like everything else.

Marcus sat, and I joined him, neither of us saying a word. Then he leaned back, tossing his head toward the fading light.

"Your eyes match the sky here. Have you noticed that?" he asked, gazing at the blue-gray cloud cover.

I looked up and realized he had a point; my sister always did say my eyes were gloomy, like the air before a clap of thunder. "I like to think mine aren't as cold."

"No. They definitely aren't." He turned his face my way. "That's not what you thought I meant, did you?"

"No." I shook my head, though lately, I was wondering how well we really knew one another. The guy I saw with his brother, the one who laughed easily, who partied often, who played the guitar and got spontaneous tattoos, I didn't know that guy. That realization hurt, like I'd been fooling myself about what we were from the beginning. "I didn't know you could play an instrument. How did I not know that?"

"It didn't come up while we were running around Europe after our siblings." He sounded like it was no big deal. Only it was.

"What else don't I know?" I shoved my hands into my pockets, squeezing them. It was time to let him off the hook, for everything. "Marcus, we met when my life fell apart. Maybe it was unrealistic to think that we could keep this going—"

"No." Marcus held out his hand to stop my train of thought. "I'm sorry for what I said. I didn't mean it."

"Yes, you did," I replied, unable to face him. There was an obelisk in front of me that had toppled diagonally onto a pedestal with a stone statue of a chalice on top. When did people stop marking tombs with elaborate monuments? Most cemeteries back home were full of flat grave markers, black rectangular stones set in grass. I'd spent a lot of time in those places, alone, grieving the end of things. I guess Marcus had picked an appropriate location for this conversation. "You were right. We never made any promises. I was never your girlfriend. It's okay, really. We don't have to make a big deal of it..."

I didn't want to embarrass myself further; begging him to feel what I felt wouldn't make it so. Now I had to hope he might still help extinguish Department D, but if he and Antonio wanted to move on, I was prepared for that, too. After all, it wasn't too long ago that Keira and I were ready to do the exact same thing. I was set to leave him. Difference was, it practically killed me to have to do it.

He grabbed my arm, pulling me until I had to meet his gaze. "I *did not* mean it. Not the way it sounded." He exhaled, flicking a look toward the sky. The light was fading fast. "*Ahnahstasia*, I know you've been through a lot, I was there for some of it. I understand what that can do to you, but you have to see this from my point of view. You don't trust me. You may not realize it, but you don't. And I never doubted Keira, not once while we were looking for her—not when we found out she was dating Craig Bernard, not even when we learned she ran that secret DNA test. You trusted her, you believed in her, and I trusted *you*. How do you think it feels when you treat my brother like the enemy?"

My body slumped as I dug my fingers into my palms, wanting to scream at full force. I didn't *want* to treat Antonio that way, I didn't want to have these thoughts, but I couldn't turn them off. "Marcus, this isn't just us, back in Boston, and me not getting along with your older brother. This is life and death. My life. Keira's life."

"What about *our* life?" He cocked his head. "I never meant that I didn't *want* you to be my girlfriend, I meant that you don't treat me that way. You're always shutting me out…"

"You're one of the only people I talk to!" I tossed up my hands. *What else can I do?*

"We talk when *you* feel like talking. How many times have I knocked on your door and you've refused to answer?"

"What you said that day *really* hurt," I yelped. I had a right to feel sad, humiliated, and rejected. I also had a right to be alone.

"I know, and I'm sorry. But when you announce that you're running away with your sister like I don't matter, when you act like I'm doing something wrong for hanging out with my brother, for trusting him, *you* hurt *me*."

My lips clamped shut, my throat constricting. I stared

at the graves. I didn't know the right thing to do or say. I wanted to fix this, fix me, fix this entire miserable circumstance, but I didn't know how, and I definitely didn't know how to be in a couple. Tears pushed at my eyes.

"You're happier with him," I blurted before my brain could take it back. "I can see it."

"No." He leaned forward, grabbing my cold hands and tugging me toward him once more. "I'm different with him, because he's my brother. You're different with Keira. You're gentler and super protective. With Charlotte, wow, you listen to every word she says, every idea. No one has more influence on you than her."

"Because I've known her forever," I said.

"Exactly." He reached for my face, wiping away the tear that fell. "I'm here, in London, because of *you*. I've never felt for a girl what I feel for you. But you've got to start letting me in."

I nodded, biting my bottom lip hard. "I know I'm being a hypocrite with Antonio. Not trusting him while I'm asking these Dresden Kids to trust me. I get that. I see that."

"Good." Marcus's eyes widened in agreement, like we were finally getting somewhere.

Only it wasn't that simple.

"Marcus, I'm a mess," I went on. "For three years, I thought my parents were dead. My sister was kidnapped. Tyson was murdered. Regina was threatened." I thought about our conversation in the hotel room, in my bed, when I pushed him away. He thought I didn't trust him, but that wasn't it. "Nothing good in my life ever lasts," I choked out.

His face crumbled, and he placed both hands on my cheeks, his touch so incredibly warm. "I'm not going anywhere. What I said, that whole girlfriend thing, *Ahnahstasia*, you are so much *more*."

My breath hitched, and I sniffled, my whole body jolted by his words. He really did care about me. I stared at his lips, at him, my heart pounding, my breath quickening. I had never wanted anything or anyone more.

"I won't kiss you, not unless you ask me to," he suddenly insisted. My brow furrowed, but I could see he wasn't playing coy; he was giving me a choice, one a lot bigger than a kiss. "I know everything that's happening with our families is…*loco*. We're going to disagree. But if we do this, then we have to do it *together*."

My shoulders fell, my entire being warring with what I wanted versus what was safest. My gut told me not to trust Antonio, but if I pushed it, I'd be pushing Marcus, too. He would never choose me over his family, any more than I'd choose him over Keira. It was a very distinct line between us, and I feared we would be crossing it soon.

"I don't want our parents, our siblings, to define who we are. Forever." My voice was small.

"Neither do I."

"But this plan, what comes next, I think it's going to get ugly. The things we're going to learn…"

"We face them together," he interjected. "We do this together. *All* of us."

The implication was clear—the Rey brothers *and* the Phoenix sisters, or no one at all.

"Okay." I nodded. I couldn't lose him, I just couldn't. "I trust you. I do. I swear. So I'll trust you about Antonio."

Marcus smiled, dimples glowing even in the darkness that had fallen around us. "I know you think I'm different with him, but he thinks I'm different with you. I'd follow you anywhere, *Ahnahstassia* Phoenix."

I kissed him. I didn't wait for permission. I didn't ask any more questions. I pressed my lips to his. It was so easy, his mouth on mine, his hair in my fists. All the grief, the fear, the complexity was gone, and my entire body filled with heat. My mind was silent. I needed this. I needed him.

Maybe cemeteries could be romantic.

Or maybe they just fit us.

"Pack up, kids! We're moving!" Julian announced the next day while we hung around his ultra modern kitchen.

"I'm sorry, what?" I asked, my fork paused mid-stab in my grilled chicken salad.

"I took the liberty of finding us a new abode." His whitened smile was so wide, it was clear he was proud of himself.

"What's wrong with this *abode*?" Marcus asked.

"For starters, it's getting rather crowded." Julian gestured to Dani and Ben, who were leaning against the granite counter.

"You want us to leave?" Dani asked.

"No, not at all." Julian swiftly held up a hand. It was the last thing he wanted. I could practically see Julian planning camera angles for their primetime special. "You and Benjamin have every right to be a part of this process, and I think it's wise that Charlotte and I take your evidence directly, record your video depositions, ensure the chain of custody, coordinate communication…"

"You're losing them," Charlotte singsonged as he rattled off procedures.

"The point is, if more of our new friends want to be involved, then my little flat isn't going to do."

"Only in your world is this a *little flat*," said Antonio

as he waved his hand around the opulent penthouse that encompassed the entire top floor of the building and had its own glass elevator.

"For once, I agree with you." I nodded at Antonio.

I even half smiled, trying to be nice. For Marcus. I was going to force myself to treat his brother the same way he treated my sister—even if I had to grit my teeth to do it. Antonio nodded in return, recognizing my effort.

"I fear there isn't ample room here, not if we have more guests in the future, so I've secured a home in East Sussex," Julian continued. "It's about an hour and a half from here. Much larger property, plenty of space, large grounds, sufficient bedrooms…"

"Home library, tennis courts, gym?" Marcus teased.

"Finished basement, breakfast nook, Olympic-size pool?" I joined in.

"Yes, yes, all of that." Julian shrugged as if we'd been serious.

"Are you kidding?" I gawked.

"About the pool? Of course, it has a pool—indoors, in the east wing." He sounded as if the feature were as standard as a garage. "The property's been in my family for generations…"

"Does that mean your dad knows we're staying there?" I looked at Charlotte, and she shook her head as if equally unaware of our moving plans.

Julian's father, Phillip Stone, had spent decades collaborating with Department D. He published their fake news stories and profited significantly from their espionage activity, so much so that he didn't help his own son when those same spies ruined Julian's career and reputation.

"Yes, my father has actually agreed to help." His voice held a mixture of shock and pleasure, like the son finally playing catch in the backyard with his father.

My brow furrowed. Did he not see what was happening here? "Julian, your dad is a part of the organization we're trying to bring down."

"My father never worked *for* Department D." He held up a finger in protest. "He was a business associate, and he insists he terminated all dealings with the organization after my...*ordeal*. He hasn't worked with them since, and he seemed quite delighted at the prospect of contributing to their demise."

"Of course he's going to say that." While I had no right to judge anyone else's family, I did have reason to be skeptical of any relative with admitted criminal ties. My eyes flickered to Antonio, then back to Julian. "Haven't you heard of the expression 'keep your enemies close'? What if your dad just wants to see what evidence we have?"

"I'm not sharing anything with him." He sounded offended.

"I'm sure you aren't, but if we're in *his* house, he could still somehow find out—"

"Not all parents are evil," Antonio interrupted, his nose scrunched like he sensed I was linking his family to the same group as Phillip Stone. I was. "People make mistakes, and not all of us knew what we were getting into. Just because your parents are still running around the world betraying you..."

"Wait, what?" Dani's eyes cut my way. "I thought your parents were dead."

Damn. I winced. All the lies were tangled in my head; I couldn't keep them straight anymore. "They are dead, at least they *were*..."

"We don't know for sure," Keira jumped in, trying to save me. "There are rumors."

"But we haven't seen them, so we don't really know," I hedged.

"You lied to me," Dani said.

"Not exactly. We buried our parents, and we spent the past three and a half years living on our own." That pain was real. The loss was real. It happened.

"Are you going to lie to all of the Dresden Kids you meet?" His eyes darkened. "Are you going to trick them into trusting you? Is that how you do things? Like your parents?"

"Hey!" Marcus stepped forward, but I grabbed his arm. Dani had a right to be angry. We should have told him sooner. Or at all. (Still, it felt good to have Marcus defend me.)

"I'm sorry you found out this way." Charlotte moved toward Dani. "If you want to leave, we get it. But you have to remember, Keira was kidnapped. Anastasia fought for her life. We have to make sure *we* can trust *you*, before we tell you everything."

"That's a rather big detail to leave out," Ben chimed into the conversation, looking as betrayed as Dani.

How could we tell them everything and then expect them to help us? It seemed smarter to let them gradually find out, after they'd gotten to know us, after they'd seen for themselves that we were on their side. Only now the omission made it look like we were trying to protect our parents, and we weren't. *Were we?*

"Their parents have not made any contact, I assure you, and we *are* trying to find them. I realize you've been through a lot, but so have *they*," said Julian, looking at Keira and me. "I promise my father has no involvement, and I have security lined up at the country house. You will be safe there."

"How do we know that's not another lie? That's all you've been doing since we met you. We can't trust you. Where's my video? I want it back." Dani shifted away from us. He was going to leave, with the evidence.

"We understand, but..." Julian's turquoise eyes bore into Charlotte.

"I don't think this is the time," she warned.

"I don't think we have a choice."

"What?" I could see the secret pass between them as clearly as if they'd cupped their hands to their mouths.

Charlotte sighed, her face begging apologies, then she turned to Dani. "Your mom did a good job of encrypting the video, but I was able to get it open. I watched it." I could feel what was coming, even before she said it and my body tensed for the blow. "The man your stepfather was meeting with, I recognized him."

No, no, no... I wanted to press my palms to my ears, block it out.

"Our dad?" Keira asked, also sensing the answer.

"Yeah," Charlotte whispered.

"So that talk about revenge on the people who did this, you still feel that way?" The hatred in Dani's voice was so sharp, it sliced into me, reopening old wounds full of shame, disappointment, and guilt. My parents looked people in the eye and ruined their lives. Did they feel nothing as they did it? Were they complete sociopaths? Would any Dresden Kid ever want to help me, given the horror my parents inflicted on their families?

"It's not your fault," Marcus whispered in my ear, a hand on my shoulder.

"It sure feels that way." I met eyes with my sister, the only other person in the room who knew how this felt. But her face was stoic, her body no longer holding the slumped posture of a victim. Instead, she looked like the old Keira, the one who could hold it together at her own parents' funeral.

She stepped toward Dani. "We told you our parents worked for Department D. We didn't keep that from you. There weren't any tricks. People have *told us* our parents are alive, but we have *not* seen them. And if they are, they definitely aren't helping us. So if you still want to bail on this, fine. But to answer your question—this changes nothing for us. *We* are going to end this. Now it's up to you. Do you still want in?"

Dani stood still, moments passing as he seemed to search for something in my sister's hazel eyes. Keira had the power to convince him. There was no doubt that she was held captive, maybe not for as long as his mother, but it still allowed Dani to believe she might want revenge. "Fine," he answered. "I'll go with you, but only to make sure that when you do find your parents, *they pay.*"

I swallowed hard, recognizing it was exactly how I felt about Craig Bernard and anyone else responsible for taking Keira. Including Urban, despite how many baby pictures he had in his arsenal. Dani's mother spent two years in a Turkish prison, and my father played a role in that. Now Dani was handing us that evidence. Would I do the same? And would I be able to convince any more Dresden Kids to do it?

Julian cleared his throat. "All right, then. I am glad you are coming with us. There are cars waiting outside, so please, everyone, pack your things."

The group dispersed in silence, but Charlotte and I held back. She inched closer to my side. "I'm sorry about your dad."

"I know." I nodded, a dark part of me thinking, *He isn't*

my dad. "Is this pointless? Why would any of them want to help us?"

"Because you are trying to help *them*. And they'll see that eventually." She rubbed my arm reassuringly.

"I don't think I would help *me*." The rage in Dani's eyes flickered in my memory, and it looked so familiar. I felt the same way most days.

"Well, let's hope the others don't share that view, because Cross sent us more names. You ready to do this?"

It was like asking, *Are you ready for your firing squad, Miss Phoenix?* How could I be? Every bit of damning evidence chipped away at my childhood like it never happened. Karate tournaments were replaced with kidnapped prime ministers, and family dinners were painted over with innocent women in prison. How bad was this going to get?

I had a feeling I didn't want to know.

But I was going to find out. We were leaving again tomorrow.

CHAPTER EIGHTEEN

Two Weeks Later…

"This house is insane!"

"Bigger than Urban's."

"Shh! We dare not speak his name."

"Why? It's their parents who are trying to kill us."

"I thought the Phoenixes were dead?"

"Uh huh, so is Tupac."

"Screw it. Let's go swimming!"

"Anyone have a wine opener?"

Our historic English mansion in East Sussex, less than a mile from Paul McCartney's country estate, was turning into a dirty frat house. Over the course of two weeks, the teams of Marcus and Antonio, and Keira and I had packed the place with teens whose families were annihilated by the work of Department D. Twelve in total. All names were supplied by Allen Cross, and so far all pointed fingers in the same direction. At my parents. All of them.

For example, Meghan Teller's father supposedly developed a "heart attack gun" that could shoot a dissolving dart into a human chest, causing cardiac arrest. He hadn't been seen in more than a decade, placed in isolation by Department D, out of fear of losing their best scientist to a competitor. His last known handler was my mother.

There was also Patrick O'Reilly, whose grandfather was convicted of kidnapping the most famous racehorse in Irish history, then accidentally killing it. Only he swore until his deathbed that the real culprits were Department D, specifically a man who looked just like, you guessed it, my father.

Benjamin Green, the first kid Marcus brought back, finally got the answers he wanted on the evidence left at his great aunt's crime scene. Charlotte linked the two sets of mysterious DNA to both of my parents.

What was worse was that not all of the evidence was pointing to crimes committed *before* my parents' supposed deaths. Some disturbingly occurred *after*.

Like Claudette West, whose mother died tragically in a mysterious plane crash last year over the Pacific Ocean. The plane was never recovered, and Claudette swore her mother's bosses were a reclusive husband-and-wife duo working out of *Cuba*, the last known place Allen Cross said my parents had lived. Claudette wasn't alone. Two other kids told identical stories of reclusive bosses working on the tiny communist island. That left all of us to wonder if my parents were running operations all this time—maybe they still even ran Department D?

"Okay, Marcello, I think that's it," Julian said as he turned off the red light on his video camera.

Julian had elevated the video depositions to include professional lighting, sound equipment, and HD cameras. The "studio" was now based in the mansion's former study, which housed floor-to-ceiling shelves of antique books that rivaled the size of most community libraries, making it one of the smaller rooms in the house. He wasn't lying when he said we'd have more space in his family's "country home." The East Sussex "Compound," as it came to be known, looked like how most people imagine the Palace of Versailles—loads of museum-quality art and furniture you were afraid to sit on. The walls were papered with fabric that looked hand painted, and the grounds were large enough to host a cross-country race that never left the property. True to his word, Julian hired men in black suits with secret-service-looking earpieces to stand watch outside every entrance. They swept for bugs daily. His father was never mentioned, nor did he stop by. Everyone felt safe, physically, from Department D's Boogiemen. They just didn't feel safe with my sister and me.

It was getting awkward.

A crowd would be gathered around a pool table taking bets on the next shot, then a Phoenix girl would enter and all chuckling ceased. When we sat down to eat lunch, the meal fell silent. Then when we got up to clear our plates, conversations resumed. I tried to talk to our guests, show them that I wasn't my parents, that I wasn't evil, that I was one of *them*. But either they were too scared to listen or too unforgiving. Eyes pierced me whenever I passed, including Dani's. He seemed to only grow more suspicious as each kid showed up pointing yet another finger at our parents. Still, they stayed at the compound, appreciating Charlotte's computer skills and Julian's over-the-top hospitality. They believed we were trying to bring down Department D, which they wanted, but they lacked a desire to spend time with the daughters of the people who created it.

"Hi, Marcello!" I waved at the latest Dresden Kid giving his video statement in the study. His father was a politician who mysteriously dropped dead right before a pivotal election. My mother was a campaign worker who served him his final meal.

"Oh, uh, hello," he replied, not meeting my eyes. He shot a quick peek at Charlotte and Julian. "Am I done here?"

"Yeah," Charlotte answered, fingers on her laptop. "If we have more questions, we'll let you know."

"Okay." He practically ran to the door, ensuring he kept as far away from me as possible—the girl with lethal cooties.

"I'll talk to you later!" I called after him.

I missed my friends. I now further appreciated the strength of character Tyson and Regina had to befriend a girl when no one else would. *God, Tyson...* My mind drifted to him and Regina every night before bed. I pictured him in that alley, fighting for his life, almost winning, until the knife went in. I imagined Regina crying into her pillow, alone in her bedroom, without any friends to comfort her, petrified that murderers were going to kill her family. She'd watched Tyson die. For thirty-seven dollars and a twisted message *to me.*

I was the most dangerous friend in the world. Maybe these Dresden Kids were right to stay away.

"They'll come around," Charlotte said, as if hearing my thoughts.

"They hate me," I replied.

"They can't hate you, when they don't even know you." She should have that printed on a button.

"They *know* my parents." I thudded my head against the wall.

"I'll admit the evidence against them is mounting." Charlotte always straddled the razor-sharp line between making me feel better and not lying to my face.

"I'm starting to understand what it must feel like to

be the daughter of a serial killer. Do you think Jeffrey Dahmer's family changed their names? So people wouldn't be afraid they'd stick their heads in freezers?"

"It's not *that* bad." Julian glanced up from his laptop.

"You mean because my parents didn't eat them?"

"Exactly. Things could always be worse."

"Julian, you're not helping," Charlotte droned, before giving me a smile so fake a politician would be proud. "The good news is the evidence we've acquired is substantial. We have collected video footage, eye witness positive IDs, and DNA linking Department D—*or more specifically your parents*—to multiple unsolved, or incorrectly solved, cases worldwide. I think we might be ready to take this to Martin Bittman and the CIA."

"Or go public," Julian suggested, his tone casual, as if this weren't the millionth time he'd brought this up.

"Are you really going there again?" I groaned.

He wasn't even trying to hide his personal agenda. I knew Julian deserved a big payout for helping us—the story of a lifetime that would lift him from laughing stock tabloid journalist to the second coming of Walter Cronkite. But it sometimes felt like he was so eager to pitch our story to the networks, he didn't fully consider what it would mean for Keira and me. No matter how often I told him.

"Hear me out, one more time!" Julian held up his hands, pleading for reason. "I know our plan has been to gather this evidence and bring it to the authorities, and I still think we should do that. But these are *conspiracy theories.*" Julian said the words like they held magic (or ratings gold). "Who knows how deep these cover ups go? What if we hand over this evidence and the authorities don't act on it, because it somehow implicates the CIA's involvement? We already know that Martin Bittman was in that original photo you found in Tuscany, of your parents with Aldo Moro, the one that was doctored to remove all of them. We can assume that the CIA would not want that evidence to surface."

"Maybe they don't. Who cares? As long as they take down Department D and everyone associated with it." I shrugged.

"What if that's not what they do?" Julian rose to his feet. "Allen Cross, an admitted card-carrying spy for Department D, called Martin Bittman, the Deputy Director of the CIA, when your sister was kidnapped and asked for his help." Julian pulled at his finger, emphasizing his point. "Then Bittman showed up in Venice and *helped.*"

Of course, I'd considered this. It was one of my arguments when Keira first tried to insist we leave everything to the CIA. Maybe the government group wasn't on our side? But at the end of the day, Keira was right—none of us were spies equipped to deal with this. So we agreed to gather evidence and trust the authorities would take them down. We had to, because the alternative was too dismal—me fighting assassins myself while wearing a tinfoil hat believing my government was out to get me. Even I could see the flaws in that. Besides, our plan did not rely entirely on blind faith. "Are you trying to tell me you and Charlotte haven't backed up every piece of evidence on a million different servers worldwide?" I cocked my head. "If the authorities don't do anything, we still have all the work we've done saved somewhere."

"That's exactly my point!" Julian started pacing, his voice high and excited. "Let's do *both*, right now. Give the CIA the evidence *and* go public with all of it. Once your story is out there, everything will be under public scrutiny, Dresden, Department D…"

"*Us.*" I glared at him.

He shut his mouth.

"Our lives will be over, Julian. Don't you get that? They may not physically kill us if you put us in the spotlight, but we'll never be able to walk down the street again. We'll never be able to—"

The sound of a muffled phone ringing cut through the room. Charlotte dove into the brown leather sofa cushions, searching wildly, until she pulled out a silver burner phone.

"It's Cross," she told us, looking at the screen.

She tucked her curly hair behind an ear, pressing the phone to it. "Hello. Yup, I have it right here." Charlotte stretched for the laptop that served as her fifth limb. "Omigod. Wow." She gave me a look that made a sickening wave break in my belly. "Okay, wow. Yeah, um, I'll show her."

What now? What other truth bomb could this man throw at my life? I fought the urge to sprint from the room and hide under my bed with the dust bunnies, but before I could, Charlotte turned her laptop toward me and mouthed the word, "*Sorry.*"

I stared at the screen.

"What is this?" I asked, blinking at a JPEG of me standing in the lobby of Dresden's corporate offices. It was clearly a still image taken from surveillance footage the day of Tyson's memorial. I was standing next to Marcus's parents in my black funeral dress and coat. "Why does Cross have this?"

"He intercepted it online." Charlotte shifted the phone from her mouth as she spoke to me. "He thinks it was sent to your parents, and he wants me to track down the IP addresses of everyone who opened it. He thinks it's some sort of threat."

"Why? What? Let me talk to him." I reached for the

phone, snatching it from her hand. "What's going on?" I barked into the receiver.

"Hello, Anastasia. I take it you've seen the photo," Cross replied.

"Obviously, but why do you think it was sent to my parents?" In the image, the Reys and I appear to be having a friendly chat; Marcus's dad is touching my shoulder, likely offering condolences for Tyson's death.

"What did I tell you that day?" he asked. "That everything Department D is doing is in service of drawing out your parents. Broadcasting a photo of you and the Reys, with them close enough to touch you, will make your mother and father very angry. Especially given the threatening message that was delivered to your friend Regina. Remember, I told you that your parents were staging a hostile takeover before their 'accident' and that most of the staff was loyal to *them*?"

"Uh huh." I nodded, trying to decipher where his thoughts were headed.

"Well, back then, there were two very important people unshakably loyal to Randolph Urban. Rosario and Carlos Rey."

"You're saying they wanted my parents dead?"

"There's only so much room at the top of the pyramid."

"So this photo is a threat? They're threatening to *kill me*?" I still couldn't believe I lived in a world where I had to ask these types of questions—of my boyfriend's parents. I felt my hand start to shake as it held the phone, my pulse accelerating. As much as I tried to act tough, a death threat was still a death threat.

"I recommend you be careful," he said. *As if we aren't already?* "And ask Miss Conner to get back to me once she has the IP addresses. I think it's in our best interest to locate your parents before they do."

He sounded like he was ready to hang up, and I jerked at the thought. "Wait! Don't!" I blurted. "Do you know about all the evidence we've collected?"

"Yes," he confirmed. "Miss Conner has kept me apprised of where you stand."

"It's pointing to my parents. All of it." I clutched the phone tighter, my hand growing clammy.

"I told you, your parents were on the ground. So the evidence is going to connect to them more than Urban or the Reys."

"But what about the recent stuff? Kids are claiming their parents were taking orders from a couple in Cuba." The vice on my stomach twisted further as I asked my next question. "Do you think it's them? Do you think my parents have been running things, like secret missions, this whole time?"

"I'm as surprised as you are about the mention of Cuba."

"Is it true?"

"A few months ago, I would have said it was completely impossible, but I fear I may be a poor judge of what your parents are capable of."

"What's that supposed to mean?" My face wrinkled. This was not a time for vague accusations. "Is it *possible* that they are still running Department D, and Urban and the Reys are completely innocent?"

"No, absolutely not. Your boyfriend may want to believe that fantasy, but I assure you that is not the case."

"But we have no evidence against anyone else!" My voice squeaked, sounding like a whiny teenager, but that was exactly how I felt. This wasn't going how I'd expected. The Phoenixes were burning, all of us. Alone. "I thought we were going to take down Urban. Because I know my parents did not kidnap my sister or kill Tyson. Whoever is coming after us, whoever gave Regina that message, is *looking* for my parents. You need to give me more, proof that Urban is behind this."

A lull fell over the line, and I could hear Cross breathing. "Fine," he finally replied. "I have some theories about what might be happening. All of the arrows pointing to your parents is far too convenient. Tell Miss Conner I will be in touch shortly with a new list of names, and be assured, at least one will point directly to Urban."

He hung up abruptly, and relief washed over me. Finally. We'd get him. No more baby pictures, no more confusion. I'd have proof that Urban was the bad guy. He'd get locked up, far away from Keira and me, unable to hurt us, and any genetic link we had would be meaningless.

I spun around to face Charlotte and Julian, feeling mildly satisfied, until I spied the collective looks of panic in their enlarged eyes. I dropped the phone. "What? Is it the photo? Of me in Dresden's lobby?" Only I knew it wasn't. Their faces wore the expression of those watching a live execution, *my* execution, utterly stunned and serious. Still, I played dumb, praying it wasn't as bad as it looked.

"Anastasia, I'm sorry," Charlotte muttered.

Blood roared in my ears as sweat broke on my forehead. *What more could there be?*

"It's everywhere," Julian replied.

Then he turned his laptop my way, and I saw it.

CHAPTER NINETEEN

*B**OSTON TATTLER**, gossip magazine*
December 8th

PHOENIXES RISE FROM THE ASHES, LITERALLY

BROOKLINE, MA—Is Keira Phoenix really dead? That is the question being asked by those closest to the mysterious family.

You may remember the case. Last year, on Mother's Day, twenty-four-year-old Keira Phoenix disappeared from her Brookline brownstone. The prior evening, she had hosted a party, alcohol was consumed, and Keira was last seen in the company of a man no one could identify beyond the first name of "Craig." The next morning, her seventeen-year-old sister, Anastasia Phoenix, found Keira missing and their bathtub full of her blood. No body was ever recovered. The case remains cold.

Until now.

Questions have recently arisen about the circumstances surrounding Keira Phoenix's disappearance, which was ruled a "probable homicide" by Boston Police.

Regina Villanueva, friend of Anastasia's and girlfriend of recently murdered Brookline Academy student Tyson Westbrook, has made a new statement to police claiming that Westbrook's mugging-gone-wrong was not accidental and was, in fact, connected to Keira Phoenix. Police have reopened both investigations, and sources tell us that authorities have uncovered a photo of Keira Phoenix holding a church bulletin, from Venice, Italy, displaying a date from *after* she disappeared. Requests to obtain a copy of this image from police were denied.

Does the photo exist? Is it a proof of life? Was Keira Phoenix really kidnapped and not killed?

And if so, was her sister, Anastasia, behind it?

After Keira's mysterious disappearance, Anastasia Phoenix dropped out of Brookline Academy and left for a "study abroad experience" in Italy, according to her legal guardians, Colleen and Sean Conner of Worcester, MA. Allegedly, their twenty-four-year-old daughter, Charlotte Conner, assumed control of Anastasia's homeschooling overseas. But recently, Anastasia sold her family home with all proceeds going directly to her.

Anastasia and Keira Phoenix were orphans. Their parents were killed by a drunk driver on Storrow Drive more than three years ago. Keira had been her sister's guardian and the executor of their parents' estate. When Keira disappeared and was declared legally dead, all finances transferred directly to Anastasia.

Now, those closest to the family are wondering—what really happened to Keira?

Regina Villanueva believes there is more to the story. "Anastasia is involved in some sort of crime, like with mobsters or drug dealers or something," says Villanueva. "The killer threatened me if I said anything, but I can't stay quiet anymore. I have to do this for Tyson. He deserves justice. Someone killed him to get to Anastasia. The killer told me so. And what did Anastasia do when I confronted her with this information? She went back to Europe. She's off on some big vacation like none of this is happening. How sick is that?"

Last month, Anastasia Phoenix returned to Boston for the funeral of Tyson Westbrook, and according to those in attendance, she openly bragged about her escapades abroad.

"She stood outside of the church, right after the funeral of her supposed best friend, telling everyone what an awesome time she was having," says Julianna Gold, a twelfth grader at Brookline Academy. "She said she was getting wasted, drinking wine all the time. She thought it was so cool that they don't card in Europe."

"She's traveling over there with her boyfriend," Villanueva reports. "They're running around Tuscany making out in vineyards while she's supposedly grieving her dead sister, while her best friend is being murdered. She's the one person connected to all of this!"

[Photo Insert of Anastasia and Marcus kissing. Marcus isn't identified.]

"She told me she smoked all this pot in Amsterdam," said Wyatt Burns, captain of Brookline Academy's state championship baseball team. "I think she was stoned at the funeral."

Adding another layer of mystery, rumors have begun to circulate in the Boston business community that Anastasia's parents, Michael and Irina Phoenix, may not be deceased. Evidence of corruption has turned up aimed at their former place of employment, the Dresden Chemical Corporation, leading to rumors that the Phoenixes faked their deaths to avoid prosecution. Police refuse to comment on the speculation, but our sources claim a connection exists between the Phoenixes and Havana, Cuba, a country that refuses extradition.

Is this a real-life story of Phoenixes rising from the ashes? In the case of Keira Phoenix, it appears so. And if you believe the proof of life photograph, two questions remain—is Keira Phoenix still being held hostage somewhere? And is her sister, Anastasia, behind it?

"What the *hell*?" I screeched, glaring at the supposed "news" article from a popular Boston tabloid. This was printed—publication date and all. That meant people read this, about me, about my family. It was all lies and distortion.

"That photo of Marcus and me was taken months after Keira was taken! *After* we were almost killed!" I shouted, pacing Julian's study and glaring at the image of Marcus and me kissing in Tuscany following our violent confrontation with Luis Basso. It took up a quarter of the page. "I wasn't off on some adventure, and we weren't having a romance! We were freaking out!"

"We know that," Charlotte said, her voice controlled as if she were talking to a woman with one foot dangling off the ledge.

"And you! They name you and your parents like you're co-conspirators because you took me in! Because you fostered me. My whole family was dead!" My sight clouded, the room tilting. I dropped my head, dark hair falling in my face, and squeezed my temples tight. I couldn't breathe.

"This would explain why my parents have been calling so much these past two days. I was so busy with Cross and the depositions, I didn't get back to them." Charlotte ran her fingers through her frizzy blond hair. "They must be losing it."

"They think I kidnapped my own sister!" I yelled, tossing my hands in the air at the ridiculousness of the idea. "What is wrong with these people? How could Regina say that stuff?"

"She's grieving. She wants someone to blame. So do we." Charlotte's big eyes were sympathetic.

"They said they would kill her whole family if she spoke. What is she thinking? You know they'll do it!" An image of Regina's little brother in a teeny tiny casket flashed in my brain. *No, no way. No more funerals.* "They act like I kidnapped my sister for money! Our parents left us with nothing but an apartment. Nothing! We ate Ramen noodles for years. How could they possibly think I had a financial motive?"

"Because most people commit crimes for money," Charlotte reasoned.

"*I* didn't commit a crime!"

"We know that."

"If I may," Julian interrupted, his British accent so annoyingly polite it made me want to hit him. "I happen to be quite familiar with being accused of a crime you didn't commit by major news outlets." He eyed me pointedly. "You must know this is the work of Department D."

I hunched over, hands on my knees. Department D, obviously, it was them. Okay, what did that mean? I inhaled slowly, trying to control my breathing, stop the spinning.

"Notice there is no mention of Marcus's name, even though he's present in the photo. His face is obscured from the image, mostly because he's kissing you, but still. He was a classmate of yours. Your friend, Regina, she knows his name, right?" Julian asked.

I nodded. Of course she did. She threw the picture in my face in the church alley. She's obviously the one who gave it to the media, to the police. *How could she not take those threats seriously? Was anyone protecting her? Her family?* I pulled at the collar of my long-sleeved T-shirt, fanning myself with the fabric, desperate for air.

"Marcus's name was left out for a reason—because the Reys don't want it published," Julian continued.

"Okay, go on."

"Think about it—the information about your parents possibly being alive, in Cuba, that didn't come from your friend. *We* just found out about that. The only people who could possibly know that information would be those working for Department D," he continued. He was on a roll, and I stayed silent, my eyes pleading for more. Answers, I needed answers. "Look at the publication—*The Boston Tattler*, it's a gossip rag. They had to place the story there because there are no facts to substantiate these claims. No reputable news outlet would print this. It's a bunch of rubbish, a Big Foot sighting, except the sightings are your family members."

"But the photo of Keira, the proof of life, that's real, and it says the police have it."

"Keira's survival is quickly becoming a poorly kept secret. The CIA knows, Department D knows, so why not the Boston PD?" said Julian. "The truth was going to come out eventually."

"But why would Department D expose us *now*?" I collapsed onto a leather couch, dropping my head onto the cushions, my brain relieved Julian was doing the thinking.

"Because it makes you look bad," Charlotte said. "All of us. This makes us look like liars."

Julian sat down on the sofa beside me, his Caribbean

blue eyes drooping with empathy. If anyone understood what I was feeling right now, it was him. "Department D must know that these Dresden Kids are here, with us, that we're acquiring evidence, and so far…Who does all the evidence point to?"

I saw the trail of breadcrumbs. "My parents."

"Exactly. This article makes your family look like it's hiding something. It makes you all look guilty of something," he explained. "When the truth about Department D comes out, the evidence is going to point to your parents, and so far *only* your parents. If it turns out your parents are alive, the spectacle that will create—"

"Added to the fact that we lied about Keira being alive…" Charlotte moaned, also catching on.

"It's your family that's going down for everything. All of you." Julian sounded truly sorry. Like he said, he did know what it was like to have his family name ruined by the press.

"Department D, Marcus's parents, Randolph Urban…" I shook my head feeling so incredibly stupid. "They're setting us up."

CHAPTER TWENTY

Keira didn't take the news of her reported resurrection very well, nor the fact that I was being accused of her fake murder. After a lifelong dream of being in the tabloids, she'd finally made it—for this.

"You really think it was Antonio's parents who planted the story?" Keira asked as we wandered through Julian's English gardens, alit with twinkling white Christmas lights put up by the caretakers. We hadn't even realized it was the holiday season. We'd missed Thanksgiving without noticing, and now the world was ice-skating toward Christmas while we were stuck in a Halloween horror show.

I pulled my new wool scarf tighter around my neck, purchased with proceeds from the sale of our brownstone. So far, that was what all that "estate money" got me— underwear, mittens, a scarf, and socks. But hey, who wouldn't kidnap their sister for that?

"The Reys were in that surveillance photo with me," I said, still strolling beside her in the frozen grass. "They work there, so they obviously have access to the footage. And Cross thinks it's them—Tyson, the message to Regina, everything. He thinks they want Mom and Dad to take the fall, and they're using us to get to them." That was our most viable theory, that I was dating the son of the people who murdered my best friend and who were trying to frame me and my family. And people wondered why I had trust issues?

"You know Marcus and Antonio don't believe this." Keira stared at her boots, hiding her eyes, likely because she felt the same way and didn't want me to see it. I wasn't the bad guy.

"No one *wants* to believe it, and I don't blame you." I shrugged, glaring at the cement gray sky. Maybe Marcus was right; maybe it did match my eyes, perpetually full of storm clouds. "I didn't want to believe our parents were spies until you were held hostage and declared dead."

Keira stopped in her tracks. "Anastasia, you said this to me once, and now I'm saying it to you." She grabbed my hand, her thick wool mitten clutching mine. "*It's time.* We need to go to the CIA. We need to sit down with Martin Bittman and give him everything we have, all the evidence, all the Dresden Kids. Then we do whatever *they* say. If they want us to go into hiding under fake passports again, we do it. This time we stay there. If they want us to draw out Mom and Dad, we do it. It's time to let the professionals take over. This needs to stop."

I stared at the Christmas lights glowing in twilight, hovering between barely noticeable and starting to shine. My nose was running from the cold, but still I insisted we have this conversation outside, away from all of the kids who hated us, all the ears that could listen. This was about Keira and me. Our family. Our decision.

"I hear you. But right now, all the evidence points to Mom and Dad. If we walk away, the Reys and Urban get off scot-free. Can you live with that? They're setting us up."

"So we tell the CIA that. We have *them* look into it." Keira shook her head with the exasperation of a person who was simply done. "It's either this, or we go public and listen to Julian. Is that what you want?"

"Don't even say that." I was not going to become a late-night punch line.

I was seventeen years old, and I wanted a life, my *own* life, on my terms, not some hand-me-down life left for me by my criminal parents, not some fake life that witness protection could offer, and not some freakshow of a spectacle that Julian would create. I wanted to be me—in college, with Marcus, and my sister back in med school. I wanted us free to make our own choices. And I wanted that for every other kid in that house.

"So what's left? What do you want to do now?" Keira flung up her hands.

I wanted to fight, all the way to the end. If we gave the CIA our evidence, *eventually* they might uncover crimes that point to Urban and the Reys, but what if they didn't? We'd be taking the chance that they might elude justice all together. After everything they'd done. Yes, these people were Marcus' parents, and yes, Urban and I shared DNA and some baby photos; but Urban also kidnapped Keira, and the Reys were the most likely candidates to have murdered Tyson. There had to be a way to implicate *them*. Not eventually. But now.

"The last time I spoke with Cross, he promised me he would send us a Dresden Kid who would have hard evidence against Urban." I looked at my sister through the darkening sky, shadows defining her deep frown and heavy brow. I could already see she didn't like what I was saying. "Let's see if Cross pulls through. If we can find *one*

case that points to Urban, then I'll be ready to go to the CIA.
But I need to know Urban will go down for something, if
not for what he did to you."

Keira shook her head, cold puffs of frozen air expelling
from her mouth as she stared at the amber lights inside
the compound, the silhouettes of the Dresden Kids moving
about behind the curtains. "I'm afraid you're going to get
yourself killed, just so you don't have to face *him*. You
can put him behind bars, Anastasia, but it won't change
anything."

I was not running from Urban, I was keeping my promise. I told Dani, I told all the Dresden Kids, that we would
make these people pay. They deserved that, and so did I.

"It's not about him." Though I really wasn't sure. Maybe
it was, but would we ever be able to live normal lives
knowing they were still out there? Right now, we had a
chance to bring them all down, to end this for good. We
had to take it.

I looked toward Julian's estate, all the shadows moving
inside. "Mom and Dad destroyed every family in there, and
they'll pay for that. I just need to make sure that Urban and
the Reys pay too. For Tyson, for you, and for me. I *need* that."

Keira shrugged, head tossed back, knit cap nearly
slipping off her head. She knew she had no choice. "Fine.
If Cross finds a kid who can point to Urban, we'll do it. But
that's it. One more try."

I nodded in agreement.

An hour later, Cross called.

Rio de Janeiro and Barcelona.

That was where Cross wanted us to go.

Charlotte and Julian gave us the news as we gathered

in the study. Meanwhile, the Dresden Kids were playing pool, swimming, and getting drunk utterly uninterested in our sudden strategy session. I, however, had become an expert on how many steps it took to get from one antique bookcase to the other—fifteen. One side of the room held leather-bound classics, like Charles Dickens and the Bronte sisters, while the other held nonfiction tomes, from scientific journals to World War II accounts. I couldn't stop pacing.

"Tell me everything," I insisted as Charlotte's fingers flew over her keys.

"Cross has two names that he swears will provide evidence against the *Urbans*, plural." She smiled coyly.

I stopped dead. *Urbans?*

"Julian and I need to verify the intel, but it appears the Rio case will connect to Randolph Urban, and the Barcelona case will connect to…wait for it…*Sophia* Urban." Charlotte pumped her brow like she knew this was the only thing on Earth that might lift my spirits from a basement of misery.

"*Sophia?* Are you kidding me?" I gasped, remembering the girl who mocked me at my parents' funeral, and throughout my childhood. She practically cooed with delight when she showed up in Rome with an evil terrorist manual, handwritten by my father, that was used to bring down Julian. We were going after *her.* Maybe there was a God.

"Yup, turns out she's a prolific flunky for Department D."

"I wonder how that strawberry blond hair will look in a bright orange jumpsuit? Just the clashing colors alone will probably torture her." I pictured Sophia's pale face, the shock of disbelief when we turned her in to the authorities, and for a brief moment I felt like we might be nearing the end of this. If we could point the authorities at Randolph *and* Sophia Urban, I could strut away with all the vindication I'd ever need. Closure achieved.

Charlotte looked at Antonio, who was leaning against the doorjamb watching us like a spectator sport, not saying a word. He wasn't inserting himself or cracking jokes or hitting on my sister. Maybe he finally realized the seriousness of the situation. Or maybe I was wrong about him all along. "Cross says you spent time in Rio last year. You and Marcus want to go there?"

His eyes met Keira's, and already I didn't like the nonverbal exchange that shifted between them.

"We were talking…" Antonio looked at me. "We think we should split up the teams." Instantly, he held up a hand like he knew my rebuttal was coming. But he cut me off. "*Escúchame.* If everything you suspect is true, and my parents really are setting up your family, do you not think you will be safer with one of us? My parents aren't going to hurt Marcus or me." He gestured to his brother for support, and Marcus nodded. Clearly, they'd discussed this without me, and I wasn't sure how I felt about that.

Marcus stepped toward me. "The article changes things. Someone is coming after *you*, directly, publicly. And who knows where they'll stop, what that message to Regina really means? I do not think you girls are safe on your own."

"I have a double black belt in karate," I said. I fought Craig Bernard and won.

"Yes, you can fight. But a karate chop is not going to stop a gun." Marcus reached for my hand, his face urging me to listen. "*Por favor*, I do not have a good feeling about this. We don't have to go."

Keira joined in, side by side with Marcus. "I want to get Urban as much as you do. *I* was the one taken from our apartment, but I'm not chained to a sink right now, and neither are you. We have other options. You can still change your mind."

They wanted me to trust the CIA, but that organization hadn't done anything for us except hand us a couple of passports and hope we led them to our parents. They didn't find Keira. I did. They didn't tell me my parents were alive. I found that out on my own. They had decades to arrest Urban, the Reys, and my parents. And they didn't.

"I can't stop when we're *this close*." I squeezed my fingers together. "I promise this is the last one, but we have to *try*."

They both closed their eyes, grimacing, reluctantly knowing I wasn't built to sit home and hope someone else solved my problems.

Antonio stepped forward. "I agree with you. I do not run from a fight either, but we must break up the groups. You are positive that your parents will not harm you, *verdad*? Well, we are positive our parents will not harm *us*."

Charlotte squeezed my shoulder. "Having you and your sister out there together, unprotected, would be a gift for someone who wanted to hurt your parents."

It had come to this—Antonio was the one person agreeing with my plan, and he was the one person in our group I didn't trust with my sister. Sure, I could pretend to like him for Marcus's sake, I could even grind my teeth and act like it wasn't at all suspicious that he used to work for the enemy, but I couldn't fake my way into putting Keira's life in his hands.

"I know what you're thinking." Keira peered at me, reading my thoughts. "And for a moment, I want you to imagine that Mom and Dad were never in a car crash, that I graduated from college, and that Dresden offered me a job in biomed at Mass General. Do you think I would have been able to turn down an offer like that? And would that have made me a criminal? Antonio was pressured by his parents, and I remember exactly what that felt like."

Keira potentially working in a medical research lab was quite different from Antonio running clean up for spies, but I knew what she meant. I watched my parents pressure Keira into medicine, and I watched them criticize her choice of specialty—pediatrics. If they had lived, if they had more time to influence her choices, she likely would have gone down the path they chose. Maybe I would have too. But I was betting we both would have drawn the line at covering up criminal conspiracies.

"It's either this or the CIA," Charlotte offered. "Both for your safety and our sanity."

Given that I was practically forcing everyone into this plan, and this was what they needed to feel safe, could I really refuse? Their logic made sense. I doubted either of our parents would want to risk hurting us. At least, I hoped not. But imagining Antonio and Keira alone in a foreign country, with no one to help her if she needed it, made my chest clamp tight.

"I'll make it easier," Antonio offered, scratching his bearded chin as he assessed my reaction. "Keira and I can take the kid in Barcelona. It's not as far away, still in Europe, and Marcus has friends there. We'll promise to meet up with them. You'll know your sister is safe. She won't just be with me."

It was a reasonable compromise, and a part of me worried it was too reasonable. Why wasn't he yelling at me? Accusing me of hating the world? *Stop it. Just say yes. You need this.*

"Okay." I nodded. It was the best offer I was going to get.

"I'll call my friends right now. Set something up." Marcus nudged my shoulder, relief thick in his voice.

"All right." Charlotte clapped once before her fingers moved back to home base on her keyboard. "I'll set up the travel plans. I think Cross expected the boys to go to Rio, because Antonio lived there, and the girls to go to Barcelona, because it's Sophia Urban and we all know how we feel about *her*. But I'll let him know we changed plans."

"No, don't." I squinted at Charlotte, pinching the headache forming above my nose. "I don't think Cross will like this whole switching teams thing. And if he tries to talk us out of it, what are we gonna do? It's what you guys need, right?"

Everyone nodded. The last thing we wanted was to fight with the one adult, the one insider, who was actually helping us.

"We'll call him when we get back," I promised. "Him and Martin Bittman. This is it. Whatever happens here, on these missions, it's over."

Charlotte printed out our boarding passes. We'd be departing on the red-eye.

CHAPTER TWENTY-ONE

Marcus and I were whizzing toward the beaches of Rio de Janeiro in the back of a canary yellow taxi, much like we had in so many foreign cities before as we searched for my sister. Only this time, Keira wasn't being held hostage in Italy. She was on the other side of the world, holding hands with Antonio.

"She's fine. They're fine," Marcus repeated.

He didn't even sound annoyed that he still had to convince me to trust his brother, which was more patience than I would ever have, especially given that I was forcing this plan on everyone and the only compromise I made was splitting up our rival crime families. We were becoming the Montagues and the Capulets, the Hatfields and the McCoys, the Red Sox and the Yankees. Though for now, the Reys and the Phoenixes were united in our common enemy—the Urbans.

Last night, Charlotte received another baby picture via email. It was anonymous, untraceable. In it, I was seated in a pumpkin patch in what looked to be Urban's backyard. It must have been part of a Dresden Halloween party, though

I wasn't sure. I looked about two years old at the time, and I had never seen the photograph before. No one else was pictured, so I assumed Urban snapped it himself—a picture of me, taken years ago, and he still kept it. Did he always know? Or maybe suspect?

Stop it. That man is not your father. He's a sperm donor. That's it.

Of course, he was also a sperm donor with an album of baby pictures that he was sending from his hideout at the risk of his own freedom.

He also kidnapped my sister. And tried to kill my parents.

I squeezed my eyes shut, wrapping my arms around my chest. Sometimes it felt like the ache on the inside was worse than anything a spy could inflict on the outside.

"You okay?" Marcus rubbed my leg.

I nodded. He knew about the photo. Everyone did. No more secrets this time, and definitely not when we were all about to hunt down two more Dresden Kids with the ability to bring down the Urbans. We debated whether the photo was a hint that he knew about our plans in Rio and Barcelona—the timing was very coincidental. But there was no threat associated with it, no message. And Cross insisted Urban wouldn't try to hurt me (or my sister) again. If anything, the photo confirmed our strategy to split up the groups—keep Keira and I separate, to lessen the chance that dangerous spies might attack. Of course, we also debated walking away; actually, they yelled and I didn't listen. Antonio was the only one who agreed with me, saying baby pictures were not the way Department D sent threats. Killing Tyson in an alley, *that* was how they threatened, *that* was their style. And that was the organization my parents created.

This better work.

"Do you want me to call my friends in Barcelona? See if Keira and Antonio checked in?" Marcus offered, squeezing my leg tighter, misreading my nerves and trying to reassure me. But that wasn't it, or it wasn't *only* it, and his touch merely made me tense further, my body fighting the urge to smack away his hand and hold it closer. I felt guilty feeling anything other than focused right now. This was *my* plan.

"It's okay. I'm sure they're fine." I shifted away, needing to force the tingles to subside.

I rolled down my window, the thick, muggy air brushing against my face with the smell of car exhaust. Outside, tin-roofed homes lined the highway, accented by colorful laundry lines haphazardly crisscrossing with a web of electrical wires. Bright graffiti decorated the crumbling facades as brown-skinned locals sat on overturned buckets and strolled down trash-littered streets with sweat seeping through their tank tops. The tourists weren't supposed to notice this part of Brazil, but it wasn't exactly hidden. The dark underbelly was always there.

"I knew it would be hot, but this…" Marcus pulled at his black T-shirt, fanning himself, exposing a strip of toned belly.

I swiftly averted my eyes. "Reminds me of Miami."

Finally, our taxi turned onto a boulevard with six lanes of heavy traffic and a stretch of white beach. *No, this reminds me of Miami.* Boxy high-rise hotels lined one side of the thoroughfare, their ivory facades matching the sand that stretched along the opposite way. Volleyball nets were staked periodically, along with white umbrellas protecting the tourists, and precisely spaced palm trees. There was nothing but tropical perfection between our car and the turquoise waves of the Atlantic Ocean.

"Well, this doesn't suck," Marcus said, the salty air coating our tongues.

"It's definitely not England," I agreed, and my shoulders actually relaxed. No more cold damp British sky. Just the sight of the ocean brought calm. How did it do that? I swore every time I saw a beach I promised I'd never live anywhere else, then I inevitably moved to another concrete city.

"I'm glad we came. You were right." Marcus leaned his head my way. "This will be good. For everyone." His dark eyes bore into me, so intense I wasn't sure if he was talking about obtaining information on Urban or sharing a romantic moment. But given the way he was staring at my lips, I was guessing it was the latter — as if the postcard locale wasn't distraction enough.

The meal was worthy of the cover of a glossy culinary magazine. Marcus and I sat in an open-air restaurant bordering a horse-racing track, which was abandoned for the evening, practically licking our plates of tender South American steak. There were candles on the tables, tropical tangerine flowers climbing up the walls, and Jesus looking down from the mountaintop. Literally.

The restaurant, which was recommended by the four-star hotel Julian had booked for our stay, sat below the elaborately lit Christ Redeemer statue, which was to Rio what the Statue of Liberty was to New York City. The cultural icon was visited by every tourist, like you hadn't really been there unless you snapped the obligatory shot. However, in Rio, the statue sat high on a hill, meaning you could see it from almost every spot in the city. Look up, and there was Jesus, his arms stretched wide as he looked down on everything you did. Even in the dark of night. With so many strobes pointed at it, his bright white presence appeared to be floating in heaven.

"I can't stop staring at Jesus," I said as I gawked at the statue in the distance.

"It is hard to miss. *Hermoso, no?*" Marcus reached for my hand.

"*Sí,* but also a bit intimidating." I pulled my hand away.

I was trying hard not to feel romantic, but Marcus spent the entire meal staring at me with eyes that practically screamed, "Say the word, and I'll tear your clothes off right now." His gaze was growing nearly impossible to ignore, particularly since he *hadn't* ever torn off my clothes. After the night I pushed him away and told him I wasn't ready, Marcus backed off. We were more focused on reconnecting and getting past my doubts about his family. Now we were alone in Rio, visibly sweating from both the heat in the air and the look in one another's eyes. I couldn't get the hairs on my arms to lie down.

"You look really pretty," he said, his eyes moving over my dress.

Our Dresden target worked as a bartender at high-end weddings. To blend with the guests tonight, I was wearing an asymmetrical, one-shoulder black cocktail dress with an incredibly short and fluttery hemline. Julian ordered it, without telling me, and had it delivered to our hotel.

"*Gracias,*" I said, my cheeks burning from the compliment. "You look handsome, too."

Marcus was wearing a trim black suit with wingtip shoes, not his standard motorcycle boots, all courtesy of Julian. He reached for my hand once more, and I sat back, practically sitting on my palms to keep from touching him. A blinking, neon, kiss-me sign would have been less of a distraction.

"I can't stop thinking about Urban," I said, forcing a change in conversation. "What if that photo *was* a threat? What if Keira is in danger?"

"Then it's a good thing she's with my brother."

My jaw tightened. He knew I didn't agree, but I didn't want to argue. Not with him, not now.

"We made our decision. Worrying about it isn't going to change things," he reasoned.

"How can you be so calm? How can you not hate me?" I blurted. "I've been a jerk to your brother, I accused your parents of being criminals, I dragged you around Europe after spies practically the day after we met, and you're still so chill. How do you do that?" I tossed up my hands, shoulders pressed high, my whole body on alert.

Marcus gave a lazy smile in return. "I'd be bored anywhere else, and you keep it interesting."

"You're crazy," I teased.

"Maybe." He glanced at my lips. "But I think you like it." The way he was staring at me was as if he wanted to flip the table over and wrap my legs around him. I could hardly breathe.

Slowly, he reached forward, and I let him touch me, a finger brushing mine. Heat instantly raced through my body. "I can't wait to see you on the dance floor," he said.

I jolted back. "What?"

Dancing? We were not dancing. We needed to find our Dresden Kid in that wedding and get out. But as Marcus paid the check, his eyes twinkling, it was clear he had other plans.

He put down the pen and stood, his dimples aimed at me like he knew the effect they had. "*Sí*, we're dancing."

I rose to meet him, shaking my head. "We might be a little busy."

"And I might have to disagree." He grabbed my waist and pulled me toward him, kissing me before my brain could object.

I didn't pull away.

I didn't want to.

And that was the problem.

CHAPTER TWENTY-TWO

I'd never been to a wedding before, so it felt odd that my first experience would be as a wedding crasher. Initially, I worried that two uninvited, non-Brazilian teenagers wouldn't make it through the doors. Then I realized the doors were a couple of stories high, set behind a set of marble columns, atop a soaring staircase that led to a massive, intricately carved mansion called Parque Lage. It was a cross between a royal palace and the Metropolitan Museum of Art. This was no intimate country club affair. Hundreds of guests strolled about with flutes of champagne, making us easily able to enter due to sheer volume alone.

Now as we moved through the cocktail area, I was worried we'd stand out because of my dress. All the women around me were decked out in floor-length ball gowns with Hollywood-styled hair, while my short cocktail number, which a moment ago felt over-the-top fancy now felt more fitting for an awards ceremony in a high school gym. *Now to accept the Physical Fitness Award, Anastasia Phoenix!*

I adjusted my strapless bra.

"You look perfect," Marcus complimented again, as if

reading my thoughts.

"It's fine," I said with a tight smile, pretending my exposed legs weren't out of place. "Let's just find the bartender."

"Follow me." Marcus extended his bent elbow to escort me toward the expansive square bar.

We nudged our way to the front, partially obscured by a floral arrangement so massive it should be called a sculpture and located in a botanical garden. An exotic blush sunflower obscured my face as I scanned the bartenders. All the servers were men, none older than twenty-five, and all were so ridiculously good-looking they must have shown professional headshots to get this job mixing drinks for Rio's elite.

I looked for the chiseled face from Charlotte's pictures. "I don't see him," I whispered.

"Me neither," Marcus replied. "There must be another bar in the reception area."

He clasped my elbow once more and maneuvered us through the crowd. Thumping samba music bounced off the marble walls, and I steered toward the beat, feeling fairly certain if there were a dance floor, a bar would be right beside it.

I glanced at Marcus, trying not to lose him in the crowd, and watched him lift a lime green cocktail from a waiter's tray.

"What's that?"

"A caipirinha." He smiled as if it were obvious. "When in Rio…" He took a large swig, and I could already smell the booze. "Want some?"

"No." I shook my head. The last thing I needed was anything clouding my judgment.

"You sure? It's very sweet." He grinned like the devil on my shoulder.

"It also smells very strong, so be careful."

We glided through an archway, and it instantly felt as if we'd stumbled onto a movie set for a royal wedding. The reception was being held in an open-air courtyard that looked like the Taj Mahal, right down to the pool of rectangular water in the center and the amber strobes uplighting the intricate architecture. There was no roof; instead, dinner was served on white linen tablecloths with tasteful gold chairs that sat directly under the stars and the watchful eyes of Jesus. Christ the Redeemer loomed on a distant mountaintop, arms outstretched, as if greeting the guests.

"Jesus is here." I pointed to the icon.

"Isn't he always?" Marcus teased as he polished off his drink in one massive gulp.

I was not going to be the grandma that told him not to drink.

I looked toward the far end of the body of water, where blinking magenta lights swirled like a beacon. "Over there." I gestured to the bar.

Marcus put down his empty cup and followed me as I tiptoed around the reflecting pool, the architecture mirrored on the water like a photo waiting to be taken. He wrapped his hands around my hips, forming a mini-conga line as he steered me straight toward the checkered dance floor.

"What are you doing?" I asked with a scolding look.

"One dance. *Por favor.*" His bottom lip protruded, his mouth pouty, but it was his eyes that wouldn't let me say no.

He pulled me close, breath in my ear as he swayed his hips to the samba beats like he'd done this dance his entire life. His hips pressed against mine, guiding me back and forth, his hands firm as he held me, sliding ever so slowly toward my rear. His stubble skimmed my cheek, and I could smell him from the shampoo in his hair to the scent of his skin.

My chin grazed the tattoo on his neck, and I closed my eyes. His body flowed against me, his grip on my hips firmer, his hands tighter, his lips closer, and the air between us growing hotter. I'd never wanted to kiss anyone more in my life. So when his tongue flicked my ear with the slightest flutter, I didn't stop him. Nor did I stop him when his mouth moved to my neck, then across my jaw, and then hovered at my mouth, a tickle of his lips against mine. I was lost, my hands clutching his hair to stay upright when he pressed his mouth against me. I could feel him moan. I pulled hard at his hair, and he bit my lower lip.

"I want you," he whispered into my kiss.

I felt out of my body. Our tongues intertwined, and he pressed hard against me. I forgot where I was. I forgot why we were here. I forgot there was a crowd of strangers around us. I forgot everything…until I cracked open my eyes.

We were in Rio.

There was a kid who could bring down Randolph Urban.

We were here to destroy Department D.

We were still in danger.

"We have to stop," I whispered, breathless, hating the words.

"Nooo," he groaned, his fingers clenching my butt. I loved how that felt.

"We have to. We have to find this kid."

"Not now," he whined, his mouth reaching for mine once more, cupping my head. I felt so *wanted*, and it was more intoxicating than any alcohol. Still, I summoned my inner responsible being and scrunched my eyes tight, forcing myself to pull away. We had to do this. It was bigger than us.

I stepped back to the face of a kid whose ice cream had fallen from the cone.

"We have to do this. Then…*later*." I raised my brows, hinting at the hotel room.

"*Later?*" he asked again, head tilted like he wanted a promise.

"Later," I promised with a seductive smirk.

And I meant it. I was practically ready to dive into the reflecting pool to cool off, so he'd better believe I felt the same way he did.

"Fine," he grumbled, finally dropping his hands from my body. I already wished he'd put them back. "I will hold you to it."

"You better," I teased. "Now let's find Paolo."

CHAPTER TWENTY-THREE

"Two caipirinhas," Marcus said to the handsome bartender with a familiar face. "You want one, no?"

I shook my head. "No." I needed to think clearly.

"I just want to have a little fun," he explained, though I didn't ask. "Don't worry."

Like that was possible. I was having flashbacks of Keira and a pitcher of lemon martinis, but still I stayed mum as I watched Paolo Striker grab some limes and a couple bottles of alcohol. His slick black hair was pulled toward the nape of his tan neck in a low ponytail that was only about two inches long. Dark wisps fell toward his perfect jawline, and he blew the strands away with a puff as he began shaking the drinks. Even in a sea of gorgeous faces, Paolo was hard to miss.

He was our Dresden Kid.

"This place is beautiful." I waved toward the palatial setting. "Do you work here a lot?"

"When I'm lucky. Not many weddings in Rio are this nice." Paolo's English had a thick Portuguese accent, but I could still understand him. "You American?"

"Yes." I gestured to Marcus. "He's Spanish."

"Spanish? You're a long way from home." The bartender cocked an eyebrow. "How do you know the bride and groom?"

Marcus and I exchanged a look. The obvious answer was—we didn't. We had no intention of even saying hello to the newlyweds. We were here for Paolo. Only now that we were standing in front of him, it seemed it might be complicated to have this conversation in such a crowded place with swanky guests jostling for the bartender's attention. I watched as Paolo turned his back to us, tossing a few more items into the shaker: some raspberries, a heap of sugar, a splash of something, and who knew what else. He was practically baking a cake.

"It's a long story…" I looked at Marcus, signaling I needed help.

"*Sí*, the bride and I go way back," said Marcus, his words soft around the edges. He was already tipsy from his first drink. "We've got a bit of *history*." He grinned suggestively, and I smacked his chest. Marcus was lying, but Paolo didn't know that. And it didn't take much wedding etiquette to realize that you shouldn't stand at a reception for a bride in white and hint that the color might not be fitting.

"You're popular with the ladies, huh?" Paolo sounded unimpressed, looking at me like I should be angry, and I was, but not for the reasons he thought.

I cleared my throat. "It's not like that."

Paolo glared like I was a dumb girl being played. Then he handed us the drinks, and Marcus quickly took a long sip. *Like he needs any more...*

I turned to Paolo, needing to get to the point. "We're actually hoping to talk to you."

"Me?" He sounded suspicious.

"You're Paolo Sousa, right?" I used his real name and

watched his jaw twitch; he didn't like it. Nor should he. His last name was practically a curse word in Brazil.

A few years ago, the Brazilian soccer team (or *futbol* team, as they say here) made it to the World Cup Championship—an event that ranked with the moon landing in regards to their national pride. Only the night before the big game, their star player collapsed with a seizure so severe he almost swallowed his tongue. But instead of sitting out, the guy played anyway—in very subpar health—and the team lost in a shutout. Paolo's grandfather was the doctor who had prescribed the athlete painkillers the night before, pills that likely caused his seizure. According to Allen Cross, Department D was hired by the athlete's corporate sponsor to cover up the fact that the star soccer player was hiding a serious medical condition that adversely mixed with the medication. Without that knowledge, the country blamed Paolo's grandfather for the team's loss. They still burned effigies in his name every season.

"It's Striker now," Paolo corrected, an edge to his voice. "Do I know you?"

"No, but I know about your family *situation*, and I think I might be able to help you."

"You don't say?" He sneered, seeming as interested as if I were selling broken clam shells on a Florida beach.

I turned to Marcus, expecting help, but he was busy "having fun" and gulping his drink. Only when the lavender dance floor lights flashed his way, his black pupils appeared alarmingly small. I pulled his drink away. "I think you've had enough."

He rolled his eyes, or tried to, but his eyeballs jerked to the left in what seemed an involuntary action.

"You okay?" I stiffened.

"I'm ffffine," he slurred, swaying to the side.

I didn't have much experience with alcohol, but it seemed like his drinks were hitting him remarkably fast. "Maybe you should sit."

"It'ssss all right. Talk to Paaaolo." His speech was slow. Then he put a hand on my shoulder, his off-kilter balance nearly knocking us over. I straightened my posture and shot him a look.

Then I turned my attention back to the bartender, whose expression was flat, like he'd expected the slobbering spectacle—occupational hazard.

"Look, I know about your grandfather." There was no longer time to build to a revelation while Marcus was swaying. "I know about the soccer game, I know he was set up, and more importantly, I know who did it. I'm here to see if you want payback."

Paolo's forehead wrinkled, his head cocked like he believed me about as much as he believed a Nigerian prince was going to deposit a million dollars into his bank account. "You're here to help me?"

"Yes," I said, glancing back at Marcus.

He was having a hard time standing upright. His knees were awkwardly turned inward, and his legs were oddly wobbling. I had to talk faster. "Let's just say I was screwed over by the same people. Me and my sister. *Thoroughly screwed.* And we're on a mission to bring them all down in a fiery inferno."

"Oh, really? What about *him*?" Paolo nodded his chiseled chin to Marcus, who was reaching out to me for stability, long arms swaying like he was on a tightrope, not on solid ground.

What's wrong with him? My limited experience with Keira coming home "over served" usually resulted in a fit of vomit. But the way Marcus was acting didn't feel right.

He only had two drinks.

I had to finish this conversation. "We're both here to help *you*. We're offering you revenge, a way to get back at the people who ruined your family, destroyed your name." My pulse accelerated as I watched Marcus's eyes dart around, pupils the size of pinheads. Should I call an ambulance? Did he need to sleep it off? I could call a cab and go back to the hotel. Maybe we could talk to Paolo tomorrow?

"No thank you." Paolo shot me a cocky smirk. "I don't think *I'm* the one who needs help."

It was his tone that sent ice water luging down my spine. Something was wrong, very wrong. Paolo seemed delighted that Marcus was struggling, but before I could say a word, I heard a thud from behind me.

I spun to find Marcus lying in front of the bar, his body seizing, limbs twitching uncontrollably, and his head thumping rhythmically against the tile floor in a manic fit. "Oh my God! What happened? Are you okay?" I dropped to my knees, cupping his head to hold him still, spit sloshing from his mouth onto my hands.

My eyes swung to the bartender. "Call an ambulance! Help! Somebody!" I shouted, tears fogging my vision.

What do I do?

I needed Keira; she was a nurse, she could fix this. My mind flicked through TV hospital dramas: Do I hold his tongue? Put a pillow under his neck? Turn him on his side? Elevate his feet?

I was completely useless. I kept holding his skull, like if my grip was firm enough I could get him to stop jerking, like I could will him to stop seizing from sheer desperation alone.

Around me, partygoers stopped dancing, and guests stepped away from the bar. Eyes turned to us, but no one moved. "Why are you all standing there? Call someone!"

I screeched—to Paolo, to anyone, to everyone. I looked down at Marcus. "Come on! Please, stay with me! *Please!*" His eyes rolled back into his head, his long lashes fluttering as his body continued to convulse. *Is he dying?* There was foam in his mouth. I scooped it away. *Does he have rabies? What is happening? Where is everyone?*

Finally, I heard the sound of a wedding guest on his phone, calling for help, and across the dance floor I saw event staff rushing our way with what looked like a first aid kit. "Marcus! Come on, please! Marcus!"

"His name's *Marcus*?" Paolo uttered from behind me, his tone off, like he wasn't simply unaware of his name before, but like he'd been *wrong*.

I turned toward him, my back ramrod straight, every gut instinct I had frantically waving a flag. "Yes, that's his name. Why?"

Paolo peered at the spectacle, his gaze full of not just confusion but something worse. Regret? Guilt?

"I…I thought he was somebody else," Paolo stuttered.

Before I could respond, security staff shoved me aside. "Miss! What did he take? What is he on?" a man asked in English as he kneeled beside us and opened a medical kit.

"Wha—What?" I asked, my mind racing in two directions: one to save Marcus, the other to question Paolo.

"What did he take?" the man asked again. "We need to know what drugs are in his system if we're going to help him. What is he *on*?"

"Nothing." I shook my head, brow wrinkling. "He just had a couple of…" My voice trailed off as I looked back at Paolo, the man who'd mixed our drinks, who was now inching away, backing from the crowd toward a rear exit.

He only had a couple of drinks, I thought.

I got up and ran after Paolo.

CHAPTER TWENTY-FOUR

I darted out of Parque Lage and into the night air, thankful that the architecture of the majestic wedding locale was uplit with so many spotlights it might as well have been the middle of the afternoon. I could clearly see Paolo, whose bartender uniform—white button-down shirt with rolled-up sleeves and formal black vest—was a stark contrast to the humid tropical setting.

The mansion bordered a botanical garden, the exterior surrounded by vegetation so lush and dense it felt entirely separate from its urban neighborhood. You couldn't hear a car honk, and the marble walls of the structure were so thick that no trace of the wedding music escaped.

"What did you put in his drink?" I shouted, kicking off my black high heels and stomping toward Paolo.

"I have no idea what you're talking about." He was trying to sound innocent, exaggerating his Portuguese accent like it made him sound cute.

"Bullshit! He was fine until you gave him those drinks!" I kept moving toward him, stopping a few paces away. "What. Did you. Put in them?" My words were clipped with rage—at Paolo, at myself. Marcus didn't want to come here. He thought this plan was a mistake. Now he was lying on the floor, choking on saliva, waiting for an ambulance. This was my fault. *If I had just listened to him, to Keira, to anyone...*

Paolo shrugged. "*Gringo* can't hold his liquor." He smiled flirtatiously, as if his good looks would have some sort of effect on this situation. Not on me.

"An ambulance is coming right now, and you're going to help me. Why the hell would you drug him?" I shifted in the direction of the street, my ears straining for the sound of a siren, but I heard nothing. My pulse felt like a stopwatch ticking off the moments I had until it was too late to save Marcus.

"*Why* would I drug him? That's your question?" Paolo tilted his head like the answer was obvious.

"Did Department D get to you?" A buzzer went off in my head.

"You could say that. Too bad for your boy. He didn't look like he was doing so good." He pretended to pout sympathetically, when really his eyes were thrilled by the fact that he held the keys to save Marcus, and while he enjoyed dangling them in front of me, he had no intention of handing them over.

We'll see about that...

I barreled at Paolo on impulse, like a hostage deciding to no longer sit quietly and follow directions. I swung a kick to his head, but he shifted, avoiding my blow, then threw a sloppy fist in return. I dodged his attack with my forearms and thrust my elbow at his jaw. The crack of bone made me smile. He attempted a sidekick, but I blocked it easily—he was turning out to be a horrible fighter—and I grabbed his left wrist, stretching out his arm and digging my elbow into a weak spot. He cried out in pain as I prepared to snap his limb, only before I could finish the job, he yanked his arm free and spun back a few steps.

Then he charged, brow low, grunting through his nose. He swung his good arm, flailing with anger, and I dodged it before landing a front kick, my bare foot square on his chest as I shoved him onto his butt.

"You know how to fight," he growled, skidding on the damp grass.

"You're catching on to that?" I was winded from the exercise, but not from the challenge. He wouldn't have lasted a day in my karate studio. My mind brought up images of Tyson, our double black belts. We first met at a tournament, and we fought at least twice a week for more than a year. Tyson could have destroyed this guy. Only he'd never have the chance. To do anything. Tyson's life was over. At seventeen.

I couldn't let that happen to Marcus.

"I'm not much of a kickboxer," Paolo admitted, staying on the ground and discreetly rubbing his arm. He was lucky I didn't break it; I only needed two more seconds.

"You suck at fighting," I said, wiping the sweat off my brow, mostly from humidity. "So unless you want me to finish this, tell me what you put in Marcus's drink."

Paolo spat, blood mixed with his saliva, which gave me a twinge of satisfaction. "I can fight. I've been fighting people my whole life."

"Maybe that's your problem, because I came here to *help* you," I hissed. "If you had just listened. Department D set up your grandfather, made him look like a quack who prescribed the wrong drugs to an athlete before the big game. Why would you work with them?"

"God, you don't know shit." Paolo shook his head, his

black hair falling loose from his ponytail. Slowly, he rose on tired legs, dusting the blades of grass that stuck to his black pants. "My grandfather wasn't incompetent. He didn't *accidentally* poison our *futbol* star." He looked at me like my intellect deserved his pity. "My grandfather was paid quite well for his services."

I gasped, too quickly to hold it in, and Paolo looked so irritatingly smug at my reaction that it reminded me of Craig Bernard on a bridge in Venice.

Paolo wasn't a Dresden Kid. His family wasn't destroyed by Department D. Allen Cross sent us after a guy whose grandfather intentionally poisoned the country's most famous athlete, a guy who followed in the family business and just poisoned my boyfriend. How could Cross be so wrong?

I pictured Marcus convulsing. I had to get back; I had to save him. I couldn't lose anyone else. I charged at Paolo, swinging a straight arm at his head, but he bobbed the blow, landing a lucky punch to my kidney. I winced at the sting and could hear Paolo cough out a laugh. I spun around and nailed him in the cheek with my elbow, then kicked him hard in the gut. He fell back onto the ground. Again.

"You're a coward! Slipping pills into people's drinks. You're pathetic." I growled, glaring down at him.

I needed answers, no more what ifs. Not anymore. "Department D, they told you to poison Marcus. Who? Specifically?"

"Fine." He shrugged with the look of a kid caught crawling through the bedroom window. "They don't pay me *that* well." He collapsed onto his back, body stretched out on the grass, his sore arm cradled to his chest and his jaw tight with pain. He was giving up. "I wasn't trying to poison *Marcus*. The man said he was Spanish, he said he was a ladies' man, he fit the profile, looks exactly like him..."

"You were after *Antonio*." Light bulbs exploded in my brain.

"I was told the guy drank a lot, had a high tolerance, so I upped the dosage."

Tolerance? I thought of all the alcohol I'd seen Antonio consume—the beer, champagne, wine, whiskey shots—all the partying Marcus said his brother reveled in. If Paolo was trying to take down Antonio, how much did he pump into Marcus?

"Wha—what did you give him?" My voice shook.

"I work mostly with Benzos and mix in some alcohol to get the job done. Makes 'em look like they partied too hard. But when I heard of the guy's stamina, I threw in a little Oxy, just to be sure." Another day at the pharmacy.

Paolo was an assassin.

Cross sent us here.

Everyone tried to talk me out of coming—Keira, Charlotte, *Marcus*. Why didn't I listen to them?

"If that wasn't Antonio Rey," Paolo asked, "who was it?"

"His brother," I whispered, barely able to hear my voice as one terrifying word echoed in my head: *overdose, overdose, overdose*... I had to tell the medics what he took.

"So he *is* a Rey? *Gracias a Dios*." Paolo sounded relieved, like he'd done his job well after all. His face pointed to the stars, long dark hair fanned on the damp grass.

Then he had the nerve to smile. Mission accomplished.

The fire burning in my gut suddenly sizzled across my skin, sweat popping like grease on a skillet.

I slid my feet back into my black high heels, eyes narrowed to slits. If he was after Antonio, that eliminated the Reys from the suspect pool. "Was it Randolph Urban?" I gritted my teeth, not wanting to say the next words. "The Phoenixes?"

"The Phoenixes?" He lifted his head. "I thought they were dead."

Yeah, so did I. An odd sense of relief washed through me as I realized my parents hadn't ordered a hit on my boyfriend. It was amazing what I considered good news these days. But that still didn't answer my question.

"Who. Was it?" I spat for the last time.

"Allen Cross." He said it like the man asked to borrow his lawn mower.

Then Paolo closed his eyes and stretched back. Discussion over, time for me to run along. He knew I had bigger problems sprawled on a dance floor choking on his tongue. And I did.

Only I couldn't move.

Allen Cross ordered a hit on Antonio? Allen Cross tried to kill one of us? Allen Cross hired an assassin? A hit man so incompetent that he almost killed Marcus by accident?

Suddenly, the blare of a siren rang out, an ambulance, drawing nearer as if pulling in front of the mansion. *Marcus! They're here! I have to help him! Where is he?* How *is he?*

I turned toward the sound, but my eyes caught on Paolo once more, outstretched on the dewy grass, resting rather peacefully, as if he no longer feared me, as if he knew I had somewhere more important to be and he was positive he'd get away with all of this.

The corners of my mouth twisted up slightly as I stared at him, so confident, so cocky.

Then I padded over to his long body, lifted my high-heeled foot, and stomped down with all my might.

Right on Paolo's crotch.

. . .

I'd never been in an ambulance before. The sirens were deafening from inside the van, adding to the noise already crowding my head as I squeezed Marcus's limp hand. I'd told the doctors that Marcus was suffering from an overdose of alcohol, Benzos (commonly known as Valium), and Oxy (or OxyContin, a painkiller as strong as heroin). They immediately started treatment.

We arrived at the ER, and a tube was inserted down his throat, pumping "activated charcoal" that the doctors said would stop the toxins from speeding through his system. IV fluids were administered through the veins in his arms. His breathing got so shallow at one point that they debated putting him on a ventilator, but thankfully after an hour of observation, his vitals improved. But he wasn't awake. The doctors didn't know when he'd come around, but they were no longer saying "if," which at least pulled my heart rate back down from panic levels. Still, the best-case scenario was that Marcus might open his eyes sometime tomorrow.

"He was lucky," they said. They'd gotten to him in time. They knew what he was on. They were able to treat him. Usually, with these types of overdoses, the doctors were too late.

I sat by his bed, his hand feeling cold and fragile, machines humming around us. The Brazilian hospital— bleached, boxy, and buzzing with fluorescent lights—looked like any other hospital in America. Only the signs were in Portuguese. Since he was eighteen years old, there was no legal requirement to call his parents. *Thank God.* But that left me alone, in Rio, dealing with what happened to him, to us.

I was the reason he was here. I was so bent on going after Randolph Urban that I ignored all the warning flares. I'd blindly sent everyone into harm's way—first, when I sent Marcus after that Dresden Kid alone; and now, when I insisted we come here even after we knew that Department D was on the attack.

I dropped my head low, squeezing his hand tighter as more tears slid down my cheeks. A hospital was a very scary place to be by yourself. The isolation from the outside world, the focus on a singular problem, and the overwhelming sense of helplessness was enough to let the funk rain down like a monsoon. I almost wanted to let it flood me, wash me away forever, then the hospital door creaked open. A middle-aged nurse walked in, tablet in her hands.

"He's improving," she said in English, checking his vitals.

I wiped tears from my eyes. *Pull it together.*

"You should go home," she said with a gentle smile. "Get some rest. There won't be any change until morning."

"What if he wakes up?" My voice cracked, and I wasn't sure if it was from agony, exhaustion, or fear. Probably all of the above.

"His body's been through a lot. He won't be awake for some time. You have until morning, maybe even lunch, at best."

I stared down at Marcus, crisp white sheets pulled high on his bare chest, tubes in his arms, monitors suctioned to his skin, bags of liquids dripping nearby, computers beeping and charting every inhale of breath, every beat of his heart. I didn't want to leave him. Not like this. Not alone.

But this wasn't over. Paolo tried to kill him. Allen Cross tried to kill one of *us*. I had to warn Keira. The hospital had no cell reception, and I hadn't felt I could leave Marcus until now. He was too unstable.

I pulled out a burner phone from Marcus's suit jacket, which the paramedics had removed. Once he was admitted, they handed me his personal belongings like I was his next of kin. I took them.

"You really don't think he'll wake up until tomorrow?"

She shook her head, sympathy in her stare. "There's nothing you can do right now but let the doctors do their jobs. And pray." It sounded like she repeated that line a lot.

"If I leave, would you call me when he wakes up, like the *second* anything changes?" I asked.

"Of course."

I typed my number into her tablet.

"Go home and get some sleep," she advised.

I nodded, knowing a peaceful night's slumber was nowhere near my future. Then I followed her out of Marcus's room and down the elevators.

I exited onto the street and dialed the only number we had programmed—Charlotte.

She answered on the first ring.

"Are you okay?" She sounded terrified. I was only supposed to use the phone if there was an emergency, which there was.

I told her everything, from the fight at the wedding to Marcus in the hospital. Thankfully, Antonio and my sister were safe. They'd checked in less than twenty minutes ago and were currently enjoying flutes of cava on *Las Ramblas* in Barcelona. She'd spoken to Keira herself, and she promised she'd let them know what happened to Marcus.

Only I hadn't yet told her the most mind-bending detail.

"Charlotte," I tried to steady my voice, my grip tightening on the phone. "Allen Cross was behind this. He ordered the hit. I need to know where he is. Right now."

CHAPTER TWENTY-FIVE

llen Cross was in Rio, which I already suspected. Maybe it was the glint in Paolo's eye, or maybe it was some innate understanding of how the business worked, but I had a feeling a hit this personal from a man that powerful wouldn't be ordered over the phone. I was right. Cross had traveled to Brazil to personally oversee the murder of my boyfriend. Of course, he was aiming for Marcus's brother, which wasn't much better, only emphasizing that spies of a certain age should probably get out of the business. There was a reason a new James Bond was hired every few years: senile assassins tend to hit the wrong targets. And now Marcus was paying the price. (Not that I wanted Cross to succeed in killing Antonio either. I might not trust the guy, but I didn't want him dead.)

I stood at the base of a soaring set of ivory stairs that led to the villa where Cross was staying. He wasn't hard to find. Charlotte was able to trace his cell phone to an exact address. He hadn't turned it off or used a burner, which seemed like another reckless oversight for an aging spy. Or maybe he didn't care. Maybe he was waiting for me.

The villa was located in Lagoa, a posh section of Rio housing the city's elite. There were hundreds of luxury residences nestled in the hills overlooking the kidney-shaped lagoon — a body of water which, according to Charlotte, was as famous for its toxicity as it was its beauty. Few fish survived in its polluted current, but wow, was it pretty. The duplicity seemed fitting. I was about to face a man who I thought was my ally, my oldest family friend, but he was really a killer who betrayed me as badly as my parents, as badly as Urban. How could he order a hit on one of us? How could I have been so wrong about him? I believed everything he said. I insisted that Marcus's parents murdered Tyson, because *Cross told me so*. What else had he lied about? Were my parents really alive? Did he actually help them fake their deaths, or was he the one who tried to kill them?

My mind was a wind tunnel tossing questions with painful debris. What if I had accepted a drink at the wedding? Would Cross have poisoned me too? Was he involved in my sister's kidnapping? Was anything true?

I clenched my fists, wanting to break him in ways that didn't involve pills slipped into a drink. I wanted to watch him hurt, like I watched Marcus — no one doing the dirty work for me. Maybe I was more like my parents than I realized.

I climbed the steep stairs to the ultra modern home, rage fueling me upward two steps at a time, coating my skin with tacky sweat from the humid South American air. The building's pearly exterior was uplit, highlighting giant boxy balconies overlooking the turquoise water. Spotlights were triggered the moment I touched the porch, announcing my arrival, but I didn't care. It was me against an old man who couldn't even manage to assassinate the right person.

I handled Craig Bernard; I could handle him.

I wiped the sweat from my brow and reached for the handle to the sapphire door. It was unlocked. The door fell open, no alarm system, no deadbolt, no chain, and no sirens. It could be a set up. Cross's phone pinged to an exact location. A smarter person would run in the opposite direction, but all I could see was Marcus's body twitching on the ground, foaming at the mouth. Cross betrayed me, like every other adult in my life. I was tired of being played; I was tired of people around me dying. I knew where this man was, and I was not going to let him get away.

I stepped inside.

The floors were marble, my black high heels clinking loudly. I looked down at my flirty dress, remembering the girl who had been on a dance floor hours before, her body entangled in a boy. A boy who was now in a hospital bed.

The great room was empty. There were white leather sofas and scarlet red pillows. There was modern art on the walls with a massive work by Mondrian. The decor was shiny, sharp, and minimalist. It reminded me of Randolph Urban's office in Boston.

I stopped short, noticing my surroundings once more.

This was a safe house. Or *his* house. Or a Department D house.

This place had Randolph Urban splashed all over it, down to the shiny glass dining room table and crimson leather chairs that perfectly matched his office decor.

"H-hello," I called, sounding like someone investigating a strange noise in the basement. They knew I was here; the spotlights eliminated any element of surprise.

"I'm outside," said the familiar voice.

Allen Cross.

My first reaction was relief. I wasn't sure why. Maybe

I was glad I wasn't standing in Randolph Urban's home having to deal with *him* right now. I wasn't sure I'd ever be ready to face him. But Allen Cross I could handle, he was why I was here, and he was the one I wanted to throw off a cliff into a toxic lagoon right now.

I followed the voice out to the balcony, so large it featured a hot tub that glowed with emerald strobes that almost matched the color of Christmas lights shining about the lagoa. *Christmas.* I'd forgotten about the holiday. Had it passed already? Was it coming up soon? It was weird that such a joyful custom was still carrying on while I was so embroiled in torment.

I walked out onto the terrace and spied an illuminated Christmas tree floating in the middle of the water. The fir's lime and violet lights reflected off the still lagoon, mixing with the tangerine beams shining from the high-rise buildings—the entire spectacle was so full of modern commercialism that it would make Charlie Brown roll over in his cartoon grave. Still, it was pretty. Department D was always big on threatening lives in the most beautiful places.

"Lovely, isn't it?" Cross said, emerging from the shadows as the lights on the floating Christmas tree shifted to crimson and gold. His mouth formed a smile, greeting an old friend, never mind the boyfriend he almost murdered.

"What is wrong with you?" I yelled, a fuse reigniting my belly. "You almost killed us! *Us! Marcus!* Why? What were you thinking?"

"I don't know," he replied as he slugged brown liquor from a crystal tumbler.

His eyes were hooded and his head was rolling unnaturally. He was drunk. Wonderful. Maybe I should top him off with a few Benzos and Oxys. Just like Marcus.

"How could you *do* that? I thought you were on our

side! Have you been lying to me this whole time? About everything?" Bile rose in my throat, and I fought the urge to spit, to rid myself of the deception that constantly poisoned me.

"No, it's not like that." He shook his bald head, knocking back the rest of his drink in a gulp.

"Marcus is in the hospital hooked up to machines! I watched him overdose. I watched him have a seizure. He's still unconscious, and they don't know when he'll wake up, all because you were *trying* to kill his brother. *Why?*"

Finally, Cross sighed like someone realizing the only option left was the truth. Good. "My wife is dead."

What?

"What are you talking about?" I rocked on my heels as aqua and yellow lights hit Cross's face, emanating from the Christmas tree floating in the lagoon, blinking on his wrinkled skin like our warped conversation was being held in a humid carnival.

"There's a lot I haven't told you." His eyes were bloodshot, from liquor or tears, I wasn't sure; and that made me nervous. "Remember that Christmas, a decade ago, when you were crawling under your Christmas tree and you heard me fighting with your parents?"

I nodded. It was the first flashback I had of him when we were reunited in Rome, but I didn't see what that had to do with Marcus foaming at the mouth.

"I told you that we were fighting because I wanted to leave the business, to be with my wife, and your parents refused to help."

"Yes. You also said you and your wife split up."

"We did. Eventually. I realized she would always be in danger. You never really leave a business like this. As you've seen, our enemies are vast and have long memories.

There will always be someone who wants to kill you." He took another sip, as if complaining about unpaid overtime at the bar with coworkers. "So I walked away from her to keep her safe. But I never stopped loving her. I never stopped looking out for her."

"That's so nice of you. Now what the hell does this have to do with me?" I asked impatiently. I didn't care about his wife. It sucked that he was grieving (weren't we all), but my boyfriend was currently receiving fluids through a tube, and it was Cross's fault. Did he really expect sympathy for *his* problems?

"Someone killed my wife," he said. "Recently. Someone from Department D."

It was a lengthy story, and he started slurring his words before he got to the end, not that it prevented him from refilling his glass. I didn't stop him. The more he drank, the more he talked. And Allen Cross had a lot to say.

Turned out he had been lying to me since the moment he resurfaced at Tyson's funeral, rescuing me from my confrontation with the Reys. But he wasn't lying about everything. What he told me about faking my parents' death and Marcus's parents working for Department D, that was true. (So he claimed.) It was the motives behind his plan that he fabricated.

Initially, he insisted he wanted to use the Dresden Kids to bring down Department D so *Keira and I* would be safe; in reality, he wanted revenge for his dead ex-wife. Esther had died only weeks before. Murdered. Professionally. Apparently, a hit on the spouse of a former top agent can't be ordered by just anyone. Her death had to be orchestrated at the highest level, and given he'd been out of the business for so long, his only recent link to espionage was aiding Keira and me in Italy. Esther's death felt like retaliation for his efforts. That meant Department D was behind it, only Cross didn't know precisely who dialed the assassin: Randolph Urban, the Reys, or my parents.

So he sent me to do his bidding, flitting around the world gathering evidence on Department D in the hope that someone would point a finger at exactly who was running things, who had the authority (and motivation) to order such a high-level, personal hit. Then all the evidence pointed to my parents.

"You think my parents killed your wife?" My tone was flat, desensitized to the sociopathic accusations so regularly thrown at my mom and dad.

"At first, it looked that way, but I wasn't certain. Your parents and I were close. *I helped them fake their deaths!*" he shouted on the balcony, like he wanted the gods and everyone else to hear. It was so uncharacteristic of the unflinching man I met in Rome. It reminded me of what the CIA director had said of Randolph Urban's actions in Venice—he was making emotional mistakes based on my parents' betrayal. Now Cross was reacting out of grief for his ex-wife. It seemed when it came to family, evil agents were as human as the rest of us. Well, except for my parents, they seemed perfectly fine living the good life while their daughters languished.

"Some of the evidence I knew was false," Cross went on. "I was there for a few of those missions, I know how the plans went down, so it was clear the testimony being provided to you didn't match actual events. The witnesses were being tampered with."

"And you didn't tell us this!"

He knew the Dresden Kids were lying? But why would

they do that? They had such good reasons to want revenge, to want to ruin Department D. Then I thought of Paolo Striker and Sophia Urban. Not all children of this organization were innocent. How many of the kids that I let into the compound were playing for the other side? And how many of them deserved stars on Hollywood Boulevard for their performances?

"Which kids? Who's lying?" I demanded.

"All of them."

My head jutted back. *All* of them? How could they *all* be agents for Department D? How could Keira, Marcus, and I be the only ones oblivious to what our parents were doing? That was impossible.

"It's not what you think." Cross read the confusion on my face as he tugged off his Christmas green bow tie and tossed it on the ground. Maybe he was hoping the alcohol would slide down faster if he didn't have any pesky constrictions around his throat. "The kids aren't agents. They don't work for us. Some of their parents did, or grandparents. But all of them really did come from families that were ravaged by Department D. They didn't lie out of espionage; they lied for the oldest reason in the world."

He glared at me, head tilted, like he'd stand there all night until I caught on.

"Money," I stated, the single word so heavy on my lips.

Cross nodded. "Money. Or more accurately, reparations, back pay, damages owed, pain and suffering. Department D delivered some pretty hefty incentives—a few had their family names completely cleared of wrongdoing, relatives released from prison, bodies suddenly located and put to rest."

"Offers they couldn't refuse," I quoted *The Godfather.*

Who the hell *wasn't* betraying us these days? Could I

trust anything Cross said?

The bitter taste of deceit flooded my mouth, mixing with the salty tropical air. I wanted to vomit. "You *gave* us those names. You knew how things really went down on those missions, and you never said a word. Were you working against us the whole time?"

He shook his head, a glob of spit flying. "No, you're not understanding." He sounded exhausted talking to a layperson. "There's a *mole* in your group. You know that, Anastasia. Come on." He pulled a face suggesting I wasn't stupid. "I gave you the names, they were all accurate, only someone was passing those names on to Department D, and they got to them first. I'll give you one guess as to who." He poured himself another drink.

"Antonio," I whispered, as if saying his name too loud was akin to screaming Bloody Mary in a bathroom mirror while turning in circles.

Cross smacked his lips in confirmation. "Like I said, Esther was killed *after* you found your sister, after Urban went on the run. So once it was apparent that Antonio was feeding his parents information on all of you, on every Dresden Kid you were going to visit before you went, it wasn't much of a leap to assume it was the Reys who killed my wife in retaliation for me helping you in Italy and for me helping your parents *fake their deaths* all those years ago!" He shouted the words again, like he clearly regretted ever helping my mom and dad. I couldn't blame him. It didn't seem like he got very much out of the deal. We had that in common.

Cross went on to explain how he figured it out. First, he hired a "Plant," as he called him, a former employee he felt certain was loyal to him. Cross then fed *us* the Plant's name as one of our Dresden Kids, and he suggested to

Charlotte that she specifically send Marcus and Antonio on his case. They went. Only a Department D agent got there first, a blond Slovakian woman, who offered cash, amnesty, and practically the crown jewels of England if he'd feed us false information and return to the compound as a spy for the organization. This was enough to confirm Cross's suspicions that our witnesses were being tampered with, but it didn't point to the exact mole. That happened when Antonio found a private moment to speak with the Plant (while Marcus was in a restroom), and Antonio admitted he was still working for Department D. Cross also confirmed that the Slovakian woman was Antonio's partner—likely the same woman I saw on the Tube staring at Antonio the first day we arrived in London. *I knew it.*

"Antonio's a spy." I bit out the words, wanting to claw out his eyes so badly I could practically feel his lashes under my fingernails. Any satisfaction I might have had at being right for not trusting him immediately erased once I realized I'd have to be the one to tell this to Marcus and Keira. *Always the messenger.* "So he was working with his parents the whole time? It was all an act? And the Dresden Kids are a bunch of lying bastards."

I thought back to the awkward moments in the compound, to all the times I felt like a high school outcast in the cafeteria. I thought they hated me. Really, they screwed me over for financial gain. In a twisted way, that actually helped my self-esteem. Their motives I understood. But Antonio? His brotherly bonding, all the guitar playing and teasing, it was going to crush Marcus more. Then I thought of how he seemed to warn Marcus away from me. He didn't want us together, because he knew I suspected him; he thought I'd figured it out. And I did, a few hours and a stomach-pumping too late.

Cross wobbled my way, his drunken legs incapable of walking a straight line. "After you *miraculously* located Antonio…" His glazed eyes suggested our Guy Fawkes encounter was no testament to Charlotte's hacker skills. Antonio wanted to be found. "He told his parents every word you said. There never was a bug in Mr. Stone's flat. They didn't need one. The Reys used their son to spoil your plans, to set you up, and to make sure it would be *your* family going down with the Department D ship. Can't say I blame them. Your parents do deserve *to burn for all this*!"

Did anyone *not* hate my parents? Myself included. *But really, did it have to be Marcus's parents?*

"So the Reys are the ones setting us up? And they killed your *wife*? Why? What does Esther have to do with this?" My face twisted, my brain frantically trying to mop up the messy details, but they were spilling way too fast.

"That's a great question!" he barked, tossing up his arms, huge pools of sweat soaking his unseasonable button-down shirt. He was growing so drunk it was hard to look at him. "Why would anyone want to kill my sweet *Esther*." He choked on her name. "Bastards. They were trying to control *me*, that's why. All signs pointed to the Reys. So you bet I thought it was them. Except it turns out, and you're not going to believe this, I was *wrong*!" he bellowed, his voice bouncing off the marble patio floor. "I almost had their son killed! I poisoned your little Spanish boyfriend for *nothing*!"

His hazel eyes looked deranged. He was stumbling, shouting, and smiling inappropriately. As much as I wanted revenge for what he did to Marcus (and I *really* did), I couldn't escape some primal instinct telling me to run. He looked out of control, capable of anything, and if this was a Department D house, there could be live grenades lying around with the teaspoons. I wasn't sure I wanted to see if I could beat a belligerent drunk before he reached for the arsenal.

I inched back, casually trying to work my way inside, snake to the front door. I'd gotten whatever answers I could tonight.

"Where are you going?" He stumbled after me, his demented expression bordering on Jack Nicholson in *The Shining*. "Aren't you going to ask who killed Esther?"

"I'm so sorry for your loss. Maybe we should talk about this later." I kept moving for the door.

"But the time is now. There won't be a later." I didn't like his tone.

"After you've sobered up. We'll talk." I reached the entry, my fingers stretching for the brass knob.

"I wouldn't take another step if I were you." His voice grew low and sinister.

That was when I saw the knife.

A shiny silver dagger was clutched in Cross's liver-spotted hand. There were jewels encrusted on the handle, like the knife belonged in a museum. I thought of Tyson, the knife to his chest, how it only took one precise blow by a trained killer. I stood motionless. If I ran, I felt there was little chance his aim was good enough to fling a heavy dagger at a moving target while he was this hammered from scotch. But what if I was wrong?

I shifted another inch toward the door, and he swiftly lifted his arm, dagger raised with the blade behind his shoulder, elbow pointed at me like he did indeed know how to throw it.

"Cross, calm down. It's been a long night. I know you weren't trying to hurt Marcus. I see that now." I tried to reason with him, my palms raised defensively as my eyes looked about for a tray, a metal picture frame, a painting, anything to shield me if he tried to impale me with a flying weapon. "I know you were after Antonio, with good reason. Antonio's a bad guy. His parents are bad guys. I'm sorry they killed your wife."

"I told you! They *didn't* kill my wife!" he screamed, elbow lifting higher like he was ready to launch the dagger.

"You're right! I'm sorry! I shouldn't have said that." I covered my face with my hands, protecting my head, like that would do any good if a hunk of pointy silver shot at my eye. "Just don't throw the knife. You don't want to hurt me. You want to hurt the people who hurt Esther. That isn't *me*."

The sound of footsteps shuffling echoed from a darkened doorway, and before I could even turn toward the sound, I caught an odd smirk on Cross's face, like he was waiting for me to look, like he was getting what he wanted, after all.

"You're right, *darling*," said a voice from the shadows, so eerily familiar, it sent the blood funneling from my head. "It was us. Now, Allen, put down the knife."

Out of the darkness, standing side by side, stepping into the foyer of an elegant villa in Rio de Janeiro, looking like they owned the place, were two people I thought I'd buried in the ground.

My parents.

CHAPTER TWENTY-SIX

I could hear myself gasp, and I could feel my eyelids fluttering uncontrollably. I could see them standing in front of me, but it was like I was watching them through a TV screen that was showing a film deemed inappropriate for children.

"Anastasia, darling, step away from the door," said my mother. *My mother!*

"It's okay," my father added.

Okay? What was okay? Nothing about this was okay.

I stood like a broken statue, unable to be dislodged, unable to process anything.

Finally, my dad stepped forward, slowly, like a hunter not wanting to startle the doe-eyed deer. He clasped my hand and gently guided me from the entry. I felt his strong fingers interlaced with mine, and I stared at the familiar hand I held as a girl crossing the street.

I stopped short. My high heels clanked on the marble floor as I yanked myself free of him.

I stepped away. Far away.

"What. The. *Fuck?*" I shouted. Because there really

were no other words.

My mother sighed as though she were expecting my oh-so-dramatic reaction. "It's good to see you."

"It's good to see me? *It's good to* see *me!*" I yelled from the depths of my throat, the words ripping their way out. The room sloped at an odd angle, all of the elegantly appointed leather furniture tilting and my parents stretching like demons. A bomb ticked deep inside, and I pulled at the asymmetrical strap of my fancy black dress like it might stop the explosion.

"Calm down. Breathe," said my father, putting a hand on my back.

I jerked, his touch like fire. *No. No way. Did he actually think he could* touch *me?*

"We realize this is a shock." There was a hint of child psychology in his voice, reminiscent of the shrinks I saw *after their funerals.*

I opened my mouth to scream, the sound halfway up my throat, but my mom held up a long slender finger, silencing me. I bit my tongue, literally. I could taste the blood.

"I imagine you have a few questions, but first, let us explain." She pulled herself up to full height and raised her brows as if to insist, *This is how things are going to be. Now hold your questions until I call on you.* Oddly, I noticed her eyebrows had been professionally groomed; she'd gone to a spa recently. "When everything—"

"No," I cut her off, finding my voice. "You don't get to tell me what to do. You don't get to tell me how *this* will go down." I gestured between the two of us. "I will ask whatever questions I want. And you. Will. Answer them."

We eyed one another, the room falling so silent I swore they could hear my heart pounding a death metal beat. But I didn't blink first.

"You've changed," she said, making a clinical observation.

"What did you expect?" I snarled. "Everyone in my life is either dead or being threatened. Because of *you*!"

Annoyance slipped into her face as she glanced at my father, like she wanted *him* to deal with me.

Dad nodded. They didn't need to speak; they knew each other so well. Yet here I was, their daughter, and it was like we'd just met.

"Anastasia, I know Allen got you up to speed on a few things, but there's more to the story," Dad began, casually moving toward me with the poise of a politician used to spin.

I stumbled a step, then another two, certain if he got any closer, the furor I was trying to restrain would break free like a feral animal.

He stopped his approach. "Our deaths, they weren't by choice. Urban had plans to terminate us, and it was either let him succeed or let him *think* he succeeded."

"Funny how neither of those options takes your children into account."

"We *did* think of you," Mom interjected. "You remember that night, when we said we were moving to Canada, and you said you wanted to stay in Boston with Keira."

Actually, I'd said a lot more than that. I'd told them that I hated them, then they died. I'd regretted those words every second of my life since. I'd apologized again and again to their tombstones, to their empty bedrooms, to the thin air, hoping it would be enough to absolve me, but the guilt never lifted. Until this moment.

Because back then, I didn't mean it. Now I did. I really, really did.

"We were honoring your wishes," Dad said. "You and

Keira staying in Boston was the right decision. It was what was best for you."

"What was best for me was having my parents, not being orphaned, and not falling into depression!" I cried, a sob lodged in my throat. "Did you really need me to say that?"

"It would have meant spending your lives on the run," Dad said.

"We had to make an impossible choice, and our options were limited," my mom continued. "There was no simple ending, and Allen's plan seemed like the best decision for everyone." She looked at Allen Cross slumped on the floor, his shoulders sagging from scotch, drool on his chin, and the dagger laying on the marble in front of his outstretched legs. He looked nothing like the controlled, unbreakable spy I'd met in Rome.

"You have no loyalty." Cross lazily lifted his chin, his tongue sounding too thick for his mouth. "Not to me, not to anyone! That's why people want to kill you, and I really hope someone finally does. You deserve to be in the ground."

He meant it. It was why he kept shouting his words on the balcony. He wanted them to know how much he regretted ever helping them, how much that decision ruined his life. Well, it ruined mine, too.

I gawked, any innocence that was left in me draining away, pooling by my feet, sliding out the door, and dripping into the toxic lagoon below. The only adult in my life I thought I could trust just wished my parents dead, and I wasn't sure I disagreed with him. "How long have you known that Randolph Urban is my father?"

The question triggered an immediate reaction. My mom cleared her voice, tensely pulling her thick espresso hair, which rippled down her back in waves, like mine. I could see myself in her, the way she tugged at her shoulders, and in the shape of her mouth, the curve of her hips. But not in her eyes. My blue-gray eyes belonged to someone else, and now we all knew who.

"It's complicated," she replied.

Hot blood rushed down my arms. I was *not* a child anymore. They'd made sure of that. Protecting me from harsh truths was no longer an option. Especially not from this, from him.

My dad reached for me, the depth of his eyes revealing that of all the accusations I could throw their way (and there were plenty), this was the one he was dreading. "He is *not* your father." His nose wrinkled in offense. It was long and pointy like Keira's. His light brown hair matched hers, too.

The years had been kind—his hairline was thinned a bit, and there were new crow's feet around his small hazel eyes, but otherwise he looked the same. And he looked nothing like me. How had I not seen it?

"*I'm* your dad," he insisted in a "biology doesn't make a family" kind of way. Only to pull that card, he needed to prove love was what bonded us together. And we both knew I didn't have much of that stacked in my deck.

"You know what I'm asking. I have results of a DNA test, confirmed by the CIA." I spat the truth. "Randolph Urban's sperm met your egg. So tell me, Mom, exactly how long were you cheating on Dad?"

I didn't blink as I said it. I wanted to hurt her. I wanted to shove at least one ounce of the pain she'd inflicted on me back onto her.

"Your father and I dealt with this a long time ago," she replied, her patience sounding thin. "I knew how Urban would react if he knew the truth, and I knew he'd never let you out of his clutches. After a lifetime in this business, I didn't want that for you. As much as you hate me, Anastasia, I was thinking of *you*. So I faked amnios; I faked blood tests. I did everything a woman could possibly do to prove you were *not* his child. To keep you safe."

"Well, you've done a bang-up job of that." I gave a bit of fake applause. "He kidnapped one daughter and had me chasing assassins around Italy!"

"You handled yourself quite nicely, I must say. Very impressive." My dad actually sounded proud, like I'd hit a grand slam in little league.

Who are these people?

"Since you brought up the CIA." Mom shifted gears, signaling to my dad that it was *time*. For what, I didn't know, but I sensed I wouldn't like what I was about to find out. I never did. "You haven't asked the big question yet, darling. Don't you want to know where we've been?"

She was right. I hadn't asked. It wasn't because I didn't want to know; it was because I hadn't thought to bring my notecards to better organize the questions I had regarding their betrayal.

She paused, the odd look on her face adding to the intentional drama. Then finally, she stepped beside my father, hand on his shoulder in solidarity. They were in this together. Them against me.

"We've been in CIA custody for almost two years now," she revealed. "We're in Rio, because we finally broke ourselves out."

CHAPTER TWENTY-SEVEN

As a teenager, there are a lot of things you aren't expected to easily understand: advanced quantum physics, open heart surgery, and Russian literature, to name a few. But nowhere on that list should be the whereabouts of your parents and your own government's reasoning for letting you think they were dead.

"You've been in CIA custody." The sentence was so heavy, it was hard to push out. I sat in an interrogation room, in Italy, with the Deputy Director of the CIA. Martin Bittman gave Keira and me falsified passports, he paid for our hotel rooms, he periodically called to "check in," and never in all of those conversations did he happen to mention that he knew for a fact that our parents were alive, because he held the keys to their cells *for two years.*

My eyes shot toward Allen Cross, who was still splayed on the floor of the entryway. "I thought you said they were in Cuba! Was everything you told me bullshit?"

"They *were* in Cuba!" he shouted with a slur in his voice. "In a top-secret black site used as a prison for high-level international criminals. Why do you think Martin Bittman was so willing to help when I called him into Venice? His most high-level prisoners had just escaped custody."

"You broke out of Gitmo?" The reality of my parents being put in the same category as Al Qaeda terrorists made me swallow down vomit.

"We weren't in Guantanamo Bay. Please." My mom scoffed like it was absurd, like out of all the things I heard today, *that* was the one that was unbelievable. "We were being held in a warehouse, off book. It wasn't exactly the best accommodations."

"Oh, gee, I'm so sorry for your discomfort," I replied sarcastically.

"After your father and I went into hiding—"

"You mean faked your deaths, in a fiery car accident, with charred bodies, that we buried," I interrupted.

She looked at me like it was time to shut up. And I did, because I needed to hear this, not because she deserved my obedience.

"We were hiding out, moving around the world, trying to stay ahead of the authorities…" she went on.

"But they caught up to us about two years ago," my father finished, "in Burma. They knew *everything,* had us on *everything.* So it was either cooperate or be thrown down a dark pit where no one would ever look."

"You should've gone with the pit," Cross hissed, his head flopping like a bobblehead.

"We chose to cooperate," my mother continued, as if she hadn't heard him. "And what they wanted was Randolph Urban. And Department D. They wanted to bring down the whole enterprise."

"This was *two years* ago?" My brow knitted in confusion. "Then why didn't you succeed already? Because it would have saved Keira and me a whole lot of kidnapping."

"Turns out we're not very good snitches," my dad quipped, like it was funny, like everything that had happened because of their choices (my sister in the trunk of a car, Tyson being *murdered*) was now a clever anecdote, something to be chuckled about over cocktails.

This could have been prevented, all of it, if they had done what the CIA wanted.

I stared him down, steam seeping from my head so intensely I was surprised the condo windows didn't fog. My father flinched.

"Darling, understand—Urban may have tried to kill us, but we *were* trying to overthrow him at the time…" My mom waggled her head back and forth like *potato pahtatto*. She sounded flippant about her own life. "We had a history with Urban, most of it good, and it wasn't like the CIA was our ally. So our loyalties were a bit divided."

"You have loyalties?" Cross jibed, needing a *ba-dum-bump* from a comedic drummer.

"The biggest factor," Dad said, ignoring him, "was what the CIA promised in return." He forced me to meet his eyes. "You and your sister. They said if we helped them, then you would never know about our pasts. They would keep you in the dark, you would have normal lives, and they would protect you at all costs, against our enemies. We believed them."

"Until Urban kidnapped Keira and the CIA did nothing," I pointed out.

Dad nodded, as if pleased I was catching on and he no longer had to build the edges of the puzzle for me.

"The CIA was getting *impatient* with our lack of progress," Mom continued, pacing the marble entry, her sky-high heels with red-soled bottoms clanking loudly. For having recently escaped prison, she seemed to have plenty of time for designer shoes and eyebrow waxing. "They told us about Keira's DNA test in Boston, and they had no intention of stopping her from running it. She would have learned everything, which completely went against their promise to keep you out of it. Instead, the CIA used her as a way of motivating us. They wanted us to talk faster, provide more evidence, build their case—so they showed us pictures of Keira with Craig Bernard; they threatened to let Keira learn the truth about our work and to make sure Randolph knew that she *knew*. That would have made both of you easy targets. So we escaped, went to Boston to stop the test, only we ran into Luis Basso first."

They were trying to protect us.

I didn't know how I felt about that. There was a sizable part of my jaded heart that swelled at the thought of parents who broke out of prison for us. But there was another part of me so blackened, nothing would ever be enough and everything would always be too late.

"You were in Boston," I repeated, my mind catching up with the timeline of events. "That test was run *before* Keira was taken. So where were you when she was kidnapped? Where were you when I was running around Italy trying to get her back? Where were you when Keira was being held *by assassins*?" I shouted, rage burning away any conflicting emotion.

Cross grunted from the floor beside me, rolling his eyes like he knew I wouldn't like the answer.

"We couldn't get involved," Dad said it as if it were a legitimate excuse. "We'd just broken out of an undisclosed black site. Rumors were spreading that we were alive."

"So you were worried about *yourselves*, about getting caught?" Their selfishness burst the tiny bubble of hope I'd felt that they might have escaped *for us*. Cross *tsk*ed in agreement.

"We didn't think Urban would hurt you or Keira. He was angry, but he was angry with *us*. So our involvement would only set him off more. We thought eventually he'd cool down, stop acting so erratically…"

"You faked your deaths and lied to him about his long-lost daughter! I don't think he's getting over that anytime soon." The words tasted rancid. I couldn't believe I was being put in a position where I had to defend that man. "Let's be honest—you stayed in hiding to protect *your asses*. You let *us* take the fall…"

"No." My father held up a finger. "We tried to intervene in Venice before you got there. We saw those proof of lifes of Keira, we knew what Urban was planning, but things didn't go well. We barely got out alive. Did you know he intended to lure us to that soccer stadium in Venice so he could blow us up? Thankfully, you were a step ahead. And baby, we are so proud!" He held up a hand like he expected a high-five for fighting Craig Bernard alone on a bridge so I could unchain my sister from a bathroom sink *before they strapped a bomb to her*. The CIA had hinted at those plans, but I didn't know Randolph Urban really desired to turn my sister into a suicide bomber who would blow up our parents.

"What is wrong with you people?" All air and reason expelled from my body.

"Urban's usually not that emotional," Mom explained, like Crazy Uncle Urban had simply overreacted. With a suicide vest. "After he found out you were his daughter, that was pretty much the tipping point. The only other time he was that unhinged was when he learned of our plot to overthrow him." She gazed at me, nudging me to *think hard*. "You were there, when we first arrived in Boston, when he gave us that housewarming present."

My mind flicked back to my entire intact family, standing on the curb outside of our new Brookline brownstone when Urban pulled up in his flashy red sports car and presented my parents with a gift. "The framed embroidery. The latitude and longitude coordinates," I recalled. What ever happened to that gift?

"That wasn't the coordinates of our home, sweetheart." Dad cocked his head. "Those were the coordinates for the meeting we secretly held to wage a coup with Department D staff loyal to *us*…"

"And where did that loyalty get us?" Cross butted in.

My father ignored him again. "Randolph knew everything."

"It was a threat," Mom added. "We started planning our escape the next day."

"Yes, with *my* help!" Cross spat, waving his drunk hand around before clutching the jeweled dagger from the ground. "And how did you repay me? By killing my *wife*!"

Cross hobbled to his feet, waving the weapon wildly, his eyes looking rabid. "I should have let him kill you!" He pointed the knife at my dad, who knocked him off balance with a single swipe.

Cross fell to the ground, but before his round belly hit, he swung out his outstretched arm and sliced my father's calf. Dad went down, blood pouring out of his torn flesh onto the white marble floor. He gripped his leg, his face grimacing. Cross stumbled back up and charged at my mother, screaming like a warrior invading the enemy camp.

I watched, stunned, as my mom's arm shot out with a speed that seemed inhuman. She grabbed an antique chair resting near the entry, turned it on its side, and stomped down like a professional wrestler, snapping off a wooden leg. Then she swung the pointed piece of wood at Cross, smacking him so hard and precisely on the wrist, he dropped the knife he was holding. The heavy metal clattered loudly onto the marble.

I had never seen my parents fight before.

I had never seen them move this fast before.

It was as if my mom's body was reacting to the threat with no conscious decisions—and the spectacle felt uncomfortably familiar, like when I tripped Wyatt Burns, attacked Luis Basso, and nearly killed Craig Bernard. On some primal level, maybe I was like them. I hated that thought.

Cross stormed at my mom, weaponless, panting through his nostrils like a wild beast. Mom rapidly struck him on the forehead with the broken chair leg, and Cross went down, falling onto this back. Then she stepped over him, straddling his body and raising the jagged end of the wooden stick above his chest, ready to come down in a deathblow.

"Stop!" I yelled, racing toward her, finally joining the chaos. "Mom! Stop! Please!"

She halted with her weapon midair, peering at me in confusion as if just remembering I was still in the room, as if only now returning to her body.

"You can't kill him," I insisted, taking in the old man on the ground, the old spy who helped me get back my sister, the old friend who gave me the answers when no one else would. Yes, he faked my parents' deaths, and yes, he almost killed Marcus, but he helped me, too. He stepped up for me in Italy when my parents were too busy protecting themselves. What I felt for him was complicated. Wasn't everything? "Let. Him. Go."

She gracefully stepped away with an empty look of remorse.

My mother was a murderer. I could see it now. She was

going to kill him. Right in front of me.

"What he said about his wife, it didn't happen like that," she pleaded quickly, palms raised, eyes not liking what she saw. She was losing me. We both knew it. She stared down at Cross. "Esther was very sick. You know that."

"Don't you talk about her! Don't you dare say her name!" Cross moaned, not getting up.

"Anastasia, it's true," said my father, now bare chested. His gray T-shirt was ripped into strips and tied around his bleeding leg. His khaki shorts were splattered with dark maroon stains, and so were his boat shoes. Gore puddled around him, but his face looked calm, like it didn't hurt, like he'd been through much worse and had this completely under control. "Once Randolph realized that Allen helped you in Italy, that he helped us fake our deaths, he was livid. He threatened Allen's wife."

"Stop talking about her!" Cross shouted.

But my mom continued. "A few weeks ago, after Venice, Randolph took a picture of Esther sitting on a park bench, proof that he could get to her whenever he wanted."

"And he could have!" Cross shouted.

"*Allen…*" My mom took on the scolding tone every disappointed parent learned to master in the nursery. "You were ready to flip sides, go back to Department D, and give us up. You were unhinged. *Look at you!*" She pointed to his sloppy appearance. If I could see how far he'd tumbled in a few weeks, then so could my parents who'd spent a lifetime with the man.

"At least I care about what happens to my loved ones." Cross sat up, suddenly seeming less drunk, as if the fight was a strong cup of coffee.

Mom's jaw tightened. "They were using Esther to get to you…"

"So you *killed* her!"

"It was what she would have wanted." Dad said this with a straight face, as if this were a solid argument and he were pleading his case to *me*. Seriously? "Esther had early onset Alzheimer's. She was living in a nursing home, and she had no idea who she was, where she was. She would have *hated* that. You know that, Allen. You weren't abiding by her wishes. We did what she would have wanted. It was a peaceful end."

"You had no right!" Cross staggered to his feet, his ailing tired legs barely able to hold him. "You weren't thinking of her. You were thinking of *yourselves*."

"We were thinking about what was best for everyone," Dad reasoned.

"What about me? What about what *I* wanted? After everything I did for you. You didn't even let me say goodbye!"

He pulled out the knife once more, no one even realized he'd lifted it from the ground, and he lunged at my mother, aiming the blade at the vacant space where her heart should be. He wanted her dead. Both of them. He wanted revenge. And with good reason.

My mom lifted the broken chair leg still gripped in her hand and smacked the dagger from Cross's fist. Before the weapon even hit the floor, she moved behind him, wrapped the wooden leg around his neck, and squeezed him in a chokehold. Cross gagged, his liver-spotted face turning purple, his hazel eyes bulging inhumanly. I raced forward, trying to intervene, but I didn't make it two steps.

I watched my father grab the dagger from the ground and plunge it into Allen Cross's chest.

CHAPTER TWENTY-EIGHT

"Is he okay? He's not dead, is he?" I heard my mouth yelp, my voice two octaves too high and my eyes seemingly incapable of blinking. "He can't be dead."

Only there was a jewel-encrusted dagger sticking out of Allen Cross's chest, and his eyes were open, glassy and lifeless, as they pointed toward the recessed lights in the ceiling. The shiny white room reeked of death, a tacky mix of blood, salt air, and sweat. I could taste it, or maybe I was chewing the inside of my cheek so hard my mouth was filling with my own blood.

"We didn't want to do that." Dad sounded like a boss during layoffs. *We regret to inform you...* Meanwhile, he was wiping his bloody hands on his already bloody shorts, and it was his death blow that put a dagger in a man's chest.

"We tried to reason with him before you got here. That's why we came," Mom said. "Our intel was that you and Keira would be in Rio, and we wanted to intercept you. We wanted you nowhere near Paolo Striker, or whatever he's calling himself."

She sounded as if her explanation mattered. They'd just *killed* a man.

"Then you showed up with Marcus *Rey*." My dad twisted the name like a curse. Marcus's name. The boy lying in a hospital bed. One of the only people I had any faith in anymore. My dad was cursing *him*. "We knew about Antonio, and we had to get you away from those boys, that family. We thought we could get Cross to back off, to stay away from you, to stop this stupid plan of his…"

"But by the time we got here, Cross was already a bottle of scotch deep. He didn't take it well when he learned what happened to your *boyfriend*." Mom didn't roll her eyes as she said the word, but she looked like she wanted to, like I'd picked a real winner.

Meanwhile, she strangled a man with a chair leg, a senior citizen with liver spots, a friend they'd cherished for decades, a man who put Christmas presents in my stocking. She was still wearing her heels. She was barely sweating. Her husband was wiping a murder weapon of his fingerprints, and her ex-lover held my sister hostage for months and left me to dig through her blood.

And she was criticizing me?

"Are you *kidding* me right now?" I screeched, baring my teeth. "Marcus was poisoned tonight! He's hooked up to tubes right now! And you just murdered your best friend!"

"You don't know the Reys. That entire family can burn for all I care."

Her words hit me so hard I feared they'd leave a bruise. This woman gave birth to me, to my sister. These people raised me, for thirteen years at least. How had I not seen the *Mommy Dearest* in her or the *Darth Vader* in my father? In *either* of my fathers. For all the harping I did about my gut, about how I was the only one who knew Keira was alive, I was so completely wrong about them. My entire life. What else was I wrong about? What else had they done?

My mother seemed to recognize the light extinguishing in my eyes, the last flicker that believed in them. Immediately, she stepped toward me, a deep frown in her forehead.

I staggered back, not letting them close.

"The Reys conspired with Urban to have us killed back then," she said. "They would have done it."

"If you weren't conspiring against them first!"

"Our problem with the Reys is long and complex." Her look was severe, as if to highlight the understatement. "They know how much we hate them, which is why they loved sending us pictures of you sucking face with their son or them hugging you in the lobby…"

I huffed. That explained a lot. Cross always suspected those photos were going to my parents. I guess he was right. Too bad I couldn't tell him. Because he was dead.

"If you say one more bad thing about Marcus, I will walk out that door, and you will never see me again." My voice was calm and controlled as I made a promise I truly meant.

Marcus was alone right now, because I was here. With them. I had to pray he was still safely sleeping in his hospital bed. I had to pray he was okay. Because I was busy confronting my non-dead parents who just murdered our now-dead ally.

"You're right. We were wrong." Dad shot my mother a worried look. "This isn't what we wanted to happen. This isn't how we planned to see you again. You and your sister were all we thought about in prison. Keeping you safe. Getting out to see *you*. We've missed you."

I shook my head in disbelief, not allowing his words to land. "You've done nothing to give me that impression."

"We never wanted you to pay for our crimes. We wanted you to have a life outside of this business. That's why we left, and that's why we tried to cooperate with the CIA. It was *so hard* to walk away." A dangerous piece of me wanted to hear the regret in his voice, wanted to see the way his eyes drooped, the way his shoulders slumped. He looked so much like Keira in that moment.

"This plan of Cross's, running around after the children of our enemies. It was going to get you killed. It's why we had to intervene now. For *you*," explained my mother, her eyes softening. "This is too much for you to handle on your own. It should never have been put on your shoulders. We thought leaving would prevent this very thing."

My hands quivered at my sides, a burn scorching from my gut all the way to my eyes. *No, no, no. They don't mean it...*

"We should have done things differently. We should have protected you more," my father insisted, slipping a key into the shackles on my wrists, trying to release me, trying to get me to let go.

I thought back to the cemetery, their names on the tombstones, the anniversaries of their deaths, the constant fights with my sister, the battles with social services. The depression. The grief. The isolation of a girl with no parents. "Do you have any idea what you put us through?"

"We are *so sorry*," Dad finally offered.

"We truly are, darling. I am so sorry," Mom agreed.

There it was. The apology I was long overdue, the remorse that was owed to me, and it changed nothing. I didn't feel better. I didn't feel relief or closure or forgiveness. The hole inside of me was still fresh. Turned out "I'm sorry" couldn't bring back my parents. The mom and dad I loved were still gone. The people in front of me now were strangers wearing their bodies as suits.

"Did you ever love us?" I asked, my voice cracking.

"Of course!"

"Yes!" they answered together.

"Then how could you let this happen to us?" I sniffled, trying so hard to hold in the tears, not give them another piece of me, but it was so hard. There was no emotional dam large enough to keep back the flood of being hit with my dead parents come back to life.

My mom and dad shared a look, then tentatively moved toward me, slowly at first, then in three huge steps. They wrapped me in a hug, four arms squeezing me tight, two faces pressing into my hair. "We love you, sweetheart," they both whispered. "We love you so much. We do. We promise we do."

That was when I lost it. I sobbed. It all came out. All the hatred I had for their betrayal, all the grief I had in their absence, all the fear I'd had for my sister, and all the love I had for my family. Something inside me fractured, wracking my body. I couldn't stop crying.

And they didn't ask me to.

They held me tighter, nuzzled me closer, and I breathed in their scent. My parents. They didn't smell like soap or perfume, nor lotion or laundry. They smelled like them. A distinct aroma that I hadn't inhaled since March eighth, the night they left us. It was the scent of their skin, the smell of their sweat; it was them. It was everything. I squeezed my eyes shut and listened to their whispers promising it would all work out, we'd be okay, they were back, and it was okay now. We were all right.

Then I opened my eyes and saw the dead body lying on the ground.

This wasn't all right.

I pulled away, stepping back from them, wiping my eyes, my nose. My one-shouldered dress was too snug to serve as a handkerchief, and my father's shirt was currently being used as a tourniquet to stop his bleeding leg.

Everything was not fine.

I gestured to Cross's lifeless body. "He was grieving for his wife, and you killed him."

"He came at us with a knife. You saw that," Mom said.

"Because you killed his wife."

"She was sick," Dad maintained.

"You said that, but you don't get to make those decisions. You don't pick whose lives are expendable and who should pay for what crimes. Your choices affect people; they affect me. Horribly." I laid it out, and for once, I heard how closely I had followed in their footsteps. I was playing God. I was running our band of misfits. I was forcing my plans on everyone. I insisted we come here. And now Marcus was lying in a hospital.

"We never wanted you mixed up in any of this." The new crow's feet around his eyes deepened. It was a new look, one I wasn't familiar with, maybe desperation?

"You should have thought about us before you became criminals. You *chose* this life. It didn't find you; it didn't happen beyond your control. You *started* Department D." I couldn't absolve them of the crimes they actively, willingly committed. "You could've gotten out after you had kids. You could have thought about Keira and me at any point, but you didn't. You got out because *your* lives were being threatened. You were thinking about *you*."

It was the simple truth, and we all knew it. It was why the shackles stayed on my wrists, why I'd never be free of this. They put them there. They bound my hands, my future, with lies. No amount of I'm Sorrys could undo that.

"Let us make it up to you." His speech was accelerating, like he could see my back turning to them. "Whatever you think about what we did, crimes we committed decades ago, you have to know this—we *did not* kidnap your sister, and we *did not* kill your friend Tyson."

"Then who did?" I cut in, realizing that there were still so many questions they hadn't answered. If they wanted forgiveness, they could start there.

My dad sighed so heavily I felt the temperature in the room change, chill. "We don't know for sure." He shook his head in embarrassment. "We know Urban took your sister, but your friend…"

"It's either Urban or the Reys," Mom finished for him. "Our money is on the Reys, after this stunt they pulled with Antonio. It's why you need to get away from those boys."

My jaw set. "Do you really think…you have any say… in who I *date*?" I bit off the words.

"It's not that. It's for your safety," Dad said.

"Come with *us*," Mom blurted, like it was time to skip to the end.

"What?" I was certain I'd heard her wrong.

"Allen was right about one thing," she insisted. "Department D, the Reys, Randolph, they're never going to stop coming after you and your sister. Not now. Not when they know we're back, when they think they can use you to get to us, like they used Allen's wife to get to him."

I knew this already. It was why I was collecting Dresden Kids like trading cards. *A lot of good that does me.*

"You know that the evidence you acquired from those kids is false," Mom went on, hearing my thoughts. "They're setting us up. Randolph and the Reys realize that Department D is tumbling down, that the CIA is too close, that too many innocents know the truth, so they're doing damage control. They've become their own client. They've started to manipulate the evidence, point everything at us, pin every crime, the entire organization on *us*, so they can walk away free and clear. You saw that news article in Boston, didn't you?"

She tilted her head, knowing the answer. Department D planted the story in the *Boston Tattler* to make my family look bad—Keira and me included. The smear campaign had begun.

"That article makes *me* look guilty," I growled. "It makes it look like I did something to my sister."

"And it's only going to get worse," Dad said. "That was the tip of Phase One."

"Unless we stop them," Mom continued.

"Come with us. Let's do this together." Dad stood in front of me like he was offering me a free trip around the world, like I should say thank you and write their names in a gratitude journal. "Let's bring down Department D. Our way. No CIA, no high school kids. Let's show them how powerful the Phoenixes really are. Together."

I half expected a locker room full of football players to burst into applause. *This is our time! This is our house! We must defend it! Go team!*

Only I wasn't inspired. I was barely standing. There was a body on the marble floor. They killed a man who had sacrificed so much to help them over the years, *and* they killed his wife. Yet they were asking for my loyalty, my trust? But…they were also the strongest, most informed allies we'd ever get. And they were my parents. They were back. They were alive. Could I really close the door and act like that didn't matter to me? Like I didn't care if someone *really* killed them this time?

They watched as I warred with myself, my mind

changing with every breath.

Then my phone rang in my pocket.

I pulled it out like I was yanking a lifeline.

It was the hospital. *Marcus.*

CHAPTER TWENTY-NINE

I sat in a taxi moving through Rio de Janeiro on my way back to Marcus. I'd left my parents in the villa at Lagoa.

This time, I'd said goodbye.

I couldn't take them up on their offer. I couldn't *be* them, mostly because I didn't know who they were. I stared out the car window as dawn broke on the city, the hazy apricot light of the wee hours exposing a side of Rio that few travelers saw. The streets were full of police.

There wasn't a riot or a crime spree. It was an ordinary December morning, with cops patrolling like armed militants. They were dressed in gray and black camouflage fatigues with black berets on their heads and combat boots on their feet as they stomped through the streets, bulletproof vests on their chests, rifles slung over their shoulders, ready to be aimed. They held German Shepherds on leashes while they cleared the sidewalks of the homeless, the poor, the drug addicted or drug dealing—any unsavory character that might scare off the tourists and ruin the *Girl from Ipanema* image of tropical paradise. It was a city skilled at duplicity, and it seemed so fitting given the parents I'd left behind.

The reality was my mom and dad were heartless, calculating, career criminals who killed people without guilt and who, for years, used their kids and their jobs as engineers to project a picture of an ordinary loving American family. It was all fake. Maybe even the love, at least for them.

I had wished when I saw them that all I would feel was a white-hot burn of hate, but it wasn't that easy, as Keira predicted. When I'd sobbed on their shoulders, it was with a mix of profound betrayal and twisted pleasure that they had broken out of prison for us. I wanted to believe they were trying to protect us, trying to destroy the organization they built, all for the well being of their children. I wanted to have a family again, and I wanted everything to be okay.

I wanted that so badly, I ran out of there at record pace. I didn't look back.

The taxi pulled in front of Rio's largest hospital, and I handed the driver cash as I stepped into the muggy air catching the stench of disinfectant and sickness wafting from the glass doors.

My heart was conflicted when it came to my parents.

But not when it came to someone else.

His eyes were open when I walked into the room.

Marcus was wearing a white gown with blue polka dots, no longer bare-chested, so the sensors must have been removed from his body. There were still tubes connected to his arms pushing fluids, and his skin looked impossibly pale, which was saying something given his already pasty complexion. But his black hair was mussed in a way that looked sexy—only guys could pull off bedhead in a hospital room.

"You're okay." I stepped toward him, exhaling a breath I didn't realize I'd been holding.

"Thanks to you." His voice was husky, like it hurt to speak.

"Are you kidding me?" I collapsed next to him, reaching my arms around the beige plastic bedrail to grip his hand, hold it tight. "I'm the reason you're here."

"You're the reason I'm alive." He tried miserably not to wince from the effort it took to talk.

"Shhh. Don't speak." I placed my finger on his lips. "Do you remember what happened?"

He shook his head "no," so I relayed his story, from the drugged drinks to me kicking Paolo in the crotch so hard he'd probably never have children. I told him what it was like to ride in the ambulance, how the doctors cared for him, and how I didn't want to leave him.

"It's okay. You needed the rest," he rasped, then he narrowed his eyes. "But it doesn't look like you've slept." He reached his hand to my face, his fingers brushing what must be massive puffy purple circles, only not from insomnia.

I searched his eyes, trying to decide if I should tell him about his brother's betrayal or Cross being dead or my parents being alive and looking to create a Phoenix Family Fighting Club. It was a lot for me to take in, and I wasn't recovering from a drug overdose. Instead, I lowered my head to his chest and rested it there. Those details could wait until tomorrow.

"I'm so sorry," I whispered, tears in my voice. "If I had listened to you, to Keira, if we'd gone to the CIA, if we hadn't come here…"

"This isn't your fault. None of this is your fault. It's okay. *We're* okay."

He stroked my hair, gently, comforting *me* while he lay in his hospital bed having narrowly escaped death. "I promise I will never do this again. I'll listen to you guys from now on. I'll trust you. I *do* trust you," I pleaded, wondering if it was even possible to express how wretched I felt.

"I know. It's okay. *I'm* okay," he repeated.

I closed my eyes. Even with the smell of antiseptic in the air, even with the beeping machines, his touch on my hair was so soothing. My breathing synced with his, my head rising and falling with his chest. After a night of stifling conversations, I felt like I could breathe again, with him, near him. My whole body relaxed, and I wanted to melt into him, fix him, heal his wounds, and let him heal mine. Suddenly I felt completely overcome, with emotion, exhaustion, and relief that I couldn't ignore the words battering inside me—collecting one, two, three—insisting they come out. They were shouting from my heart, and I had to say them. I wanted to say them.

"I love you," I whispered, eyes still clenched.

I'd never said the words before, not to a guy, and it took more guts and bravery than anything I'd done since I'd left America, more strength than fighting any spy. I'd walked away from the two people who left me, abandoned me, and did nothing to teach me what those words meant. I had to find that meaning on my own.

I could hear his heart pound faster in his chest.

His lungs hiccupped. "I love you, too," he rasped, then he pulled at my head, urging me to face him. When I did, there were tears in his eyes, and I knew they weren't from pain. These were the words he wanted to hear, he needed to hear, and I couldn't do it before. Now it felt so real, so honest.

I slowly lowered my head and kissed him carefully on the lips, barely touching him, afraid to hurt him.

"I love you so much. And I trust you, with everything." I breathed against his mouth.

He nodded in return, pressing his forehead to mine.

We stayed like that, forehead to forehead, hands clutching one another's face.

This was what I wanted.

CHAPTER THIRTY

Our black town car pulled in front of the East Sussex Compound. We hadn't rushed back. After Marcus was released from the hospital, we decided to wait until he "felt strong enough to travel." Really, we wanted time in the sun, fingers entwined, with the sound of the surf crashing and the feel of the salt air curling our hair. We even bought bathing suits from a street vendor and swam in the bath-water-warm turquoise ocean, my legs wrapped around Marcus's waist as we kissed in the waves. I never saw my parents again in Rio. I wasn't sure if they'd left for their evil hideout under a volcano or if they were lurking behind palm trees following us in trench coats, but I was with the person I wanted to be with.

"You ready for this?" Marcus asked as we stepped out of the luxury car that Julian had sent to Heathrow Airport to retrieve us.

"No, but does it matter?" I cocked my head, my dark hair falling over my shoulder. "Are you?"

"Not at all." He shrugged.

It took a full day for me to tell him about Antonio.

I couldn't bring myself to do it, to break him further. I waited until we were sitting on the beach, our toes in the sand. Then I finally faced him and told him the whole story:

"Charlotte booked our airfare," I began, knowing our paradise would be coming to an end eventually and dreading every tick of the clock that brought us closer to that reality.

"Let's stay here forever," he moaned, rolling over on his lounge chair and reaching for my leg, sticky with the sunscreen he'd rubbed on it.

I took a breath so big, my chest lifted a couple of inches. "There's something I need to tell you."

Marcus blinked his eyes open, alarm already present as he squinted in the tropical sun. *"Que?"*

"I didn't want to tell you earlier, because you were still recovering, and I don't want to hurt you more, cause a setback. And I know how it might look, the history that's there, the way I acted in the beginning, but it's not about that…" I rambled, staring at the moons of my fingernails as I delivered the blow.

"Say it. You're scaring me." Marcus sat up, his legs long in front of him.

"It's Antonio." No turning back now. "He's still working for Department D, for your parents. All the Dresden Kids lied; their evidence is fake. They were paid to say the things they did by Department D. Agents got to them before we ever showed up." I grabbed a fistful of beach towel, twisting the terry fabric between my hands so hard the rough texture was leaving a burn. "Department D was able to do that, *your parents* were able to do that, because Antonio gave them all the names of every kid we were going to meet. He told your parents every word we ever said. He helped them set up my family, plant that news article. He's still one of them."

I watched Marcus pale, his body empty out so fully he slumped back on his recliner like a raft that deflated. His eyes closed.

Then I waited. There was a lot more to say, about how Allen Cross had figured it out, about how he didn't tell us we were being misled, about how Charlotte and Julian had kicked out every Dresden Kid the moment I called with the truth. But he didn't need to hear that right now. He couldn't hear it.

"Are you sure?" he asked, eyes still scrunched.

I nodded though he couldn't see me. "Yeah. I'm *so sorry*."

His long lashes shot up. "Why are *you* sorry?" he snapped. "*I'm* the idiot! I'm the one who believed him. I'm the one who begged you to trust him! This is *my* fault!"

"No, it's not. He's your brother." I understood that sibling bond more than anyone. You do stupid things for family, like chase after assassins.

"I should have known better. I should have known *him*." He punched the plastic slats holding the beach chair together, holding us up. "*I begged you...*" His voice trailed off, so full of shame it sent a piercing ache through my chest.

I reached for his hands and pried his palms open, pressing my thumb until his fists released. "You love your brother, and he hurt you, betrayed you. If there's anyone who knows what it's like to be betrayed by family, it's me." I let out a dark chuckle. "There is no judgment here. We are equal members of the Evil Family Club. I'm just sorry you had to join."

We talked about it more (and more and more) as the hours blended together in the sun. But anytime anyone's mood got too dark, brow got too heavy, the other always found a way to squash the conversation. Usually it involved a pair of warm lips.

Now we were going to have to face them, face everyone, and no kiss would save us.

We walked to the compound's soaring wooden door. I placed my hand on the brass handle, and we stepped inside.

"You're back!" Charlotte and Keira squealed in unison as they rushed toward me. My sister hugged me first.

"Are you okay?" she asked in my ear.

"No," I answered honestly. Physically, I was fine. Mentally, I was in need of a wheelchair.

"I want to hear everything *again*," Keira said, her hazel eyes reminding me so much of our dad's, *her* dad's. "How did they look? Really?"

"Exactly the same," I answered truthfully. "With maybe a few extra wrinkles. Oh, and Mom stopped to get her brows waxed. You know, priorities." My voice was cold.

"You still hate them." It wasn't a question.

"I don't know." I shook my head, feeling uncertain if the sky was blue. "It was *Mom and Dad.*"

Keira hugged me once more. "It's okay to be happy to see them."

But was it? After everything they'd done?

"I don't know how you were able to walk out of there and not go with them." She wasn't judging me; she sounded in awe.

"You didn't see what they did to Cross." I pulled back from her embrace with a steely look. "The way they moved, fought, it was like nothing I've ever seen. I couldn't believe it was them doing those things. I couldn't put the parents I knew in those bodies."

To anyone else, that wouldn't make sense, but I knew my sister would understand. And she did. She nodded, her eyes drooping like our dad's. *Her* dad's. How had we not seen it before?

"I wish I could have been there. For you. To see them."

"I know. It sucks. It isn't right." I squeezed her hand. Keira had earned that confrontation through three years of social service visits, teacher conferences, and electric bills. She needed her moment to let that all out, and I suspected one day she'd get it. I just wasn't sure I wanted to be there for it.

I looked at our friends, standing back a few paces, giving us space. "I should have listened to you. All of you. We shouldn't have gone to Rio. You shouldn't have gone to Barcelona. If anything had happened to you, it would've been my fault. Because I was stubborn, because I *had* to keep going. I still can't believe Marcus—"

"I'm okay," he repeated for the millionth time.

"And *I'm* the one who needs to apologize." Charlotte looked at Marcus. "I'm so sorry. My intel on Paolo, I should have done better. I should've known better. I trusted Cross—"

"We all did." Marcus smiled in forgiveness. He wasn't angry with her. How could he be?

"I'm glad you made it back safely." Julian clapped a hand on Marcus and my shoulders. "I had the master suite made up for you, Marcus, or whoever you want to share it with." He winked in the least subtle way possible. "I'll sleep in a guest room. You deserve some peace and quiet."

It was so Julian; it was what he could offer—money and comfort. "Thank you," I said.

That was when I noticed Antonio in the doorway. I guessed it would have been too much to have expected him to leave, given that it was his brother who was poisoned and pumped full of life-saving charcoal, but still, it took guts for him to stand in this house and face us like he wasn't the ultimate traitor.

I gritted my teeth to keep from running at him full speed with a scissor kick to the head. Marcus gripped my forearm, pulling me back, sensing my reaction. He always did. Maybe we shared my parents' unspoken communication, only without the intent to murder.

"Let me talk to him," he whispered to me.

I nodded, not taking my eyes off the brother who sold us out to his parents.

"Hermano, lo siento. Lo siento mucho," Antonio started in Spanish, tears welling in his dark eyes as he took four long strides to Marcus and gripped him in a bear hug. Marcus actually embraced him back. I wanted to scream, rip them apart, and claw Antonio's beard off.

But no, Marcus was giving him a hug.

"I didn't know what I was doing," Antonio continued in Spanish. "It was Mom and Dad. I listened to them. I didn't know! What happened to you... I'm so sorry!"

"I know, I know." Marcus nodded, listening as he pulled away.

"If I had any idea that kid in Rio was dangerous, I never would have let you go," Antonio continued to rattle in his native tongue. "I wanted to stop, but I didn't know how to get out. If I stopped giving Mom and Dad names, I would have tipped them off. So I thought I'd try to make things safer, send you and Anastasia together. I knew the Phoenixes were drawing close. That was who I saw as the threat, who I *still* see as the threat."

We all paused at the mention of my name. Even Charlotte and Julian, who couldn't speak Spanish, understood that much.

"I thought with the girls separated, us separated, it

would stop all of our parents from doing anything crazy," Antonio reasoned. "Mom and Pop, I swear it's not as bad as it sounds. They're not evil."

I understood every word, and so did Keira. And I couldn't stay quiet anymore.

"They're not *evil*? They killed Tyson," I snapped, eyes blazing.

"You don't know that! I swear, they're not killers!" Antonio spun my way, flicking a tattooed arm in the air. I wanted to scratch it. "There is no proof of anything. It could have been your parents or Urban."

Technically, this was true. My parents swore it wasn't them, and given the message was directed *to* them, I had to admit in this instance, they were the least likely culprits. That left Randolph Urban and the Reys, both motivated to get to my parents, and both amoral enough to use children. But the Reys were the ones who were running operations lately, and that was all the evidence I needed. Clearly, Marcus and Antonio felt otherwise.

"Antonio, you lied to us! You betrayed us. Just like *them*, just like our parents." I was not offering any Ghandi-like hugs of forgiveness, and I knew it would hurt Marcus to attack his brother, but he didn't see the person he loved twitching on the ground. "Marcus could have died."

"I know! I'm sorry! *Dios mio!* But my parents have made me feel like an idiot my whole life. Antonio, the screw up. Then they got me this job, and all of the sudden they were proud of me. I was good at it." Antonio pumped his broad shoulders as if he had no other choice. Had he heard the way his parents talked about him in Boston, that their opinion of him hadn't changed, he probably wouldn't be defending them now.

"Your parents suck. Join the club. I hope your spying

made them proud." I offered a sarcastic thumbs up. "Now, get the hell out!"

Unfortunately, I knew exactly what it was like to have horrible parents who did horrible things. The difference was when faced with the opportunity to help with my parents' crimes (or help them get away with their crimes), I walked away.

"Anastasia, wait." Keira pulled me back. "Antonio told me everything in Barcelona. As soon as we heard about Marcus in the hospital, before you even talked to Cross or Mom and Dad. I'm not defending him—obviously—but I think everyone should know that in the end, he came clean."

Is she kidding me with this? Like that matters?

"He came clean after his brother almost swallowed his tongue!" I swung my hand at Marcus, who snatched my palm and held it close to his chest.

"It's my turn to speak." Marcus's voice was still hoarse from the tube shoved down his throat, which only illustrated my point.

"I know what you did." Marcus looked at his brother. "And I know what Mom and Pop can be like, the pressure. But you *lied* to me, and I *defended* you. Over and over." His eyes screamed apologies for insisting I trust his brother, but as far as I was concerned, Marcus didn't need to apologize for anything, ever. Not after what happened in Brazil. Not after I made him go there.

"I know." Antonio hung his head, itching his beard in a nervous tic. "But I am still that guy, your brother. From the moment you showed up on bonfire night, from the moment I met Keira"—he looked at her, and she had the good sense to step back—"I wanted to somehow stop all of this. But I did not know how. You think *you're* being set up." He glared at me. "I think *my parents* are being set up. They haven't done the things your parents have. I know it! I swear it. And I could not let them be blamed for everything."

"From over here, it sure looks like they've done a lot," I snipped. They almost got their son killed. They sent us running around the world on wild goose chases. They planted fake news blaming me for Keira's kidnapping, and they very likely killed Tyson. "We got lucky that none of the other Dresden Kids tried to kill us. Paolo Striker, Sophia Urban, they work for Department D. Paolo *kills* for them. These weren't innocent missions that you let us go on, and you let these kids live here. They could have done anything!"

"Speaking of which," Julian piped up. He slid an envelope from the breast pocket of his blazer, because of course Julian wears a jacket in the afternoon in his own home. Everyone looked at me, already knowing what the message held. "This is for you. From Dani."

The Dresden Kids left before Marcus was discharged from the hospital, all swiftly packing bags and none offering any defense. Apparently, except for one.

I slid the letter out of the envelope, with a trembling hand and a racing heart. It was handwritten:

Anastasia,

I didn't want to skulk away. I'm not a coward. I wanted to face you, but it was clear I was no longer welcome. So I am forced to settle for this—what I told you wasn't a lie. Not all of it. My mother spent two years in a Turkish prison. I lived on the streets after my uncle abused me. My stepfather worked for Department D; he had my mother thrown in jail.

However, I don't know if your parents were involved

in what happened to my country, to my mother. The video of your father meeting with my uncle, that was given to me by the Department D agent who showed up before you did, a woman, Slovakian.

Antonio's partner, I thought to myself, teeth grinding.

While that one bit of evidence may have been fabricated, everything else I told you was true. Our lives were destroyed. My mother wakes up every night screaming with nightmares. I have scars all over my body from what my uncle did. We left Turkey with no money and no family. Then a woman shows up and gives us cash and a gold watch.

I remembered his mother's Rolex, the "gift from her lawyer." *I knew it wasn't fake!*

She cleared my mother's name, and already my mom is working as a reporter again, doing what she loves, and making more money than she ever did before. When you met us that first day, you promised revenge. You promised we could get back at the people who did this to us. Your parents are not good people. They started Department D. They ran that organization. No one asked us to bury an innocent bystander under false evidence, like they did my mother. Getting back at your parents, meant getting our revenge. You must realize there is no difference to any of us Dresden Kids between any of your parents.
So we enjoyed our time here while we were together, a group of kids who had all been through the same

thing, wronged by the same evil people. Not one of us felt guilty for the things we said or the false evidence we gave. You might not have done this to us, but your parents did.

I truly hope you bring down Department D one day, and I wish you no ill will. I hope you don't wish any on us.

Sincerely,
Dani

"Shit," I muttered, dropping the letter to my side.

"We read it already. I hope you don't mind." Charlotte exhaled, even her breath sounding apologetic. "None of this is about you, Anastasia. You or Keira. They get that. We all get that. And we *will* bring them down."

"How?" Keira asked, voicing the question on everyone's mind. "All the evidence we thought we had is fake."

"We don't know for sure." Charlotte squirmed in her fuzzy socks as she looked at me with guilt in her eyes. "I gave everything to the CIA. I know they had your parents in some secret black site, but we're outmatched when it comes to computers. That video of your dad looked *real*."

"I'm working to get us better equipment," Julian offered, like that was the problem.

"Some of that evidence *could be* legit. We don't know. We need their resources. Besides, at least now we know everything. We know why the CIA has been so eager to help—because we were either building a case against your parents or we were leading them *to* your parents. Now it's out in the open, and maybe they can really help end this—"

"Before anyone else gets hurt," I finished for her, agreeing. The CIA wasn't our enemy. We needed help.

Or a new plan.

I glanced at the broken faces in our group. We'd all given up so much, from Keira's kidnapping and anxiety, to the career Charlotte put on hold, to Julian's public shaming in the media, to Marcus's hospital stay, to even Antonio's twisted family loyalties. We were all damaged. Including me. Especially me.

Maybe we couldn't bring down Department D on our own. Maybe it was too big for a bunch of teenagers to handle from the shadows.

I thought back to that Boston news article. They were coming after us—not my parents, but *us*. Like my mom said, Department D had become their own client, and they knew quite well how to manipulate the press, how to convince the world of their version of the truth before anyone had a chance to prove the opposite. They were making the world think I killed my sister, or kidnapped her, or faked her death. I'd been blamed for Tyson's murder, and they'd already planted the seed that my parents were alive. We looked guilty.

They would keep coming at us with these stories. They'd convince the world that the name Phoenix should go down with Benedict Arnold. No one was ever going to believe us.

Unless we spoke up.

Unless we changed the game with something completely unexpected.

We needed a new plan, and maybe we already had it.

For months, my friends had been asking me to trust them, to listen to their ideas. They pressed me again and again. I always said no. But maybe the time had come for one of those ideas; maybe it was time to say yes.

"Julian." I looked at him, power in my voice. "Where's your camera? I think it's time for me to give you my deposition."

THE TRUTH

Evidence of a fake Turkish Coup plot, supposedly orchestrated in 2003, was first published in newspapers in late 2010. Code-named Operation Sledgehammer, the hypothetical coup was designed to overthrow the newly elected, Islamic-rooted government. Evidence detailed plans to bomb mosques and shoot down planes in an attempt to create such chaos that the military could take control of the government. By 2012, more than three hundred people were sentenced to prison, including military officers and journalists. They were held for years without trials, until it was proven that the evidence of the supposed 2003 coup was created with a 2007 version of Microsoft Office. The entire plot was fabricated, with most theories pointing to the Gulenist movement, which hoped to promote their own senior officials to the top ranks of the military. To date, no one has been charged for creating this conspiracy. In preparation for this novel, the author spoke with Dani Rodrik, a Harvard Professor whose father-in-law, General Cetin Dogan, was among those falsely imprisoned.
-The Chronicle of Higher Education, October 2015

...

Hilda Murrell, aged 78, was sexually assaulted and murdered in Shropshire, England, in March 1984. Her body was left abandoned in a field, and a lone sixteen-year-old boy was convicted of the crime. However, Hilda, an outspoken activist against nuclear power, was scheduled to give a very public speech highlighting the dangers of Margaret Thatcher's nuclear power policies and was murdered before she had the chance. Additionally, Hilda's nephew, Robert Green, was an admiral in the British Navy and head of a nuclear submarine during the 1982 Falklands War that reportedly sank a non-threatening Argentinian ship. The international scandal, involving his nuclear sub, not only cast doubts on Margaret Thatcher's leadership, but gave weight to Hilda's stance against nuclear proliferation. Many conspiracy theories exist regarding her death, and her nephew has written a book about the case.

-The Guardian, 2012

...

The 1998 World Cup Final featured France beating Brazil in 3-0 shutout. The night before the game, star player Ronaldo Luís Nazário de Lima, suffered a seizure so severe, teammates described him as foaming at the mouth and nearly swallowing his tongue. He was removed from the team line up. However, an hour before the game, he was added back to the team roster. The team lost badly, and many conspiracy theories exist as to why Ronaldo returned to play—from Ronaldo not remembering his seizure, to pressure from a corporate sponsor, to the player hiding a secret medical condition. None have been proven, and Ronaldo has been inducted into the Brazilian Football Museum Hall of Fame.

The Bleacher Report, 2013

ACKNOWLEDGMENTS

I've learned to depend on every person in my village as I've brought Anastasia Phoenix to life. First and foremost, thank you to Lawrence Martin-Bittman, otherwise known as Agent 006.5, for the espionage inspiration that led to the creation of Department D and its specialty — disinformation. When I wrote the first draft of Book 1, *Proof of Lies*, disinformation was not a word I'd ever heard before. Now, fake news is everywhere. Thank you, Larry, for being ahead of the times.

Thanks to my agent, Taylor Martindale Kean, for your editorial feedback, which has made this series so much stronger, and for your support as you've championed every step of this publishing process. To my editor, Alycia Tornetta, you've helped me grow Anastasia so she's both strong and caring, snarky and sympathetic. Without you, her story wouldn't be the same.

I am grateful to all the people my husband and I met during our travels, who gave us advice and local information that has added depth to my international settings. Specifically, thank you to our lovely B&B host in Lewes, England, Angela Wigglesworth, for welcoming us into her home on Bonfire Night; the doorman at the NeoBankside Apartments in London, England, Clio Asolfi, for letting me sneak up to the penthouse floor for a peek at Julian's view; and to the dread-locked twenty-something guy we met at a bar near the Tate Modern, for recommending we go out to Zone 2 and visit the "best Irish pub outside of Dublin" and the old cemetery across the street. My British scenes wouldn't have been the same without you.

Special thanks go out to Ric and Leticia Ochman for hosting the most amazing wedding at the Parque Lage in Rio de Janeiro, Brazil. I don't know how this book would have ended without you. And thanks again, Leticia, for all the help promoting *Proof of Lies*.

I am indebted to everyone who helped market this series through their personal and professional networks, specifically: Jenee Chizick, Riley Londres, Tom Gailey, Eric Smith, Jennifer Rodriguez, Ben Reynolds, and Marissa Nicole Rodriguez. I love visiting schools, and I am grateful to all of the teachers, librarians, and administrators who have allowed me to speak to their students. It's always a blast. Special thanks to Harvard Professor Dani Rodrik for speaking to me about the conspiracies and crimes in the Turkish government, so I could plausibly insert my characters into those events.

A shout-out to my talented friend and photographer Chris Klock for taking all of my author photos, and special thanks to those who have offered their homes for quiet writing retreats, including Cristina and Matt Wallach, Paula and Larry Wallach, and Marguerite and Mike Sheehan. Without those weekends away from my little people, my books would not be written.

To my friends and family who traveled from all over to celebrate the launch of *Proof of Lies*, thank you for making the party so awesome! It's a night I'll always remember. Without my Ridley Girls, BU friends, and neighbors, I'd have a lot less laughter in my life.

I have fantastic in-laws who not only lend me their homes to write, but also do some serious copyediting. Thank you to Paula and Larry for catching all those typos.

I am who I am because of my Rodriguez Family. Our relatives struggling in Puerto Rico following Hurricane Maria showed us what family really means. I am now positive that if I am ever trapped in a collapsed building, one of you will find a congressman to email a nonprofit who will call a colleague who will somehow get me out. So to Lou, Natalie, Nicole, and Prao, thank you for being such caring and generous people. And to my parents, thank you for encouraging me every step of the way since the first day I told you I got an agent. Every time you show up at my events, I feel less nervous. Thanks!

To my husband, Jordan, you believe in me more than I believe in myself. You make my writing dream possible, by not only supporting me, but by being an excellent, calm, creative, there's-always-a-way husband and father. We've taken this journey together, literally around the world, and I love you for that.

To Juliet and Lincoln, showing you *Proof of Lies* on the shelf of a bookstore meant more to me than you realize right now. I can't wait for you to one day read these novels, just not for another ten or twelve years.

DON'T MISS THE
STUNNING CONCLUSION TO THE
ANASTASIA PHOENIX TRILOGY

THE END OF THE LIE

Hollywood comes calling after Anastasia and her friends take their harrowing tale of espionage and near-death experiences public. While their newfound celebrity status raises their profiles so high Department D can't possibly touch them, it also takes an emotional toll. Plagued by constant online threats and struggling to bring down the parents who abandoned her, Anastasia wonders if she'll ever be normal again.

When an old friend takes to the Internet with viral videos unloading all the Phoenix family's darkest secrets, Anastasia fears her parents might do anything to silence the truth, maybe even murder. Aided by Marcus, the handsome bad boy who has supported her since the beginning, Anastasia grows even more determined to find her parents—but can she really turn them in? As more spies from their past emerge, leading them on a treacherous trail from Poland to Prague, Anastasia begins to realize how far people will go to protect themselves…including her.

AVAILABLE IN 2019

Grab the Entangled Teen releases readers are talking about!

Pretty Dead Girls
by Monica Murphy

In Cape Bonita, wicked lies are hidden just beneath the surface. But all it takes is one tragedy for them to be exposed. The most popular girls in school are turning up dead, and Penelope Malone is terrified she's next. All the victims have been linked to Penelope—and to a boy from her physics class. The one with the rumored dark past and a brooding stare that cuts right through her. There's something he isn't telling her. But there's something she's not telling him, either. Everyone has secrets, and theirs might get them killed.

Wicked Charm
by Amber Hart

Nothing good comes from living in the Devil's swamp.

Willow Bell doesn't think moving to the Okefenokee is half bad, but nothing prepares her for what awaits in the shadows of the bog—or for the boy next door, who might just be the trouble people speak of.

Beneath his wicked, depthless eyes and the allure that draws girls to him, Beau Cadwell is mystery to his core. Where Beau goes, chaos follows. *His lips are full of twisted grins and lies*, the girls say. *He's evil in disguise*, warns Gran.

It isn't until girls wind up dead in the swamp that Willow wonders if maybe Beau is more intense than she can handle. His riddles tell her that he's someone to be wary of, but his touch tells her that she can trust him. Problem is, which is true? It's hard to tell with a boy like him…